MISSING TEETH AND WHAT LIES BENEATH

The Tooth Fairy Chronicles

Book Six

Victoria Rocus

Serenade Publishing

Serenade Publishing

www.serenadepublishing.com

VICTORIA ROCUS

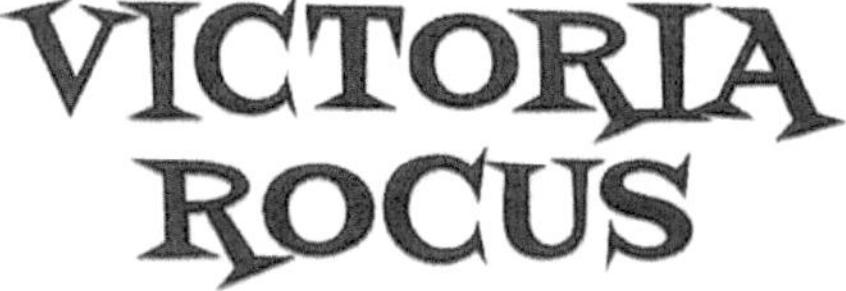

WISHING YOU "MAGIC" IN EVERY PAGE. THANKS FOR READING!

GLOSSARY AND PRONUNCIATION OF ANCIENT OTHERWORLD GAELIC

Aistriú na Foirme – (ASH-tree-oo nuh far-may) – the ability to shift physical form, a high-level Otherworld magical skill

An Banna Siora – (On Bon-nå Shear-ē) - "The Eternal Bond" - an unbreakable vow of commitment that follows a couple into the Afterlife. It is sealed through the application of magical ink added to the original bond

Aoibheann - (Ay-veen) a feminine name meaning "radiant beauty"; the name of Crann Bethadh's head housekeeper

Athair - (ă-hair) - "father" - when capitalized, used as a formal title

Avalon – (Av-uh-lon) – a kingdom south of I Idir and ruled by The Lady of the Lake, Dr. Brannigan's Great Great Grandmother. Avalon has always remained neutral in the battle between the Mundanes and the Fae, but has recently begun supporting The Morrigan's view

Bairn - (bĕrhn) – baby

Bás Beo – (BAWS-bow) – a codicil added to the An Banna Siorai that states that if the female partner in the bond joins the Afterlife during child bearing years, the male partner assumes the life of "the living dead' and virtually "ceases to exist" in society. The reasoning behind this ancient amendment has since been lost to history, but is believed to have been added to protect the female partner's inheritance rights

Badh - (bod) – an ancient Tuatha de Danann House that serves as part of I Idir's Ruling Council. The Morrigan originally descended from this line before starting her own as Otherworldly Queen of I Idir

Balfour – (BAL-fuh) a groomsman at Dun Siorai who cares for Dylan's pony, Toirneach. He is a participant in Samhain's Wilding Night festivities

Banphrionsa - (bon frún-sa) – royal title of Princess

Beltane - (bee-awl-tin-ya) A sacred Otherworldly holiday held on May 1 st , halfway between the Spring Equinox and the Summer Solstice, celebrating fertility and new growth.

Birgit – (beer-gît) – a variation of the name Bridget, meaning "help" or "salvation; The name of Dylan's scathach.

Blasta Fianain – (BLAS-tuh FEE-uh-nin) – a tasty cookie or biscuit

Brabúsaí – (bruh-BOO-shee) – a profiteer, someone who benefits from the pain of others

Bréagadóir Salach - (brig-a DOOR sâ-LEK) – a "dirty liar," considered a scathing Fae insult

Buaf – (boo-êf) – toad; the original name given to Oisin at birth by the staff of Dun Siorai

Cac – (kak) -a vulgar slang word for "shit"

Cairde – (ka-ir-yeh) – friends

Capall- (KAH-puhl) – horse

Caoimhin – (Kwee-vin) – the Gaelic pronunciation of "Kevin." The name of the Prince of I Idir, a Roman Catholic priest who prefers the title "Fr. Kevin; brother to Maureen Beckett, the Banphrionsa of I Idir

Cara is Dílse M'anama – (ka-ra DEEL-shah uh-nuh-ma) translates to "dearest one of my soul," a phrase Declan uses to describe Rosie

Cerridwen Prep – (kerr-ID-wen) – a school whose name is derived from an ancient Welsh goddess worshipped as the keeper of "the cauldron of knowledge." Cerridwen Prep is a private primary and elementary school in Salem, MA, one that specifically caters to Fae children living in the Mundane world. The curriculum is patterned after similar Mundane schools, with the addition of specific courses of study in I Idirian and Sidhe history, culture, language and politics

Cillian - (Kill-ee-an) – translates to "bright-headed" in reference to war or strife. Cillian Mac Badh is the young heir to House Badh, a cousin to the Queen of I Idir, and Declan's long-time nemesis.

Ciúbanna siúcra – (Koo-bahn-ah shoo-kruh) - sugar cube

Comortas Capall – (KUH-mer-tus KA-puhl) – a horse tournament or race that takes on the sabbat of Samhain. Among the Sidhe, it is a race that is highly anticipated

Comrádaí mo Chroí – (kum-RAW-dee muh-kree) – translates to "friend of my heart." The title the young Mairead Beckett gives to Dylan on their first day of school, one which Rosie finds disconcerting in children so young

Crann Bethadh - (Krŏn Bĕ-hĕ) - "Tree of Life" - the royal

seat of The Morrigan, Queen Maeve, built out of a giant, ancient oak; sometimes referred to as "The Raven's Nest"

Cruinniú Teaghlaigh – (kr-in-yoo tyah-ligh) – an informal family or clan meeting

Cuach an Fhithich – (koo-ahk ah vih-hih) – translates to "Raven's Hollow," and is the estate belonging to House Badh, an important member of the Ruling Council with direct family ties to The Morrigan

Dearthái – (JAR-haw-ihr) – brother

Deirfuir – (DER-fuhr) – sister

Dochtuir – (duhk-toor) – doctor

Dylan – (Dee-ol-oon) – the Gaelic pronunciation of "Dylan," a Welsh name meaning "son of the sea." The name of Rosie and Declan's oldest son

Dubnos – (dŏv-nus) - the Fae version of the Underworld

Dun Siorai - (Dune Shear-ē) translates to "Eternal Fortress:" House Nuada's ancestral home

Éabón – (AY-vawn) – translates to "ebony." The name of Rosie's mare

Fabht – (fowth) – bug

Fiadh – (Fee-ah) – a female name meaning "wild fawn." The name of the woman who represents House Nuada in the Comortas Capall

Fómhar – (FOWV-er) – Autumn or harvest time

Gaoth Dorcha – (Gwee Dorka) – translates to "Dark Wind," the name of Mairead Beckett's pony

Glóhach – (GLEE-ah) – a gelding or castrated male horse

I Idir - (ē ēdar) – translates to "In Between," the Fae kingdom in the Otherworld ruled by The Morrigan, Queen Maeve, as its monarch

Lammas – (la-mus) – a Fae sabbat celebrated on August

1 st , marking the first harvest of the year. It is traditionally known by the ancient name of Lughnasadh- (LOO-nuh-sah) in honor of the immortal god, Lugh - (LOO)

Laoise – (LEE-sha) – a feminine name meaning "light." The name of Oisin's "lady love" in I Idir

Leanaí – (lan-nee) – children

Leanbh na Lamh Airgid – (layn-uv nuh lahv ar-gid) – translates to "Child of the Silver Hand" and is a title The Morrigan uses to address Declan. It refers to his royal lineage, descended from the first king of the Tuatha de Danann and possessing a silver hand. By using this title, the Queen is insinuating Declan has an important but difficult "path."

Liam – (lee-uhm) – A shortened Gaelic version of "William," that means "strong-willed warrior." The name of Rosie and Declan's second son

Mac - (mc) - "son of"- a title given to an eldest son and heir of a Ruling House

Macha – (MOT-cha) –The Morrigan's sister, who was executed for treason against the Throne. Macha's great, great grandson was also beheaded by The Black Knight (Ted Beckett) for the same crime (Trick or Treaty: Book One of The Morrigan Tales October, 2026)

Mairéad – (MAR-uhd) – a feminine name derived from the English, "Margaret," meaning "pearl." The name carries connotations of beauty, purity and rarity, and is the name of Ted and Maureen Beckett's eldest daughter, who is currently a Princess of I Idir, and named heir to The Throne (Stupid Cupid: Book Three of The Morrigan Tales, February, 2027)

Mathair – (mă-hair) - "mother" - when capitalized, used as a formal title

Mhamai – (whu-mee) – translates to "Mommy," a child's version of mathair

Milseán – (mil-shawn) – candy or sweets

Mo Ros Milis – (muh rohs milish) – translates to "My Sweet Rose," one of Declan's favorite pet names for Rosie

Mo Shiorghra - (mō hear-gra) - "My Eternal Love" - a fated mate in magical Fae tradition, wrought through a magical spell and destined by the Universe

Niamh – (neev) – a feminine name meaning "bright" or "radiant." The name of the Fitzpatrick's second scathach nanny; cousin to Birgit, and another granddaughter of Declan's childhood nanny and scathach,

Nuada - (new-a-da) - the name of an ancient Celtic king who possessed a silver arm; a major House from his bloodline within I Idir's Ruling Council that currently has Declan as its Lord after the treacherous behavior of his father, Callum Fitzpatrick

Oíche Fiáin – (EE-ha FEN) – translates to "Wilding Night," an ancient evening celebration of the Samhain sabbat originally centered on the rites of fertility. Over the years, the observance has taken more of a "rave" like atmosphere of pure abandon, centering on the goal of personal pleasure through drinking, music, dancing and sex. Children conceived on Oíche Fiáin are still believed to be especially blessed by the Universe

Oisin – (OSH-een) – translates to "little deer." The name given to Declan's half-brother by The Morrigan in reference to his deceased mathair who was allegedly murdered

by his father, Callum Fitzpatrick. The child's name at
birth was Buaf

Otharlann – (uh-her-lon) – infirmary or hospital

Peadar – (PAD-êr) – translates to "Peter" or "Rock." The
name of thegroomsman who takes care of Rosie's mare,
Eabon

Pionós – (pyuh-nohss) – a punishment, specifically one a
parent would give to a child

Réalta Dorcha – (RAY-al-tuh DOR-uh-khuh) Translates to
"Dark Star" and is the name of *Oisin's* stallion

Riail an Tiarna - (ree-al en cheer-na) – "The Lord's Rule;"
an ancient law of I Idir allowing a House's reigning Lord
to override the decisions made by the lower-ranking
heads of households within his bloodline.

Ronin – (RHO-nahwn) – a male name that translates to
"little seal." It is the name of Rosie and Declan's youngest
son, who Rosie jokes was most likely conceived near the
Irish sea shore

Samhain – (SAH-win) – a Fae sabbat of major importance,
signaling the end of the harvest season, and the beginning
of the New Year. It is a time for meditation and memories
of the family members who have moved on to the Afterlife. It is also a time to look forward to the future, and the
period when the Veil between the two worlds is at its
thinnest.

Samhradh – (sow-ruh) – Summer

Scathach - (skah-hak) – an elite group of trained Fae
female bodyguards hired by Ruling Class Houses to care
for their infant heirs. These positions are usually
passed down

Seamus – (shay-mus) – the Otherworld name for "James"
or "Jamie;" the name Oisin has given his dog.

Sidhe - (shē) - the term used for the Fae race in Celtic
mythology, as well as the forts and mounds they once
lived in during ancient times; the Sidhe possess higher levels of magical skill, and thus are considered part of
Fae higher society

Siobhan - (shiv-awn) - a Celtic female name meaning "gracious gift"; the name of Declan's mother

Siúlóid Machnaimh – (shoo-luid makh-niv) – translates
to "Walk of Meditation." Refers to a contemplative walk
or hike of a spiritual nature, usually taken alone

Súile – (soo-luh) - eyes

Súile Lofa – (soo-luh luh-fuh) – translates to "Rotten Eyes,"
a highly contagious bacterial infection, similar to human
conjunctivitis ("Pink Eye"), that the Fae are susceptible to
catching

Stór Mo Chroí – (ah stohr muh kree) – translates to "Treasure of My Heart," a title Declan often gives to Rosie

Striapach – (stree-ap-ukh) – a trollop or strumpet; "loose"
woman

Taibhse – (tiv-shuh) – ghost or departed spirit

Tir na Fathach – (cheer nah vak-hakh) – a mountainous
piece of sacred, undeveloped property on the outer
border of I Idir near Dun Siorai. Owned by The Throne,
but under the guardianship of House Nuada, its name
translates to "Land of the Giants" based on the ancient
tale that a race of Otherworldly giants are buried beneath
it. Rosie and Declan had their first "date" on Tir na
Fathach

Toirneach – (tarn-uhk) – translates to "thunder" and is the name of Dylan's beloved pony

Toirpíní – (TUR-pee-nee) tadpoles

Uncail – (un-kehl) - uncle

GLOSSARY AND PRONUNCIATION OF ANCIENT OTHERWORLDLY NORDBOERNE WORDS

Asgard – (As-gart) -a *Nordboerne* Elven Otherworld kingdom just north of *I Idir*. The two kingdoms share a border, and after years of peaceful co-operation, are currently not in agreement over The Morrigan's determination to keep the Mundanes from crossing the Veil. The philosophy, culture and magic style of the *Nordboerne* peoples are similar in many ways to that of the Fae

Dökkálfar – (dol-kal-far) – translates to "Dark Elves" and refers to the *Nordboerne* Elven race of darker-skinned inhabitants who lived unground or in cave homes built within the sides of the earth in the upper most Northern areas of *Asgard*

Jotun – (YOOT-uhn) – a type of dark sorcery believed to have been first established by a race of evil-purposed, ancient *Nordboerne* giants; it uses "soul magic" as part of its ritual, and the practice of it has officially been outlawed in most Otherworldly kingdoms.

Ljósálfar – (lyohs-ahl -farh) – fair-skinned Elven people physically and magically similar to the *Sidhe* Fae; the

Ljósálfar and the *Dökkálfar* make up the majority of the citizenship of *Asgard*, though over many centuries, a small portion of the *Ljósálfar* have taken up residence and built family units in *I Idir* among the Fae

Nordboerne – (NOR-bo-ren) – translates to "people of the North," and refers to all the races, Elven and other, who can trace their bloodlines to the kingdom of *Asgard*

Seior – (SAY-der) – the style of magic practiced by all types of *Nordboerne* people; similar to *Sidhe* personal magic but associated with a larger degree of ritual spell casting

MISSING 1

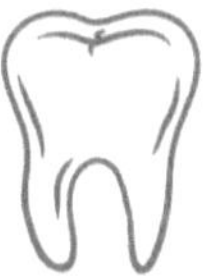

Sharing Family News

Five Years Later… **July 28th**

Motherhood is best suited to younger women. That's what I tell myself as I wrestle the wooden handle of Declan's favorite shaving brush from the mouth of my toddler, while my youngest yodels for his feeding in the arms of his nanny. "Liam…Sweetie, give that to Mommy. That's yucky. Your Da doesn't want teeth marks in his shaving brush."

The two-year-old looks at me and grins. "Da no here!" he says, plucking the handle of the brush from his mouth and holding it up to me, then snatching it away and sitting on it as I reach to grab it from his hand; typical Liam behavior.

Meanwhile, Ronin lets me know that he is in need of his mother's immediate attention with such a high-pitched howl that no doubt every canine in *I Idir* will be called to *Dun Siorai's* gates by his human dog whistle. "Da' ya' wish for me ta' just try and fix him a bottle, ma' Lady," *Niamh*, our second *scathach* nanny, asks. "Just ta' tide the wee *bairn* over until ya' ken' set' a spell?"

"No. I'm ready for a break anyway. I'll take Ronin from you if you take Liam off to the kitchen for a snack. I know Cook has made some raisin cookies for him. That should keep him out of trouble for a while."

"What da' ya' say ta' some *blasta fianain* (yummy cookies), Master Liam? Shall we hurry off ta' the kitchen and visit with Cook?" the *scathach* asks my second son. The young nanny, cousin to *Birgit*, hands Ronin to me and holds out her hand toward Liam.

The tyke immediately jumps up and grabs *Niamh's* offered hand, Declan's shaving brush all but forgotten. As he reaches the door to our suite, he turns around and gives me the most innocent of smiles along with a cheerful wave, always the charmer of our "little man clan."

Ronin and I settle in my favorite bedroom nursing chair, the baby happy to be fed, myself grateful to be off my feet and not bending over the massive travel trunk. Although I'm excited at the prospect of returning to Salem, packing for the fall semester in the Mundane world is always a chore, made even more difficult today by the addition of a colicky baby. Peering into the tiny red face, I can't help but smile. Ronin is the child that looks most like me and my dad, the same round head, turned-up nose, and apple-shaped cheeks that give testimony to his Mundane Eastern European background. I wish my father could have seen him before he passed. Despite the illness that took his memory, I believe with all my heart that Edmund Parker would have still recognized Ronin as his "own" through the "call of the blood."

That's not to say that our newest son is a tooth fairy like his Mama. As it was with Dylan and Liam, except for a few human facial features, Ronin Alasdair Fitzpatrick *Nuada* falls heavily to the *Sidhe* side of his genetic make-up, complete with high forehead, slightly pointed ears, and, if the Houses mages are to be believed, an impressive vein of magical ability. It seems that Fate has destined me to a family experience centered on male testosterone and Fae magic.

It also wasn't any kind of "plan" that gave us three children in five years. Four, actually, if you count my Tax Man's half-brother, *Oisin,* who we consider as one of our "own." Truthfully, because Declan and I "found" each other later than sooner, children were never a guarantee in our relationship. Issues with infertility have run rampant among Fae couples for at least three Other-worldly generations, and if conception does miraculously take place, it's usually for parents under the age of 30, even those with a partially Mundane bloodline like the two of us share. We were over-the-moon grateful when Dylan was born, and doubly thrilled when his brother Liam followed a few years later. But at the ages of 40 for Declan and nearly 38 for me, ages considered to be long-in-the-tooth for Fae baby-making, we were both amazed when Ronin came to be, conceived on an anniversary trip to the Mundane Irish shore, and born earlier this Spring. No one can say that Lord and Lady *Nuada* aren't doing their patriotic duty for the future population of *I Idir*.

I am interrupted in my thoughts by a knock at our bedroom door. Throwing a blanket over myself and Ronin, I answer, "Come in."

Dylan pushes his way into the room, wearing boy-sized leather boots and little leggings coated in a thick layer of mud, with *Birgit* right behind him. "Look Mama," he says with a dose of pride as he shoves a glass jar toward me, "I've caught two fine tadpoles! *Birgit* promises they will become big fat, croaky frogs someday. Please ma' bestest Lady *Mathair*, ken' I keep 'em, least 'til they change? I promise they will not escape. I will fix a fine home and take real good care of 'em, Mama."

I look inside the jar. The poor things are very small, and if I recall a random zoology class I took during my undergraduate years, it takes about fourteen weeks for the metamorphosis to take place. We'll be gone from the Otherworld in less than two. I break the news as gently as I can. "Dylan...Honey...it will take the tadpoles another two months or so to change into their toad bodies. We're leaving for the Salem house in eight days."

Disappointment paints his little face, a younger match to my husband's own, right down to the "Cranky Declan" look. "I would rather stay here and take care of the tadpoles, Lady *Mathair*. I donna' want ta' go ta' the Mundane house."

"I thought you were excited about going to a Mundane school like your *Uncail Oisin*. They don't have kinder-garten here in *I Idir*," I counter.

My eldest ponders this statement. Sticking his bottom lip out further, he says, "Then I will just have to take my tadpoles with me to the Mundane world."

"You know that isn't possible, Sweetie. Animals born in the Otherworld can't survive in the Mundane. That's why *Oisin* has to leave Seamus here when we return to Salem," I explain.

In typical five-year-old fashion, his voice takes on a whine. "But why, Mama? We are living things and we can survive in the Mundane world. Why can't Da make it the same far' ma' tadpoles. Ken' he not try some magic on them? He is LORD *Nuada*, after all."

If Declan were here at this moment, I'm sure he'd get a proud papa chuckle over his son's glowing confidence in him. He'd also immediately shut down any of Dylan's whining, an argument tactic the Tax Man has no patience for in either children or adults. And, because he is LORD *Nuada*, his simple "no" would have been the end of any discussion about not returning to Salem and taking tadpoles with us. But Mom was obviously the soft touch and everybody knew it. "Magic isn't the answer to every problem, Dylan. It's important you understand that. Your magic is a gift from the Universe, given to you to use for the good of all; not a free-for-all method of gaining everything you think you need."

"I must know everything about magic, Mama, if I am to be ma' Da's *Mac Nuada*" he says, his little boy chest comically puffed out.

It's hard not to smile at his bravado. If I ever wondered what my Tax Man was like as a boy, I have his mini me standing in front of my eyes. The two of them are so alike in appearance, temperament and personality, I contemplate if, somehow, my half of our son's DNA went AWOL. I look up at *Birgit*, who is working to keep a grin off her face lest she hurt Dylan's pint-sized pride in his heritage. "I thought *Oisin* was going to take him to the creek to look for tadpoles. How did you get roped into the job?" I ask. "I remember you wanted to visit your mother this afternoon."

"That was the plan," the *scathach* replies with a shrug. "However, it seems Master *Oisin* has a "lady love" in the village. He promised Dylan he'd return directly after lunch, but as of yet, he hasn't returned. The little one was growing vera' impatient and I was concerned he'd wander off to the creek on his own, so I took him myself."

Puberty had hit *Oisin* hard. According to Doc Brannigan's age assessment and our desire to give the boy a "real" birthdate, Declan's half-brother had turned thirteen last December, complete with all the growing pains that come with that particular life stage. In line with Fae culture, *Oisin* was only a few months away from full manhood, and although as a second son he wasn't required to partake in The Ritual, the day was considered a milestone and would be celebrated accordingly. The fact that the kid had already begun to "sow his wild oats," literally, all over *I Idir,* made me a tad nervous about returning to the Mundane world with its entirely different view regarding sexuality and reproduction. I was counting on Declan to give his half-brother a good talking to on the subject before the kid embarked on a new adventure in Mundane Junior High School.

As if he'd realized he was being talked about (and

perhaps he did; we weren't completely sure of all magical traits the boy's Elven DNA provided), *Oisin* appeared in the doorway of our bedroom suite. "There ya' be, Dylan! I've been lookin' all over the estate far' ya'. I thought me and you was gonna' go look for *toirpini* (tadpoles)?"

"*Birgit* and I have already gone, *Uncail*," Dylan sniffed, not bothering to hide his hurt feelings. "Ya' took too long ta' come back from the village." He held up the jar to show his treasure. "We found two big ones…but ma' Mama says I ken' no take them with us to Salem."

The teenager's face was flushed and sweaty. I didn't want to even think about the reasons why. I'm pretty sure it wasn't from his guilt at disappointing Dylan. "Aye, yar' Lady *Mathair* is right, wee *Mac Nuada*. Otherworld creatures ken' no cross the veil. 'Tis why I must leave ma' good boy *Seamus* here at *Dun Siorai* when we cross over, though I miss him vera' much every single day."

Oisin is the only one who calls Dylan by his birthright title. Traditionally, that moniker isn't used until the heir completes his Ritual at age 14. All children from titled House families, male or female, are awarded the addition of "Lord" or "Lady" on the event of their fourteenth birthday. Neither my husband nor I truthfully understand why *Oisin* is insistent on using it for Dylan at such a young age, though I suspect it has something to do with the teenager's reluctance to accept the title himself as a "bastard" son of Lord Callum Fitzpatrick. I know for a fact Declan will offer the title to the boy on his next birthday, though I have my doubts *Oisin* will graciously accept it.

"Then you and I should no go ta' Salem, *Uncail Oisin*. We could stay here at *Dun Siorai*! You could stay with

Seamus and I ken' stay with ma' tadpoles! 'Tis a simple fix. You are almost ta' yar' manhood. You ken' be ma' guardian." Dylan suggests, crossing his arms with the bravado of a stubborn five-year old.

Oisin looks at me hopefully. "'Tis not a bad idea, Lady Sister. I could stay right here and care far' our young Lord *Mac.* I'm sure the Academy Headmaster would accept me into the next level of Academy studies earlier than tradition dictates. As you know, I excel in my studies. I would undoubtedly learn more things of importance than within a common Mundane classroom."

"Here now, there'll be no stayin' behind at *Dun Siorai* far' anyone," a male voice interjects from the doorway behind the teenager. "The Mundane school year begins in three weeks and both of ya' lads will be there on the first day, showin' the fortitude and hard work I expect from a son of House *Nuada.*"

MISSING 2

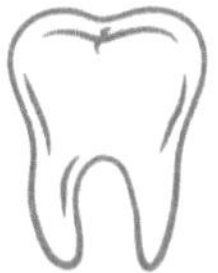

The Lord States His Views

"My Lord, it's good to see you home so early," I answer. "I didn't expect your return until after dinner."

My husband maneuvers through the crowd at the door and bends down to kiss me. "Tis always a pleasure ta' return home, *mo Ros milis* (my sweet Rose), though had I known there was a family meetin' afoot I would have urged my harse' ta' gallop at a faster pace."

I laugh. "No family meeting. Just a friendly discussion between its members."

Declan stands up to address the two boys, his arms gathered at his back in lordly pose. "I hope neither of ya' have been given' ma' Lady a hard time about returnin' to Salem far' yar' Mundane school year. We have discussed at length the importance of ya' both acclimatin' ta' the ways of Mundane culture. If House *Nuda* is ta' be ready to move forward into the future, its sons must be comfortable and competent in both worlds."

Five additional years have done nothing to diminish my Tax Man's physique or vigor. If anything, spending more time here in the Otherworld, where top-notch physical prowess is the expected norm for its leadership, my husband of five years and one month has packed on more muscle mass and strength than when I first met him. And though it can be said that the Tax Man looks mouth-wateringly delicious in his Mundane Brooks Brother business apparel, there's something extra hot about the man in Ren Faire style Otherworldly garb that always gets my libido going.

Both Dylan and *Oisin* look to my husband with the wide eyes of hero worship, though because he is five, my son is the first to raise his concerns, Dylan's comfort level with his "Da" making him more at ease. He shows his father the jar with the blasted tadpoles that started this whole discussion. "I have a pair of *toirpini* (tadpoles), *Athair.* I vera' much wish ta' watch them change into lovely frogs. I have even given them names; *Mairead* and Liam."

All three of us fight not to laugh at the boy's choice of names. Declan is biting his lip as he says, "I see. Those be fine names, lad, but do ya' think it is quite proper ta' name a pair of creek frogs after the Princess of *I Idir* and yar' younger brother? They may take offense at bein' named after yar' water-dwellin' pets."

Dylan has a love/hate relationship with both afore-mentioned children. The youngest granddaughter of the Queen is our eldest son's nemesis and has been since the day he was born. Princess *Mairead* seems to absolutely dote on my boy, but also works very hard to "best him" at every turn, whether it be a game of checkers, simple magical spells, or horsemanship. As for his relationship with his younger brother, when I was pregnant with Liam, Dylan was thrilled at the prospect of being a big brother. Unfortunately, the reality of having a new baby in the house wasn't nearly as fun as Dylan thought it would be, and Liam was, and still is, a thundering mass of constant energy that drains everyone around him, while at the same time, is too young to act as a satisfying playmate for his older brother.

"'Twere it me, ma Lord, I would be most chuffed ta' know someone had named a *torpini* as lovely as these after me. I ken' no see why they would take offense at it."

His Lordship Daddy rubs a hand over his face, which I know from experience is his way of keeping a poker face. "Perhaps ya' are right, son. We once had a piglet that I thought was especially fine. I named him McGibbons after our barn man. The gentleman seemed quite agreeable to the honor."

"A piglet, *Athair*? He must be a fine hog by now. Da' ya' still have "Piggy McGibbons?" Can I see him?" Dylan asks in youthful innocence.

It's my turn to rub my face. I can only imagine what happened to the "Piggy McGibbons." My husband circumvents our son's question, a direct clue that I'm probably right about the history of the pig. "Oh, I was only a vera' wee lad when McGibbons was around. Alas, the hog has passed on to the Universe many seasons ago."

"Passed on to your breakfast plate, I'll bet," I tease mentally. *"Bacon, anyone?"*

His laughter echoes in my head, a sound that always

goes directly to my nether regions, reminding me that my Forever Mate has been gone from home far too many days. Some quality personal time later this evening is a must for the two of us.

I don't bother shielding these thoughts so his laugh drops a few suggestive octaves lower. *I've missed ya' too, Rosie Lass. Perhaps we ken' squeeze in some "alone time" long before evening."*

"Maybe someday I can have a piglet too, Da?" Dylan asks, interrupting our mental sexy talk.

"We will see, lad, though barn animals do not make good pets. The Universe has given them other purposes. Perhaps we can find something else for ya' ta' care far'?" the Tax Man suggests.

"Truly, Da?" he asks in amazement. "Ken' I get a puppy like *Seamus*?"

"One dog in the house is enough, I think. I donna' imagine that *Seamus* would care much far' any competition. I was thinkin' ya' might like ta' train yar' own hawk or falcon…when you are a bit older, of course, and have the strength ta' handle such a bird of prey."

Our eldest claps his hands in glee. "A hawk or a falcon? Of ma' vera' own? Would he wear a little hood like the birds in the Beltane tournaments?"

"Hoodin' yar' bird is part of the trainin' far' both ya' and the bird. When the time comes, ya' will learn everything ya' need ta' know," Declan tells him. "Our Master Gillis is one of the best falconers in *I Idir*. He will guide ya' through every step and help take care of yar' bird while ya' are away at school. But ya' must understand, son, that buildin' a connection with a bird of prey is no easy thing.

Ya' must be vera' dedicated and work vera' hard at it if ya' wish ta' be successful enough to compete in the Beltane tournaments. Are ya' up to such a task?"

"Oh yes, *Athair!* I will follow all of Master Gillis' words and train with ma' bird every day! I promise."

"That is good to hear, son. But first ya' must faithfully attend to yar' schoolwork, both in the Mundane world and at the Academy here in *I Idir.* A son of House *Nuada* must be ready far' anything that he encounters walkin' his path and a good education will be his greatest asset."

My little man puts his hand over his heart and gives Declan a child-like bow. It is the *Sidhe* gesture of love and respect an heir gives his Lord Father. I hadn't even realized that someone had taught Dylan this traditional response. Our son's reaction hits my mate straight in the "feels." I know because I'm feeling it all as well through our personal bond.

"Did ya' hear, Mama? I am ta' get a bird of ma' own when I am bigger! Da says so!"

"Yes, Dylan. I heard. That's very exciting. But remember, your father also said you had to do well at your schoolwork. That includes starting kindergarten on time in Salem."

"I know, Mama. I will be the best *Sidhe* boy in ma' class. Number one!"

"That's lovely to hear, Sweetie, but Da and I only need you to try your very best. You don't have to be 'number one' all the time," I reply, lest we turn our son into another over-the-top competitive soul like his sire.

"On no, Mama. I am to be *Mac Nuada* when I reach

manhood. I must be number one all the time," Dylan says, in all seriousness.

Birgit apparently notices my startled expression because she jumps into the conversation and changes the subject. "Master Dylan, shall we rid ourselves of these muddy clothes and find a more suitable home far' yar' tadpoles? That jar seems much too small far' such grand specimens. By the time we are finished with all that, it will certainly be time for yar' evenin' meal."

"Aye, Birggie," Dylan answers, using his baby name for the nanny. "You are right. This jar is much too small. Will I see you later, Da?" he asks Declan.

"I will come to the nursery before yar' bedtime, lad. I have been savin' up a good tale just for tonight," his father says.

"Will it have pirates?" our son asks.

"Aye...pirates and sea monsters," Declan says with a grin.

"That sounds vera' fine, Da! I ken' hardly wait! Maybe *Liam* will like this one and not bother us like he usually does," Dylan replies, a reference to his younger brother's tendency to lose interest in things and make his own fun.

"I believe even our Liam will love this story," their father answers.

Happy with Declan's promise, our son scuttles over to hug his father and kiss me before joining the nanny at the door to our suite. "Will ya' be wantin' afternoon tea, ma Lord?" the *scathach* asks my husband.

"That would be perfect, *Birgit.* Tell Cook that I'd prefer a heavy afternoon tea here in our quarters rather than a formal evening meal in the dining room. We are no expectin' any guests at *Dun Siorai* this evenin' and after a day's hard ride, I am mostly lookin' forward ta' a quiet evenin' with ma' Lady and our family," his Lordship advises. "If she has already prepared a grand table, tell her to share it among the staff. I should not want any food ta' go ta' waste."

"I will let her know, ma' Lord," the nanny says with a ghost of a smile, knowing full-well that Declan has been away for several days and that the two of us want time alone together. Our passion as bonded mates is no secret at *Dun Siorai* and I've long gotten over being embarrassed by it. Most couples would be green with envy over what my Tax Man and I have together. I remain forever grateful to the Universe for matching us, and five years later, I'm still head-over-heels in love with the man, as I believe he is with me.

Birgit and Dylan exit the room, leaving us alone with *Oisin*. "How fare thee, brother?" Declan asks. "Have you finished your summer session at the Academy yet?"

"I am well, ma' Lord. The summer session ended a week ago. I expect a most satisfactory review from my Master Mages," the teen-ager says. *Oisin* shifts position and looks away, a tell-tale sign that I've come to learn means he has something to say that he knows one or the other of us will take issue with. Declan sees it too.

"Is there something on yar' mind, brother?" my husband asks.

The boy shifts position again. "I was hoping I might convince ya', ma Lord, ta' let me stay at *Dun Siorai* this fall and winter instead of returning to Salem."

Even though the boy has already brought this idea up,

it shocks me that he continues the discussion after Declan's negative response. Not only is it unusual for him to counter his brother's agenda, it's odd because *Oisin* has always loved his time spent in the Mundane world. After the hard-fought treaties finally allowed us the safety of returning home, Declan's half-brother became a number one fan of the technology and freedom from Fae protocol that Salem offered. He'd done amazingly well education wise in the private Fae grammar school in which he'd been enrolled and seemed to have a normal amount of peer socialization among both his Fae classmates and human friends. I wondered if this unusual request had something to do with his new beginnings at Salem's large, public high school, though *Oisin* himself had been the one begging to leave the security of the Fae private school for a public education along the lines of what Declan and I had experienced.

"Does this have anything to do with starting at the public school, Hon?" I ask. "There's no shame if you don't feel quite ready to attend an entirely Mundane school. There's a private Fae junior high school in Swampscott. You'd have to take the bus there every day, but maybe you'd be more comfortable within a school of Otherworldy kids."

The thirteen-year-old gives me one of those adolescent eye rolls that began about the time he turned twelve. "My Lady, you insult me by your insinuation that I am fearful of mingling with Mundanes. It is a ridiculous statement."

Apparently, my Tax Man doesn't like the tone his younger brother is taking with me. He raises that one damn eyebrow and in full Lordly voice declares, "I might suggest you lose that disrespectful tone with ma' Lady, Master *Oisin*. You are fully aware that your Lady Sister has only your best interests at heart. It is she alone that you should thank for getting you to this point in your education."

Oisin flushed a deep red. The boy worships Declan and to be scolded by his Lord and brother cut him deep. "I meant nothing rude toward ma' Lady Sister, ma' Lord." he turns toward me and takes my hands in his. "Truly, dear Rosie, I mean no disrespect. I am just frustrated that everyone at *Dun Siorai* continues ta' treat me like a child when I am only four months from manhood."

"If that's what you feel I am doing, *Oisin*, then I am sincerely sorry. I suppose the *mathair* in me is finding it hard to let the little boy in you go. That doesn't explain, though, why you've changed your mind about returning to Salem with us," I say. "You've always seemed so...so happy there. Why the sudden change?"

He turns a deeper shade of pink. "I have found a Lady of my own. I believe she is ma' 'one and only.' Ma' true love."

"I see," my husband replies. "Findin' yar' soul mate is no small feat, brother...especially with so few years behind ya'."

The teen interrupts before Declan can finish, something he rarely does which is testament to how passionate he feels about the situation. "I know ya' believe I am too young ta' have such strong feelins', ma' Lord. Yet, I swear ta' ya'...what I feel far' *Laoise* is the real thing. We are both mad in love. She lives in the village. Her father and brothers are metal workers."

The Tax Man, ever blunt, asks, "Have ya' laid with this girl, *Oisin?*"

The kid looks at me and then at my husband, mortified that his brother would ask such a personal question about sex in front of me. Unfortunately, sometimes Declan can be...well...Declan. "There is no reason ta' be embarrassed over this conversation, *Oisin,*" he says. "The joinin' of a Fae couple is as natural as breathin'. 'Tis the will of the Universe. Besides, we are all family here. What ya' say ta' me ken' be said ta' ma' Lady as well. We are Eternally Bonded and have no secrets between us."

At this point, I'm pretty sure the poor kid wants to be anywhere but here. "No, ma' Lord," he mumbles into his chest, too embarrassed to look anywhere but the floor. "We have yet to join. *Laoise* believes it is best ta' wait until I reach the age of manhood and am eligible for handfastin' Then she says we will make a sound decision about ar' feelings' far' one another."

Laoise sounds like one smart cookie. I like her already. Still, I hope with every maternal bone in my body that my mate doesn't ask the kid what I think he's going to ask him. *"Don't you dare ask him if she will be his 'first,' Tax Man. He's mortified enough!"* I hiss at him in his head.

"Duh," He responds. It always throws me off a bit when his Lordship uses modern Mundane slang. It's so out of character with the Otherworldly Fae Lord personae he takes on when he is in *I Idir.*

"I respect yar' honesty, brother, and I have no doubt that what ya' feel far' *Laoise* consumes yar' every thought'," he tells the boy. "Still, yar' education needs ta' be yar' life's focus. Ta' be able ta' study within the Mundane world is a fleetin' gift, and you, months away from your manhood and yar' title, should understand that yar' first responsibility lies with *I Idir* and yar' House. You will travel to the Mundane world with yar' family and begin yar' secondary studies as planned. If this girl shares yar' feelin' as ya' say she does, then she will wait ta' see ya' at *Samhain*."

Oisin opens his mouth to protest, but then abruptly closes it. Anyone who truly knows Lord Declan Fitzpatrick *Nuada* is fully aware that once he's made a decision, he will never change his mind, and to try and force a different outcome means taking on the risk of incurring "Cranky Declan." "As ya' wish, ma' Lord," the teenager says, then gives my husband and I a curt bow before stomping out of the room.

"Well, that went well," I say with sarcasm.

"'Twas no reason ta' sugar coat ma' answer, Lass. No doubt the girl will be his first, and I wad' guess sooner than later if Nature has its way. 'Tis simply the will of the Universe. He will forever remember her, but I still hold to the belief that she is not his 'one and only.' And if I am wrong, and she is exactly that, then the two will find each other no matter what transpires in between. Ya' know as well as I that this ability to travel back and forth between the two worlds could change at any time. The treaty is a fragile promise, especially with my *athair* working covertly behind the scenes to cause mayhem."

Under the shadow of the blanket, Ronin has finished nursing and fallen into his late afternoon nap. Of all of my three, this wee boy is the one who is most happy on a set schedule. You could set your watch by when Ronin is hungry, sleeping, or pooping. I get up and lay him in the family cradle near our bed where I guarantee he'll snooze peacefully for a good two or three hours before needing another feeding.

Declan has slipped off his shirt and locked the door to our bedroom in anticipation of some "alone time" for he and I. "You do realize they're going to deliver the tea tray you ordered," I tease.

He grins as he kisses the back of my neck and begins to undo my braid, one of his favorite foreplay activities. "Aye. And they will note the locked door and leave the tray outside in the hall. As they always do."

Ronin isn't the only one with a "set schedule." "I thought you said you were hungry?" I ask.

"I am hungry...only not far' tea, *banrion mo chroi* (Queen of my Heart)," he whispers in my ear as he gathers me up under the knees and heads for our bed.

MISSING 3

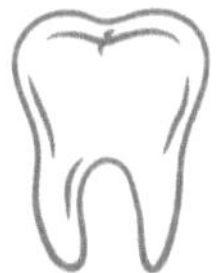

Bad News on Wings

I'm enjoying a twilight style, post-coitus doze when I feel the weight shift on the mattress, then hear Declan as he slips on his pants. He pads across the room, careful not to wake the still napping Ronin, and retrieves the tea tray outside our bedroom door. Opening one eye, I watch him place the tray next to the bedside table. "Shall I fix you a cup, Love," he asks?

I stretch and yawn before sitting up. "That would be lovely, thank you. I suppose we can't just lie around here naked for hours, can we?"

My Tax Man shakes his head. "Sadly, no. I promised Dylan a bedtime story and no doubt *Liam* will expect his nightly ride on ma' back. Then, I'm ta' meet Duncan so we ken' go over the border schedule for next week, all while still leavin' some quality time for Ronin. But, I am willin', ma' Love, ta' take a rain check on naked loungin' later tonight if yar' up far' it." He leans across the bed and hands me my cup and saucer. Sipping it, I make a sour face before answering. He notices and frowns. "Is that a 'no,' then…ta' ma' offer of a rain check?"

"Oh, heavens no, Sweetie. Of course, I'll take your rain check. Always. I only made a face because the tea is cold."

"Ah," he answers, then waves a hand across my cup and the tea pot itself. Steam rises from the spout. Testing a sample, I reply, "Perfect. Thank you, Tax Man." The fact that Declan uses his magic to warm my tea is a big hairy deal and part of his "love language" towards me. My husband makes it a point to limit the use of his powerful magic for everyday "chores," finding it "disrespectful." His metaphysical abilities are sacred to him, a spiritual gift he doesn't take lightly, and his willingness to share them for my benefit is endearing.

He tucks into his food and I consider asking him to fix me a plate so I don't have to get out of bed, but decide against it. A cup of tea is one thing, but crumbs and grease stains among the bed linens would be abhorrent to my "Mr. Clean." Instead, I reach for my robe and join him at the table. It's only then do I notice how exhausted he appears; the dark circles under his eyes, the slouchy posture, the grim expression. "Tough few days?" I ask.

Knowing it's my favorite, Declan slices a hefty wedge from a small wheel of Irish Gubbeen and hands it to me. Sighing, he says, "Aye. There were three more Mundane deaths on *I Idir* land; two men and one woman who appear ta' be from somewhere in the Middle East, though none of us could positively identify which specific country they call home. They carried no identification, so attemptin' ta' send back the remains becomes nearly impossible. According ta' Robyn, they'd been dead about 18 hours, meanin' they must have arrived in the Other-world earlier in the week."

"Why do they keep coming if they know full well they'll sicken and die?" I comment, frustrated at the blatant stupidity and greed exhibited by our human counterparts. "I had hoped these tragedies would end with the signing of the treaties."

"That was the hope, Lass, but so far, that has proved ta' be a false assumption. In truth, the commitment of the Mundane world leaders towards the treaties they signed with *I Idir* and Avalon is lukewarm at best, and that fully includes the United States. After The Morrigan's demonstration of her power and what havoc it ken' rend ta' their precious technology, those larger countries had little choice but ta' agree ta' her terms. Although the documents seemingly protect the sanctity of life of the Fae living and doin' business in the Mundane world, it does nothing ta' curb the Mundanes' all-encompassin' desire ta' breach the Veil. No doubt they believe if they ken' take The Morrigan on in her own space, they will have a better chance of being successful in claiming *I Idir* and Avalon as one of their own colonies. 'Tis nearly impossible to take control of a kingdom that you are unable to physically spend time in. It makes invasion of a foreign land impossible."

I shudder at the word "invasion." The thought of hordes of armed Mundane soldiers claiming the peaceful *I Idir* countryside is abhorrent. "You think they would've learned their lesson," I say, adding a slice of thinly shaved smoked goose to my cheese. "With all the chaos Herself rained down on them."

Six months after Declan was rescued from the North Koreans by The Morrigan, who, at that time, had succeeded in decimating their cutting-edge genetics lab in the capital city of Pyongyang, was also able to crash several of their "Dear Leader's" financial holdings. Thinking they could prevail where the North Koreans had not, Russia and China both decided to kidnap a large group of mixed Fae blood persons off the streets of Washington D.C., Paris, and London, all for the sole purpose of harvesting Otherworldly stem cells. Moved to fury, the Celtic Goddess of War and Destruction hit the Mundane world in retaliation; not with fire and destruction like she did with North Korea, but with a total disruption of their technology network using a powerful type of magical magnetic interference.

On this occasion, Herself didn't limit vengeance to the main culprits, but incapacitated technology worldwide, basically shutting down all their satellites and networks. Life for the Mundanes across the globe came to a screeching halt. In less than three days, a treaty had been hammered out by the world leaders, the Mundanes absolutely reliant on their technology and desperate to keep knowledge of the origins of the disaster, as well as the reality of an Otherworld dimension, a locked secret from their populations. It was for this reason alone that our little family was allowed to safely return to Salem. At the time, I wasn't completely naive enough to believe that this would end all the dysfunction between the two worlds, but I was grateful to at least pretend things would be okay…if only for the time being.

"The Mundanes have been determined ta' conquer the Otherworld for at least four hundred years, Love. It is part of their human culture, this need to conquer at the misery of others. I donna' believe they will ever stop tryin' ta' take what is not theirs," his Lordship pontificates as he loads a scone with fresh goat cheese and honey.

When Declan says things like this it always stirs up my human loyalty. Granted, I've come to have more affection and respect for my Fae roots than I had before meeting my husband, but I also witness plenty of the same exact behavior from his Otherworldly counterparts. There is no limit to the bickering and backstabbing between the Houses of the Ruling Council, and the neighboring countries surrounding *I Idir* would like nothing more than to see The Morrigan knocked off her high pedestal.

The Tax Man and I have had this go around before, and I'm not in the mood to debate this evening, especially when he's so physically tired. Taking on the mantle as House *Nuada's* Lord has been a big change for all of us. True to his word, Declan has done everything possible to try and make this work for our family, which is no small feat. We both firmly believe that a dual education in both the Mundane and the Otherworld is the right choice for our children.

Therefore, we return to Salem every August for the beginning of the traditional Mundane school year. Although Declan goes back and forth between worlds every few days, I stay in Salem to keep a regular schedule for the kids. However, we still return to *Dun Siorai* for all the Fae holidays as well as the Mundane sanctioned school breaks. Come May, when Mundane school lets out for the summer, the children and I travel to *Dun Siora* and *Oisin* begins a summer session at the Academy to reinforce his magical abilities. Our boys will all do the same when they reach the required age of eight.

In my case, I wisely took on two more pediatric dentists to my practice, as well as four more hygienists and an assistant for Mel, with the understanding that from Mid-May until August, Dr. Rosie Parker-Fitzpatrick, would be unavailable to her patients, too busy "visiting" my husband's extended family "in Ireland." I still do some work with the Tooth Fairy Corps, mainly with training, and of course, there's our never-mentioned-out-loud "spy work" for the Black Knight. Yes, it's a crazy, busy schedule, but not unlike the problems faced by most working parents in the Mundane World. Thank the goddesses for *Birgit* and *Niamh*. They make this so much easier for our clan and give Declan and I a much-appreciated piece of mind regarding the safety of our four children.

No doubt my husband can sense my annoyance over his Mundane prejudice. I rarely shield anything from him. Thankfully, he takes the same high road as myself and doesn't bring it up. Instead, he changes the topic to that of the upcoming *Lammas* festival. "Is the House ready far' the celebration in a few days? I am sorry, Rosie Lass. I realize that, as of late, I have been away more than I have been home, and the hospitality duties of House *Nuada* have mainly fallen ta' you. I hope ya' will forgive ma' lack of participation."

Lammas is a Fae holiday celebrated on the first of August commemorating the harvesting of the first grain, mainly that which is used for wheat and corn flour. Its ancient name is *"Lughnasadh"* after the old god, Lugh, and it is a day dedicated to honoring his spirit. The celebration includes feasting with friends and family, a table heavy with grain-based delicacies, along with harvest altars, crafts, dancing, and, of course, tournament games for the ever-competitive Fae population. Whereas the games at Beltane are focused on the men's sports, *Lammas* features *I Idir's* women competing against one another.

I have never been the athletic type. Never once did I go out for any teams during my school days, nor did I play "just for the fun of it." My favorite position is, and always has been, "Left Out." When I became Lady *Nuada,* as well as an active member of the Black Knight's espionage network, it was imperative that I learn to at least properly defend myself like any titled Fae woman. I trained daily with Duncan and the Lord Warrior for several months, both of whom showed a mountain of patience and graciousness with my novice standing and lack of physical agility.

Now, should the need arise, I can at least handle my own with a dirk, use a women's weight longsword, and if necessary, arm myself with the bow and arrow, though my draw arm is weak due to a bad break I experienced in high school. I'm no expert by any means, and I sure as hell don't belong in any public tournaments showcasing my lack of skill. In the past, because of the timing of my pregnancies and post-partum limitations, I could only participate in one *Lammas* Games, that competition taking place a few months after Dylan's first birthday. It was an embarrassing disaster with me coming in last place in all three events. I was deeply mortified with my showing despite the Tax Man's reassurance that he was ever so proud of me "far' givin' it an honest try."

Since he's brought up the holiday, I try to focus on the other aspects of the festival. "It's fine, my Lord. I fully realize you have your hands full. The rest of us have it covered. Cook and I have already developed a fabulous menu for the banquet, *Birgit* has organized a group of House ladies in the making of the corn husk dolls and wheat wreaths for the altar, and I'm nearly finished with the needlework piece I plan on gifting the Queen as House *Nuada's* royal token. You needn't worry about a thing, Hon."

He leans across the small table to kiss me, tasting like honey and goat cheese. "House *Nuada* is blessed ta' have such a clever and capable Lady at its helm. And I am the luckiest soul in the Universe ta' share ma' humble life with ya."

I can never help blushing when Declan says mega-romantic stuff like this. It makes me want to crawl right back in that bed and forget about food and drink. "You make my head spin, Tax Man. I might just have to interrupt your meal…if you get my drift."

He laughs but doesn't stop filling his plate. The man wasn't kidding about being hungry. I don't have time to try another seduction tactic because the next question out of his mouth dampens my libido like an ice-cold shower. "Will you be enterin' the games this year, Rosie Love?"

I start by licking my lips, then realize it's my "tell"

when I'm about to fib. Changing tactics, I look him straight in the eye, put up my very best shield, and try to look believably sad. "I'm afraid I won't be able to participate this year, Sweetie. Sadly, when I delivered Ronin, I… uhmmm…strained some muscles in my pelvic floor. Doc doesn't want to see me doing any additional damage so… uhmm… any strenuous exercise is probably out for now."

It wasn't a complete lie. Ronin did have an exceptionally large head, and Robyn was forced to use forceps in those final minutes. Plus, it is true that I strained some muscles down there, but the Doc never mentioned a word about limiting activity. In fact, he suggested a list of exercises I might do to strengthen that area. Still, I'm pretty sure Declan won't be up for discussing my lady parts with his comrade in arms so I'm convinced that I'm "safe" with my stretch of the truth.

When his expression turns to one of alarm, I do feel a tad bit guilty, but damn, I really don't want to suffer through those games again. "Oh Lass, I'm so sorry," he says, putting his hand over mine. "I didn't know ya' had hurt yourself deliverin' our wee boy. Ya' never let on." Like a lightbulb going on his head, my husband looks over to our messy bed and adds, "Hell, Lass…I'm not hurtin' ya' when we…" he lets the words trail off, his face a mask of concern.

Good grief. I should have realized the Tax Man would make a mountain out of a molehill over any perceived issues with my health. That's just the way he rolls, and I don't relish the idea of forced celibacy or even tentative lovemaking with an overly cautious hubby. That whole way of thinking needs to be immediately nipped in the bud. "Oh, gracious no, Declan. You're not hurting me in the least. Sex uses different…muscles." It sounds dumb even to my ear, but I'm too far in to stop now. "It's… strenuous activity…stretching and pulling …that sort of thing that the Doc wants me to try and avoid."

My husband tilts his head and views me questioningly, and for a second, I think I might be busted. But then he just shrugs and says, "Of course, Lass, you must do exactly as Robyn tells ya'. No games far' you this year! Should ya' even be strainin' yourself with all this packin' for the trip home. Perhaps I should have the staff come do it far' ya'?"

Packing for Salem helps me mentally prepare for the next several months "at home," and I like the job of doing it myself. Besides, the Fae are terrible gossips, and I don't need the whole staff discussing my "broken lady parts." "That's a nice offer, Sweetie, but I'm taking it slow and easy. I promise I won't exert myself. I want to be sure I'm taking everything we need."

Once again, I realize I sound lame, and I have a huge amount of guilt about feeling the need to fib, but the Tax Man nods and goes back to eating his meal which hopefully means the end of this discussion. We enjoy the lavish spread in content silence until there is tapping at the window glass, signaling the arrival of a raven-gram. Declan automatically rises and walks to the window to receive the message, knowing full well I detest those beady-eyed harbingers of mostly bad news.

He scans the parchment and makes a face. "Who's it from?" I ask, suddenly not hungry anymore.

"It's from my *mathair*. She wants to meet with us both this evening after the evening meal," he says.

Initially, I inwardly groan. "After the evening meal," in Fae culture, means late; 10:00 PM or after. Declan and I had hoped to share quiet time as a family and a couple, even opting for a heavy afternoon tea rather than the late-served evening meal. His mother's request puts an end to that. Then, another thought pokes at my brain. "Why such formality? Lady *Siobhan* is here regularly to visit with the children. Couldn't she just talk to us while she's already at *Dun Siorai*? It's odd for her to send a raven-gram in advance of a visit. She usually just shows up without even asking if it's a good time while expecting us to drop everything and accommodate her." All my red flags are flying over this odd message, and I can't help but ramble.

"It is because she is asking far' a 'formal' meetin' with Lord and Lady *Nuada*…not with her son and daughter-in-law."

"Whatever does that mean?" I ask, a sinking feeling building in my stomach.

"Nothin' good, Lass. Nothin' good." he answers.

MISSING 4

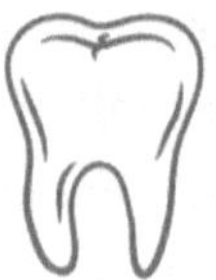

Asking Motherly Things

I AM one hundred percent NOT a morning person. I'll hit that alarm at least four times before I get moving, and even then, I'll need a long hot shower and plenty of caffeine to begin to feel ambitious. With that in mind, one would assume that I would naturally be a night owl, capable of all kinds of useful nocturnal activity. Wrongo. By 10 PM, I fight to keep my eyes open during formal, evening meals. Nowadays, when the kids are all finally down for the night, their sleep-loving Mama is always right behind them, hoping to get a few solid hours before Ronin wakes for his next feeding. This is the reason I'm over-the-top annoyed with my mother-in-law for not only demanding this ridiculous meeting so late in the day, but even more so because she's unapologetically late.

It is nearly 11:30 PM before Lady *Siobhan* Donnely Fitzpatrick *Nuada* graces us with her presence. In keeping with the Fae culture of hospitality, Declan's *mathair* is offered an array of late evening refreshments, which in turn, keeps the kitchen staff up past their usual working hours, a situation I will definitely hear complaints about in the morning. How my husband can remain so patient while Dragon Mama sips his best port and calmly nibbles on summer grapes and toasted hazelnuts is beyond me. *"Can't you do anything to speed her up?"* I mentally ask. *"We're both dead on our feet."*

His Lordship frowns. I'm not sure if it's meant for me or his mother. "Perhaps ya' could get to the reason ya' wanted ta' meet so formally with ma' Lady and I, Lady *Mathair*. The hours is late and Ronin will be needin' his feedin' soon."

Siobhan sighs and places her near empty glass on the table. I hope to hell my husband doesn't offer to refill it. "I certainly didn't mean to keep you from your chamber, Lord and Lady *Nuada,* though it would have been entirely rude of me to not accept your gracious offer of hospitality."

"I ken' no understand why you would need a meetin' steeped in protocol," Declan counters. "Since ya' have moved ta' *Crann Bethadh,* ya' have had free reign ta' come and go within *Dun Siorai* as ya' please, *Mathair*. Could ya' not have just spoken up on one of those occasions? I must confess that the formalness of yar' visit has caused me some concern."

My mother-in-law glances cautiously towards me and then back at my husband, which I'll admit, gives me apprehension as well. It's my guess she's here to ask for money, which is never an easy subject with my Tax Man. I won't go as far as to say he's cheap, but he does keep a tight rein on his financial holdings. If only it had been as simple as that.

"Do you remember, my Lord, when you were being held by those vile terrorists and I came to the Mundane world to care for your *Mo Shiorghra* and unborn heir?" she questions.

The Tax Man frowns again. This time I know it's directed toward her. "Of course, Lady *Mathair*. I could never forget your devotion to ma' own. I have repeatedly offered ya' ma' gratitude along with the best racing mare in my stable and her newly born male colt, who has since become *I Idir's* most coveted stud. Is there something more ya' desire far' protectin' yar' first born grandson?" I hear the steely edge in his tone. Lady *Siobhan* has made a sizable financial gain from those two horses, not to mention the ever-important Fae bragging rights when the stallion takes first place in every race. I'm sure my husband thinks his "debt" has been generously paid over something his *mathair* swore she did out of the concern in her heart.

In return, His Lordship receives an equally scathing look that resembles his own. "I am insulted to think my own son believes me to be a crass *brabusai* (profiteer). Dylan is of my bloodline, my first-born grandchild, and heir to House *Nuada*. To say I would not sacrifice my life for him is slander."

Confusion crosses Declan's face. He doesn't under-stand where his *mathair* is going with this conversation any more than I do. "I apologize if I have jumped to false conclusions, Lady *Mathair*. I am lost as to why you'd bring those horrid days to mind. I would hope you might get to the point so I ken' understand what it is ya' want from me."

"It pains me to know that no matter what I say or do, you will always think the worst of me, *Deaglan*. Still, I suppose I should explain my need to return to such painful memories. I did what I did during those dark days for your Lady and your heir because I am your *mathair*, the one who brought you into this world and the one who only seeks the best Path for her bloodline. Despite the poison your damned sire poured into your heart towards me, a mother loves her child from the moment he or she is conceived. I need for you to fully understand this."

In all the time I've known both Declan and his mother, I have never heard her use the "L word" in regards to my husband. Or the rest of her children, to be brutally honest. Though Lady *Siobhan* constantly coos and cuddles all three of her grandsons, never raising her voice and spoiling them on every occasion, I have never heard her tell any of them that she actually loved them. The fact that she's using the word now causes me no little consternation.

Her declaration also brings on the Tax Man's poker face, the one he uses when he doesn't wish to share one iota of what he's really thinking or feeling. Plus, he's pulled up one hell of a mental shield, ten times stronger than anything I could ever conjure up, locking me completely out. "I am losin' patience with yar' word games, Lady *Siobhan*. State yar' request of House *Nuada's* Lord, or be on yar' way back ta' *Crann Bethadh*."

I've heard mother and son go at each other on so many occasions that I've lost count. Despite the tentative truce they forged after Dylan's birth, they still bring out the worst in each other, while being more alike than they'd ever care to admit. But my husband's words are spoken in a voice so cold and commanding, without a shred of empathy, that I can't help but recall memories of his father, Callum Fitzpatrick. It's a thought that makes my stomach roll.

Even Dragon Mama appears a bit stunned at her son's frigid demeanor. This is definitely a Declan she hasn't faced before. "Very well, Lord *Nuada*. I will state my request. I am here to ask your consideration in rescinding your sister Meghan's exile; I need you to let my youngest daughter...your own sister...return to her rightful home and title."

I have grown in my "Fae skin" since handfasting Declan, and even more so since becoming Lady of House *Nuada*. Even so, I don't believe I will ever be able to reign my emotions in as tight as the *Sidhe* are able. I don't need a mirror to know that every ounce of shock, revulsion, and fear is written plainly across my face.

Meghan is Declan's youngest sister. The one who tried to kill me before my handfasting to her older brother. Not once, but three different times; first by poisoning my salad with a toxic bug, secondly by cutting the straps holding my horse's saddle, and thirdly by attempting to put a venomous snake in my bed. Her reasoning for such vile actions? I was "taking up too much of her brother's time" and she was jealous.

Because I was the *Mo Shiorghra* of House *Nuada's* heir, his "One and Only" Fated Mate and essential to the House's bloodline, it was my right, under *I Idir's* sacred law, to ask for either her execution or her exile from the kingdom. There was no way I would ever be party to capital punishment of any kind, so Meghan Fitzpatrick was exiled to Avalon, forbidden to return to her home country or to use her House title as "Lady," and for five years, this had been her fate. Now, her formidable and politely active mother was rallying to her cause, seeking some kind of pardon from my husband and I, though it was clear she was mainly directing her monumental request towards him.

I was expecting Declan to be firm in his negative response. Or at least register some shock at this ridiculous notion, telling her, "You're joking, right?" Or something along that line. Instead, he answers blandly, his masked emotions still in place. "You have wasted yar' time in coming here, Lady *Siobhan*. Meghan was sentenced by Her Majesty. I have neither the power nor the right ta' commute her punishment. Ya' best be takin' yar' beggin' ta' the Queen."

It wasn't the answer I'd hoped for. Not this bland, half-hearted excuse. The Tax Man was basically "passing the buck" when he should have stood firm with a strongly worded, negative response. *"Seriously, Declan? That's the best you can do?"* The question bounces off his mental shields and echoes in my head. I give him my best stink-eye which he purposely ignores. Dragon Mama doesn't look my way either. No doubt she has known from the start that I wouldn't be in her corner over this topic.

"I have spoken to Her Majesty. As I belong to House *Nuada*, she has decided that the decision must be made by the Lord and Lady themselves," his mother explains.

"*Of course, she did,*" I tersely think, then wait for Herself's response in my head. None comes and I am unsure as to whether it's because The Morrigan is simply ignoring my sarcastic comment, or the spell she used to enter my mind when my husband was kidnapped is slowly beginning to fade. In the beginning, I heard her all the time. Over the past year or so, her comments, scolding and laughter have slowly begun to decrease. One can only hope this is the beginning of the end. What I did for Declan's safe return I'd do again in an instant, but it hasn't been an easy ride having the goddess of war and destruction in your head at every turn.

If his Lordship is annoyed or surprised at The Morrigan's dropping the problem in his lap, he doesn't show it in any form. His face is expressionless and his voice is without emotion. "I see. Then you should know, Lady *Siobhan*, that my Lady and I are not prepared to make a decision of such magnitude so quickly. We both shall require time and discussion before giving you an answer."

"I've expected as much, Lord *Nuada*," Dragon Mama says, playing the protocol game as artfully as her son. "I appreciate that you are willing to give my request such honest consideration. Meghan is heartily sorry for her actions toward Lady *Nuada*, and makes the claim that it was her traitorous sire who pushed her to do what she did. She is nearly 21 years old now and sees things as an adult. She has been shunned in Avalon and has little chance of finding a proper mate or the possibility of offspring. She needs to come home to *I Idir*, to her mathair and *deirfuiracha* (sisters), in order to have any chance at a happy, fruitful future. Surely, she has suffered enough for the sins of her damnable *athair*? That foul male has always been at the center of all of House *Nuada's* troubles."

No one has more reason to detest…no hate…Callum Fitzpatrick more than myself. The evil bastard offered up his child…his only son and heir…to the North Koreans as a lab rat. He willfully killed *Oisin's* mother and ripped the boy from her womb. Then, a few years later, impregnated and murdered Marcy Kilcrabtree and her unborn child in cold blood. I look forward to the day the former Lord of House *Nuada* pays for all his hideous decisions. I may even disregard my moral aversion to capital punishment and be fully present when he loses his traitorous head under the Black Knight's sword. Still, I call bullshit on Lady *Siobhan's* claim that her father was the sole reason Meghan Fitzpatrick tried to murder me. The kid was a complete narcissistic psycho and I have no reason to think she's become a different person while in exile. Over these past five years, I've heard plenty of nasty gossip about her outrageous behavior in Avalon. A leopard doesn't change its spots. Especially not a *Sidhe* one with both Callum's and *Siobhan's* DNA in her bloodline.

"We will take that into consideration, ma' Lady. But as I have said, we are not willin' ta' make a decision this vera' evening," my husband replies.

"Do you know when you might? Make a decision, I mean," she asks, not bothering to hide her impatience and frustration.

Declan finally shows some emotion by narrowing his eyes at her. "Why the rush for an answer, *Mathair*? What is it you are not telling me?"

Lady *Siobhan* doesn't wait for her son to refill her glass, instead reaching for the crystal decanter herself and pouring a generous ounce into her snifter that she drinks in one gulp. "I've had the runes read for Meghan. The House mages have foretold that your sister's Path lies here in *I Idir* and that she must return to her place of birth as soon as possible to fulfill her destiny."

"How convenient." I think to myself.

I open my mouth to express my opinion but the Tax Man cuts me off. "And you have told Her Majesty this vera' thing? About the prediction of the mages?"

"Aye. All she would say was that she trusted Lord and Lady *Nuada* to make the right decision. You know 'tis best not to pressure her for more than she is willing to give. Meghan's very future rests with you and your gracious Lady," Siobhan replies.

"Hmmm...I'm suddenly 'gracious' now, am I?" I smell a set-up, but with everyone's shields at mega-brick-wall-status, I can't get my thoughts to my husband's mind without Dragon Mama hearing them as well. Nor can I get a better read on what's really going on here. If I've learned anything about Fitzpatrick family dynamics, it's that you watch every word you say publicly because they all come back, at some point, to bite you in the ass.

Declan glances at me and lowers his mental shields. *"I know ya' are bustin' at the seams with your feelins', Rosie, ma' Love. 'Tis best ta' wait until we are alone. Confrontin' ma' mathair when we are both exhausted and emotional will not help the situation."*

I can't help but frown. Okay maybe it was more like a pout than a frown, but hell, I've held my piece long enough. *"I can't believe you didn't just tell her no from the very start...Meghan can absolutely not return to I Idir! She tried to kill me, Declan! Three different times! And as far as me being emotional...well damn! Don't you think I have every right to be?"*

My One and Only doesn't answer me. He addresses his mother instead. "As I said earlier, Lady *Siobhan*, ma' Lady and I will carefully examine all that has been said here this evenin'. As Lord of House *Nuada*, I will give ya' our decision soon."

"How soon?" his *mathair* asks, because, like her only son, Dragon Mama never knows when to leave well enough alone.

"Before *Lammas*," his Lordship replies. "I donna' wish to have this hangin' over the House before the start of a sacred holiday."

Lammas is in three days. In my opinion, we don't need a full three days to make such an obvious decision. My mind is made up, and I can't see Declan disagreeing. He was, after all, the one who said publicly he never wished to see his sister again. However, I don't say a word. I will grant my husband this token of patience, so I just stand there with my lips pressed in a thin line.

"That is most agreeable, my Lord. I believe in my heart that you and your *Mo Shiorghra* will make the right decision," *Siobhan* says, as she stands to take her leave. She kisses her son on the cheek, and then me, an action I construe as part of her "loving mother act," then quickly lets herself out of Declan's study to return to *Crann Bethadh*.

MISSING 5

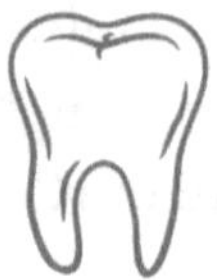

From Night to Light

I HAVE ENOUGH OTHERWORLDLY savvy to know not to discuss sensitive topics in the halls of *Dun Siorai*. The Tax Man and I remain silent on the trek back to our family quarters, both mulling over his *mathair's* bold request. Truthfully, my husband is the one mulling. Me? I'm fuming.

I plan on hashing this out as soon as we have some privacy, but Fate, and Ronin, have other ideas. I can hear my infant son's wailing even before we reach our door. *Niamh* meets us with our very unhappy son on one arm, a standard Mundane baby bottle in the other. The poor girl looks completely flustered at her inability to soothe our youngest son.

"I am vera' sorry, ma' Lady. I have tried everythin' I know to comfort wee Master Ronin, but he will not settle, nor will he take ta' the rubber nipple. Even ma' dear cousin could offer no solution. He seeks only his beloved *mathair*."

"It's okay, *Niamh*. Hand him to me. He's the most stubborn of our three about taking to bottle feeding," I offer. "I'll have to see about finding other possible nipple brands when we reach Salem, otherwise the return to my practice is going to be a nightmare. Maybe Doc Robyn will have a suggestion."

"Aye, ma' Lady," the nanny says, "I hope the good *dochtuir* (doctor) ken' find some *bairn* (baby) magic that will please Master Ronin when his *mathair* is unavailable."

I take the baby from *Niamh* and head for my favorite chair in our bedroom suite. Declan follows me and while I settle in to feed our son, he yawns and says, "I know we have much ta' discuss, Love, but not over the head of our blessed boy. I have some contracts I need ta' look over. Once ya' get our wee one settled, we'll talk."

"We most certainly will, Tax Man," I reply, not terribly confident that by the time I finish and head to bed, my exhausted husband will still be awake.

As predicted, by the time I feed Ronin, change him, and get him settled in for the night, or at least for three or four hours until he's due for his next feeding, I find my *Mo Shiorghra* sound asleep and snoring away, a pile of papers still resting on his chest. I don't have the heart to wake the poor man, just so we can spend the rest of the early morning hours embroiled in this dysfunctional family battle. I remove the papers and stack them on the nightstand, pull our light comforter over him, then slip into our bed on the other side. What needs to be said can keep for a few more hours.

* * *

I wake to a sun-drenched room, which, in my current life stage, is the absolutely wrong scenario. Ronin was due for his next feeding between 4:30 and 5:00 AM, long before the rays of dawn normally appear. Now fully awake with Declan' side of the bed empty, I check the baby's cradle, only to find it empty. It doesn't take long to find them both in our bedroom's sitting area, the baby resting in my husband's lap, and an empty bottle on the side table next to them.

Declan puts a finger up to his mouth to suggest silence, then puts a sleeping Ronin back into his cradle. He returns with a steaming mug of what I can smell is fresh, hot coffee, a Mundane weakness I still can't forgo, and hands it to me. "Thank you, Sweetie. It's just what I needed," I say, taking the chair opposite of the one he was sitting in. "You let me sleep in."

"Aye. 'Tis the least I ken' do after ma' *mathair* kept us up so late. I am sorry I fell asleep befar' ya' came ta' bed, Lass. 'Twas especially dry readin'.'"

"It's fine. What I really want to know," I say, lifting up the empty baby bottle, "is your secret on how you got our Master Ronin to take the rubber nipple."

The corners of his mouth turn up. "'Twas a simple fix, Lady Wife. I just explained ta' our wee lad that he must learn ta' share his *mathair* far' the good of the House, and that sometimes, one must be willin' ta' conprinise on things they find…disagreeable." He says this with a perfectly straight face so I'm unable to tell whether he's just teasing or being completely serious, or if, perhaps, he's talking about something entirely different than Ronin's feeding. The Tax Man has always had this unusual way of seemingly communicating with all of his infant children, even when they are in their earliest stages of development and shouldn't be capable of such skill. To this day, I still don't understand if the phenomena comes through the *Sidhe* bond, or within his paternal one, but Declan seems to reach his children on a very personal level long before most experts consider this even a possibility.

"And now that you've explained this all to Ronin, will he take the bottle from anyone, or just his commanding Lord Father?" I ask.

"I suppose we shall soon see if ma' wee boy holds true ta' his pledge ta' be mar' acceptin' of anyone but his beautiful *mathair.* Hopefully, this vera' afternoon," my husband answers.

"This afternoon?"

"Aye. I need ta' ride south toward Avalon ta' check on some foals I plan ta' purchase once they are weaned. I was vera' much countin' on ya' riding' out there with me. I am aware that we yet need ta' talk about Lady *Siobhan's* request and I'd rather not do it here at *Dun Siorai.* The sky shows a pleasant enough day; dry with moderate temperatures. Do ya' think you are up ta' a few hours in the saddle, Love?" he asks, knowing full well how I feel about bouncing around on horses.

Despite my feelings about equine travel, spending a whole afternoon alone with my husband is an infrequent treat I'm not willing to pass on. Between his duties as House *Nuada's* Lord, his business and financial ties in the

Mundane world, and his work for the Black Knight, Declan is away from us more than he is home. Five years ago, when my *Mo Shiogrha* took on the title of Lord *Nuada*, there needed to be a lifestyle change that I worked hard to both understand and adapt to, definitely something easier said than done. Even though I've come to accept our hectic schedule, a whole afternoon without having to share my Tax Man's attention is a gift, even if Dragon Mama's ridiculous request might cast a shadow on the day. "Of course, I'll ride with you, Sweetie…to the ends of the earth if necessary," I tease.

Declan gives me a sexy grin, one that makes my toes curl in my slippers. "Then ma' day is made perfect, Lass. We will leave later this morning…once we finish with the trappins' of family life."

MISSING 6

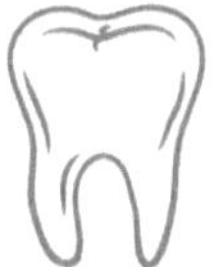

Some Afternoon Delight

EVEN AFTER FIVE years as the Tax Man's mate, I still don't "get" the Otherworld's insistence on horse travel. I suppose in some environmental way, I understand their reluctance to trade eco-friendly horses for carbon-spewing, gas or electric burning automobiles. However, one would think that with so many of the Otherworldly residents possessing various levels of magical gifts, they would prefer to move themselves in that much easier manner. The exact opposite is true. Nearly all the kingdoms in the Otherworld chose the more traditional four-legged mode of transportation, believing it exemplifies their devotion to their various mother goddesses, while leveling the "playing field" for diversity of magical ability. However, like their counterparts in the Mundane worlds, the citizens on the other side of the Veil have plenty of loop-holes and counter excuses to go against these norms if and when they desire to do so.

Still, the Fae folk of *I Idir* consider excellent horseman-ship a badge of honor, especially among the hoity-toity, ruling class. It was expected that as Lady *Nuada*, I would, at the very least, have my own horse and the most basic skills in riding it. My *capall* (horse) is a beautiful, coal black gelding by the name of *Eabon*, which appropriately means "ebony" in the old language. The horse was a belated Beltane gift from my Tax Man in the same year Declan became Lord of House *Nuada* and I its honored Lady, a not-so-subtle hint that my days of staying clear of the stables for anything other than secret, lustful rendezvouses, were over.

During the past five years, *Eabon* and I have developed a genuine affection for each other, and the horse has become more like a family pet than "transportation." Unlike my husband, I don't exercise the gelding daily, relying on *Peadar*, his stable lad to do so, but I make sure to visit him a few times a week while we are living at *Dun Siorai*, always with an apple or carrot in my pocket, a treat my horsey friend has come to expect.

Today, when I arrive at the stables, I find Declan already in the process of saddling *Eabon* up for this after-noon's adventure, a chore that usually falls to *Peadar*, who stands back, looking quite put-out at being replaced. I consider asking his Lordship why he's stepped on the stable lad's toes, but then a lightbulb goes on in my brain. All this talk about Meghan returning home to *I Idir* has stirred up bad memories in my Tax Man's thoughts. It was here, in this very stable, five years ago, on the eve of our handfasting, that his youngest sister had cut the strap holding my horse's saddle in place in hopes that I would be thrown and trampled, the second of her three attempts on my life.

Declan's aurora is a smokey, purple and gray color, proof that his mood is troubled, and I re-evaluate my original plans for a positive discussion regarding his mother's damnable request, along with any notions of a romantic get-away. Nonetheless, reneging on his invitation won't help the situation at all, so I shield any misgivings and put on a happy face. "*Eabon* and I are lucky to have our Lord personally looking after us," I say, a tad too cheerful to be believable.

I get a raised eyebrow in return, along with a half-smile that doesn't reach my husband's eyes. "*'Tis wise to never leave anything ta' luck, ma' Love. The past comin' back ta' haunt us is a stark reminder ta' remain on guard,*" he says to my thoughts. I'm not sure how to respond, so I don't. Instead, I step forward so Declan can put his hands around my waist and lift me into the saddle. "Are ya' ready for a day together, ma' Lady?" he asks.

"Yes, my Lord. We should leave as soon as possible, though, before someone or something puts a kibosh on this outing before we even get started." A million possibilities race through my mind. Running a House and an estate this large is a never-ending carousel of problems requiring immediate attention.

"I agree," he replies, putting a booted foot in the stirrup of his own stallion and settling himself in his saddle before we venture out of the stable and through the metal gates of *Dun Siorai*.

I decide to let my husband be the one to bring up his *mathair's* ridiculous request. Maybe that makes me a coward, but I don't relish the idea of an entire afternoon of "cranky Declan." We ride side by side through the countryside, rich with the floral bounty of late summer. As predicted, the weather is perfect; cloudlessly mild with just enough breeze to keep the sweat off one's forehead. We'd gone about a mile or so before the Tax Man turns to me and says,"I suppose there's no use puttin' off this discussion, Lass. Lady *Siobhan* will expect an answer sooner or later."

"Truthfully, Declan, I'm not sure what there is to discuss. Your *mathair's* request is outside the bounds of family or House loyalty," I state. "The laws of *I Idir* are clear regarding an attempted murder, especially of a Fated Mate. This so-called 'repeal' of her sentence has no business even being considered. Lady *Siobhan* perfectly knows this herself. I'm not sure what she hopes to gain by even making such an outrageous demand."

"I agree, Love," the Tax Man replies. "There is no feckin' way I could ever trust ma' sister livin' among my mate or ma' children. Even if what ma' *mathair* says is true…and that is a big 'if'…that it was truly ma' sire behind Meghan's evil acts, it does not mean she could not be swayed to act against us in the future, as she has proven herself to be weak of mind and will. Callum Fitzpatrick still walks freely between both world, usin' his hideous black magic to shield his identity while he works to bring about the downfall of *I Idir*. There is no reason ta' deny that he could vera' much be behind this attempt ta' bring Meghan back within the walls of *Dun Siorai*."

"You don't really think Lady *Siobhan* would work with him to harm us," I ask, horrified at the notion.

"Truthfully…no. She hates the man with a passion so great it frightens me, though 'tis not impossible, I suppose. Things in *I Idir* are never what they seem. However, I donna' believe ma' *mathair* would betray The Morrigan. She is far too smart and too much of a Ruling Class survivor ta' take such huge risks. Besides, when everything is said and done, I believe she cares deeply far' the grandchildren of her line. She was devastated when Tessa miscarried and then never conceived again. I believe her when she says she would give her life far' Dylan. Or any of our children, far' that matter."

"Then why is she pushing so hard for Meghan to return to *I Idir?* I wholeheartedly agree with you: Your *mathair* has always been wickedly smart in plotting her own place among the Ruling Class and it's unlikely she'd want the wrath of the Queen to fall on her head. It doesn't make a lick of sense for her to aid your father in any way. I swear she'd take him out herself if she thought she could get away with it. What is this request really about?"

"That, ma' Love, is the question to answer. And if Herself has determined that you and I should make the decision about Meghan, then ya' ken' believe without a doubt that 'tis all a scheme The Raven wishes to keep her hands clean of," his Lordship offers, as he leaves the open road and comes to a stop within a thick grove of rowan trees. "Rest assured, Love…the safety and well-being of you and our children is ma' only concern. I will give ma' *mathair* her answer late tomorrow and it will be, of course, a resoundin' 'NO'."

"Thank you, Declan. That puts my troubled mind at ease, though I'm not sure why you're waiting until late tomorrow to tell her. Wouldn't it be better to get it over with as soon as possible?"

Declan maneuvers off his stallion and pulls a wool blanket out of his saddle bag, setting it in place on the ground before answering. I'm liking where I think this is going. "Lady *Siobhan* is a high-ranking member of House *Nuada* and I am its Lord," he explains. "She is entitled ta' come ta' me with any demands she has of the House, and in return, I am expected to give har' requests and concerns my full consideration. I ken' no have it seem that I have jumped to a preconceived decision without properly weighing her needs against those of the House."

That's the way Declan Fitzpatrick rolls. He takes his leadership responsibilities as Lord of House *Nuada* with shoulder-crushing seriousness. Plus, my Tax Man has, and always will be, a devoted rule follower. "Of course, my Lord. Tomorrow is soon enough." Noting the blanket, I ask with more innocence than I'm feeling, "Are we stopping here for a bit?"

"Aye, ma' Lady. I believe we are in need of relaxation after such serious House discussions," he replies with a smile. A bottle of chilled summer wine and two glasses appear on a flat rock near his Lordship's chosen spot. He helps me off *Eabon* and ties the horses to a tree near a small stream before joining me on the blanket.

"This is lovely, Sweetie. Thanks for planning it."

"'Tis as much a treat for me, Lass, as it is far' ya'. Plus, I've gone ahead and checked with Robyn about yar' pulled lady muscle and he assured me that any lovemakin'…"

I don't let him finish. "Wait…you talked to Robyn about

that? About the two of us…" The thought that the doctor is privy to the knowledge that I'm the kind of person that lies to their Eternal Mate makes my stomach drop.

My feelings of panic must show on my face. Declan's half smile and raised eyebrow is an indication that he's just teasing. Apparently, the gig is up on my *Lammas* games tall tale. Or maybe it was never a "gig" to begin with. Part of me is relieved he didn't really go to Doc Brannigan with my ill-conceived lie, and the other is annoyed that I'm being called out about it. It kinda' ruins the sexy vibe going on here. "So, you knew all along I was lying about the pulled muscle."

"Not initially, but ya' seem far too…how shall I say this delicately…'painlessly flexible' to be sufferin' from any kind of groin injury. I've experienced such a thing ma'self during past *Beltane* games. Afterwards, I was forced ta' be vera' tentative about how I sat and walked for a long time. 'Tis doubtful ya' could ride me as wonderfully hard as ya' do while sufferin' such…tenderness in that area," he says, not bothering to hide his shit-eating, I'm-Lord-*Nuada*-I know-everything grin.

Now I'm just embarrassed. Not only because I've been busted, but because the Tax Man just made me sound like some sex-craved, porno-star-acrobat. "Well, aren't you just Mr. Sensitive."

"Yar' a vera' passionate woman, Rosie, and I am the luckiest man I know to be able to share ma' life and body with ya'. Surely ya' already know that ya' own ma' complete soul along with the rest of ma' parts. I'm simply tryin' to be open and honest, Love," he counters.

"Which just comes across as a reminder that I am not. Being honest, I mean."

I get that single eyebrow again, a sign that the Tax Man has no plans on backing down. "Truth be told, Lass, it gives me pause ta' think that ya' would fib ta' me about something as silly as this. If ya' didn't want ta' participate in the games, then ya' should have just been upfront and told me so."

"Easier said than done, Tax Man! You can be quite… persistent. Plus, I know how competitive you are and how much it means for you to have House *Nuada* in the winner's circle. I suck at those kinds of things, Declan. I'm just not athletic. I don't want to let you down. Ever." I squeak the words out, a physical reaction to the guilt that's creeping over me about lying to him.

My One and Only blinks, then reaches across the blanket and pulls me into his lap. "Feckin' hell, Rosie…you could never let me down. Ever. Yar' ma' Eternal Mate, ma' *Mo Shiorghra*… the woman who pulled me from the vera' brink of despair. I donna' care about the feckin' games. Yar' happiness…and the welfare of our family…are foremost in ma' mind. I swear ta' ya' there isn't anyone or anything that could change that for me. Not in a hundred lifetimes."

MISSING 7

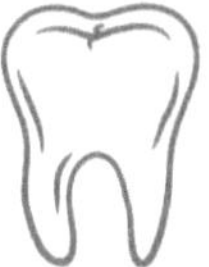

The Raven Commands

ALL THAT TALK OF "HARD RIDING" could only have one result. For a good hour, we forget about facing Lady *Siobhan*, forget about the *Lammas* competition, forget about the state of things between the worlds. Instead, we focus on the two of us as a couple, Rosie and Declan Fitzpatrick, out for some quality time together. It appears that my Tax Man thoroughly enjoys my being a sex-craved, porno-star-acrobat. I rather like it myself, and note that if there were competitions in this arena of skill, I, Lady *Nuada*, would undoubtedly take first place.

We are relishing both our carefree abandon and the last of the summer wine when we hear the sounds of people on horseback not far from where we are relaxing. It's a chaotic dive for our clothes as we scramble to make ourselves presentable before two large stallions enter the grove my husband promised me was "well-hidden."

I recognize the horse before its rider; I'd spent hours

in a pillion behind Declan on the pitch black, magical stallion during that awful "mission" to *Asgard* five years ago. Hades is not the kind of Fae animal one easily forgets, especially when his Mistress is the goddess of war and destruction. However, Herself seeking us out in the middle of nowhere is not a good omen.

I can hear his lordship swearing under his breath as he tries to put himself in enough order to face his Queen. There is no way I can attend to all the laces and buttons of my Otherworldly undergarments in the short time it will take Herself and her consort, the legend warrior, *Chu Chulainn*, to reach us, so I settle for simply covering myself up, and shoving my "unmentionables" under the blanket.

By the time Her Majesty and escort reaches us, Declan and I are dressed and standing, though anyone with a half brain could deduce what the two of us have been up to here in a hidden grove of trees along the roadside. Declan bows and I drop a curtsy, hoping that my face isn't as red it feels.

"I hope I'm not interrupting anything of importance, Lord *Nuada*?" the Raven Queen asks, a knowing half-smile playing on her lips. Less polite, her male consort looks at me with a huge grin, then winks, and now I'm absolutely sure my face is beet red.

"No, Your Majesty. My Lady and I were just taking a short respite on our way to Avalon. I have business I must attend to there," my husband says with an air of confidence and calmness I don't share. "May I offer Your Highness some late summer wine from *Dun Siorai's* vineyards?"

he asks, raising the bottle that has magically refilled itself in the last twenty seconds.

"Thank you, Lord *Nuada.* Some other time perhaps. My time is limited and I need to discuss some business of great importance with you and your Lady."

I don't need Fae mental telepathy or a degree in *I Idir* politics to know what Herself's "business" consists of. The Queen's tracking of us on the road to Avalon is almost certainly related to Lady *Siobhan's* request to release Meghan Fitzpatrick *Nuada* from her sentence of exile. Declan has the same thoughts and I can feel him tense up, then slam a shield firmly down on his thoughts, though we are both fully aware that The Morrigan can easily breach most attempts to hide what you want to keep secret. I don't bother with a shield; instead, I attempt to empty my mind of all my emotions. In return, I hear the tinkling of bells.

"If I can be of service ta' you and *I Idir,* ma' Queen, then please speak yar' mind," Lord *Nuada* replies.

"I am aware that your Lady *Mathair* has come to you regarding the release of your sister, Meghan, and that you promised her a decision very soon."

"Aye, Your Majesty. Your information is correct," my husband says.

"And what will your answer be, Lord *Nuada?* the Raven Queen questions.

"I am afraid that I ken' no agree ta' such a request, Your Majesty. For the safety and peace of mind of ma' Eternal Mate and our children, I must refuse my Lady *Mathair's* appeal on my sister's behalf." He quickly adds, "As is my right as Lord of House *Nuada.*"

The Morrigan narrows her eyes and stares at the two of us before speaking, while the Lord Warrior remains passively neutral, though I have no doubt he is here to help "convince us" to agree with whatever the Queen decides. "I am afraid I will need you to reverse your decision, young Lord. For the good of *I Idir*."

As I may have mentioned before, Declan Fitzpatrick *Nuada* has a very wide stubborn streak. Once he's made up his mind, my Eternal Mate almost never changes it. I worry that Declan is walking on thin ice with regards to the goddess of war and destruction, who, everyone is aware, is also determined in getting her own way.

"I beg Your Majesty's pardon, but I donna' understand how releasing a convicted murderer free in *I Idir* helps the kingdom. It, in fact, such action makes it substantially less safe," he replies, and even I am shocked at the boldness of my Tax Man's answer.

The ground around us vibrates with the Raven's displeasure at being questioned, but Lord *Nuada* gives no indication that he's been convinced to change his mind. I know it's nothing more than a glamour magic illusion, but the face of the Fae woman on her horse slowly shifts into that of a fierce black bird with glowing red eyes and sharpened beak. At least I hope it's an illusion. Thinking back, I do recall the time the Queen flew into my room at *Dun Siorai* as a bird, so I suppose shape shifting isn't out of the realm of possibility, and frankly, it scares the shit out of me.

"I'm afraid this is not a request, young *Nuada*. You will do as I ask because you must. Your sister is key to us locating the traitor you call 'sire.' Finding him means finding the head of the Mundane cabal that drives these attempts to breach the Veil. Up until now, your personal loyalty to the Throne of *I Idir* has never been questioned despite the actions of your evil sire's bloodline. I know you value the future happiness and longevity of your own line. It would be most unfortunate should you lose all that you hold dearest."

And there it was: the ever-present threat that, in *I Idir,* The Morrigan rules. It didn't matter that my beloved Tax Man had made countless sacrifices for Her kingdom, going as far as being captured, tortured, and experimented on by Mundane terrorists. His debt to the Raven Queen for saving his life would never be fully paid. Ever.

If I can see Lord *Nuada's* rage simmering in his aura, then without a doubt those two supremely powerful beings sitting atop their magical horses could see it as well. The fear overwhelming me is so heavy I feel as if I will suffocate on it. I brace for even more threats from the goddess of war and destruction. Instead, what comes next confuses me.

The Morrigan suddenly appears on the ground in front of my Eternal Mate. She has his full attention as she quietly says to him, "I know you simmer with anger over the seeming injustice of my decision and the cruelty of my threats, *Nuada*; you who are courageous of heart and pure of soul. The blood of ancient kings runs through your veins and you feel the ties to this world more acutely than most of your generation. What I do to save *I Idir* comes with a price that even I, a goddess of the old times, will share, but one that cannot be avoided. If the Fae are to exist into the next millennium, then we must proceed with blunt-edged determination. If it offers you comfort, *Leanbh na Lamh Airgid* (Child of the Silver Hand), know that if you stand with me, so shall I stand with you when your own bloodline is tested." When she finished speaking, The Morrigan touched her forehead to my husband's.

The air around us crackled and for a moment, and just like it did on that awful day in the north lands, time as we knew it seemed to exist in a vacuum. When the void finally broke, the Queen and her consort were gone, leaving Declan and I alone in the grove, deeply troubled over this grim turn of events.

And that, dear friends, is how my murderous sister-in-law returned to the halls of *Dun Siorai*.

MISSING 8

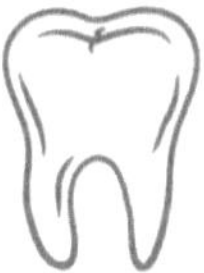

While The Sister Demands

IF THERE WAS anything positive about Meghan's return to *Dun Siorai*, it's the fact that I only had to live with her vile presence for a few more days. After a short discussion, Declan and I have changed our plans to leave *I Idir* and return to the Mundane world earlier than expected, saving me a few extra days of having to constantly watch my back. I know what you're thinking. My take on this whole thing does make me sound overly dramatic, and perhaps there could be the teeniest, tiniest chance that my psycho sister-in-law has done a complete turn- around while in exile and is no longer intent on putting me six-feet under. But I have my doubts. The Tax Man once harangued me over the topic of how a "leopard never changes its spots" in regards to his mother, and thus, I refuse to let *Dun Siorai's* newest red-headed *panthera pardus* (leopard) catch me off guard.

Not that his Lordship would ever allow his sister easy access to his family. The children and I are never alone. If Declan is unable to be at our side himself, that responsibility is taken up by either his cousin, Duncan, Mac Kelly, or Connor Dell, all of whom my husband considers his inner circle. Having a "shadow" when I'm as busy as I am, both with the impending *Lammas* celebration and the move to Salem, is not totally convenient, but my husband will not hear not a word of my complaint. I've also noted that both *scathach* nannies have added an extra layer of blades to their usual weaponry and that all three children spend most of their day being entertained within the confines of our family quarters. Lord *Nuada* may have been forced against his will to release Meghan from her exile, but he's refused to hide his obvious feelings about having to do so.

On the morning the youngest of *Siobhan's* daughters arrived at the estate, she was met by her Lord brother and a small retinue of *Dun Siorai's* most-trusted security detail. I offered to accompany my mate to her "homecoming." In return, I was graced with a very "cranky Declan" look and a terse "not a feckin' chance, Rosie." That was the end of the discussion. If the gossip I heard from the staff who witnessed the homecoming is true, his Lordship "was so cold in his greeting ta' his *deifiur* (sister), 'twas a surprise that the lass's nose dinna' completely freeze up and fall off har' face."

Meghan is assigned living quarters, not within the family section of the estate, but rather at the far end of the sprawling grounds where untitled guests of the House are usually sheltered. Per the staff gossip, if his Lady Sister was upset by her brother's less than warm welcome, she didn't let on. In fact, the tattle-talers were heartily disappointed that the meeting between the two siblings was, at best, rather bland, and that the lady involved showed a complete lack of emotion to her supposedly much-desired homecoming.

As it came to be, I found myself face to face with my would-be murderer simply by chance. No. I take that statement back. This wasn't an unfortunate piece of bad timing. We believers of The Old Ways don't hold to such things. Rather, this was surely the Universe letting me know, in no uncertain terms, that I couldn't hide from my past, because, damnit, here it was, in the kitchen, large as life, staring me down and smirking like some evil clown in a horror movie.

Cook and I were busy going over last-minute details regarding the timing between various courses to be served at the evening *Lughnasadh* meal. With the arrival of our newest "guest," House *Nuada* anticipated approximately sixty-four adults and eight children of assorted ages for the traditional celebratory meal, which was to be held in the estate's massive banquet room. Cook stopped speaking in mid-sentence, her eyes wide and focused over my head toward the doorway. I was about to ask her what was wrong when I heard a female voice behind me.

"I hope I'm not disturbing anything important," she asks in a voice layered with false saccharin.

This is the second time in less than a week someone has asked that silly question of me, fully knowing their intrusion was entirely unwelcome. I don't bother turning around so I can't tell whether my husband's sister flinches when I dispense with the use of her formal title of "Lady." "What is it you need, Meghan? Cook and I are busy."

If Meghan doesn't flinch at my lack of House protocol, Cook sure as hell does. The poor woman is thoroughly rooted in the scraping and bowing the Ruling Class Houses require of their staff and my blatant disrespect toward a descendant of the *Nuada* bloodline shocks her, even if said descendant is a certified psychopath. Wisely, Cook has come to know and respect me enough not to undermine my frosty greeting to Declan's sister by saying anything herself.

My back is still turned to her when Meghan asks, "I was hopin' I might seek an alternative breakfast ta' the array served in ma' quarters? That one was...unsatisfactory."

Cook's face flushes a deep red. As well as the woman knows me, I know Cook. The portly Brownie takes her position as House *Nuada's* culinarian very seriously. I have no doubt that our House chef went out of her way to provide our unwanted guest with a most lovely selection of choices despite her diminished status, and Meghan's disapproval deeply embarrasses her, especially as it comes in her Mistress's presence. I finally turn around and face my long-time nemesis. "Unsatisfactory, you say? I can't imagine any of Cook's fine repertoire of recipes to be anything other than hearty and delicious."

I haven't seen my sister-in-law since that dreadful incident the day of my handfasting. At the time, she'd been a mere girl of sixteen, albeit a very pretty one, but still in the throes of adolescence. The woman in front of me is a stunning beauty, even measured by Fae standards, and if my Tax Man had been born with two xx chromosomes instead of his xy combination, I have no doubt his feminine version would have appeared exactly like the vision in front of me. For a heartbeat, I'm too stunned to speak as they look so much alike, but then I see the tightly pressed lips with the crooked half-smile of a fully developed smirk, and my shocked surprise evaporates like rain on a hot pavement. "'Tis not that the selection is poorly made, Lady *Nuada*," Meghan replies. "I am sure it's all quite tasty. My dislike centers on the over-abundance of unhealthy and fattening choices." Like her mother and brother, she raises that one damnable eyebrow and adds, "I realize your Ladyship has happily taken on a more… matronly appearance these past five years. No doubt gifting ma' Lord with three strapping sons in such a short period of time has taken their toll on ma' Lady's shape, and it's quite commendable that yar' are at ease with yar' motherly visage. I, however, am in the prime of ma' maidenhood and yet without a mate. Plus, I am told I will begin weapons training soon. I need ta' respect ma' body and its beauty with a sound and healthy diet."

As long as I live, I will never understand a woman's desire to body shame a fellow female. Trust me when I say I've had more than my share of nasty, demeaning comments about my less than svelte figure, and I've always been unable to comprehend why anyone with any kind of reasonable knowledge of polite behavior would publicly remark on someone's physical appearance. I always told myself that this need to negatively comment is born of their own insecurities, but as I've aged, I've come to the conclusion that sometimes people simply suck.

"But I have such a pretty face, right?" I say, a sarcastic response to the hundreds of times it's been insulated that if only I were thinner of body, I'd be considered "passably attractive."

Declan's youngest sister has spent only the smallest amount of time in the Mundane world, so the sarcasm of my comment rolls right over head. Like my husband sometimes does, she takes my words at face value, tilting her head and looking at me. "I suppose ma' Lord finds yar' face appealing, Lady *Nuada*," she says, "since he desires ya' enough ta' have produced three children."

With the conversation quickly deteriorating to both TMI and mean-spirited rudeness in front of Cook, I decide to put it to rest. I keep my facial expression and tone blandly neutral. "In that statement you are correct, Megan Fitzpatrick. Your Lord Brother finds me impossible to resist. We are now Eternal Mates and, since you are a new part of the household, you will undoubtedly be privy to the magic our passion produces. Therefore, I suggest you work to hold your tongue of such caustic and demeaning comments. As a woman, you surely realize the sway and hold my...feminine allure has with his Lordship. If you hope to experience even the slightest feeling of... hospitality within the walls of *Dun Siorai*, I suggest you remember that I am now its Lady with all the power and respect that comes with that title."

I see the storm brewing in her eyes. If I had any doubts about Meghan Fitzpatrick *Nuada's* current feelings about me, they are gone. My husband's sister hates me as much as she did five years ago. Nothing at all has changed during her years in exile. If anything, the five years of simmering anger towards me has reached a boil, and if I'm not careful, it's good ole' Rosie who will end up being burned.

MISSING 9

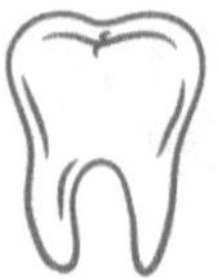

The Girl Has Skill

LIKE THEIR COUNTERPARTS in the Mundane world, the habitants of the Otherworld love a reason to celebrate. Every race of people on the other side of the Veil observe their own holidays and holy days based on individual culture and belief systems, but the heart of all of them almost always focuses on building a sense of community within worship and festivity. The Fae Folk are no different; the sabbats of the "Wheel of the Year" are meant to encourage a sense of deep commitment to the gods and goddesses of the land that feed and nurture their people, along with the energy of interconnectedness that binds all Fae together regardless of their individual magical gifts.

The sabbat of *Lughnasadh*, or *Lammas*, as it is modernly called, pays homage to *Lugh*, the ancient god associated with the sun, the harvest, craftsmanship free of magical intervention, and a love for the various arts. Of all the sabbats, this one is my personal favorite. Maybe it's the "crafty girl" in me, this whole idea of inborn creativity that draws me so deeply to this late summer celebration. Or truthfully, it might just have something to do with the fact that *Lughnasadh* is usually the prequel to our family returning to the Mundane world, our last big *samhradh* (summer) 'hurrah' in the Otherworld before going "home." I just feel freer to celebrate knowing I mentally have one foot across the Veil.

Don't get me wrong. I no longer despise any time spent in *I Idir*. If my relationship with Declan was ever going to be built on solid foundation, I needed to move past my long-held prejudices regarding life in the Other-world. Still, despite the monumental task of getting everyone and everything ready to cross, going "home," and knowing I'll be in Salem during my absolute favorite season of autumn, always lightens my heart.

As tradition dictates, the day begins with a sunrise spiritual meditation led by the House's mages in *Dun Siorai's* sacred grove. This year, for the first time, Dylan is allowed to attend and I think the laces on my Tax Man's ceremonial doublet will surely burst from the pride he's holding over our little man's behavior. It's hard to say how much of the spiritual part Dylan can comprehend at the age of five, but, dressed in "big boy" House attire rather than his everyday leggings and tunic, and doing his very best to stay still and quiet, little Lord *Mac Nuada* makes an adorable picture.

When we return to the estate, Cook has a breakfast prepared that is worthy of the ancient god, *Lugh*, himself. In keeping with the harvest spirit of the sabbat, grains hold center stage in a wide array of baked goods, cereals, and bread puddings, along with the very best of the late summer harvest of fruit. I note that even the supposedly carb-conscious Meghan heartily partakes in these festival treats, piling her plate high with an array of tiny pastries and rustic bread. Thank the goddesses that there is no interaction between my husband's sister and our family, with my nemesis deciding to carry a tray back to her own quarters rather than joining us in the family dining room. I welcome that decision. I'm in the best mood I've been since Lady *Siobhan's* late night visit and I'd rather not have to view Meghan's alternating scowls and smirks as a side dish to my lovely breakfast.

For most of the population of *I Idir*, the favored part of the day's activities are the annual women's games. Though glad not to be participating myself, I share the excitement throughout the stands as the crowd waves maroon and gold banners in support of the members of House *Nuada* who are scheduled to compete. I know that *Birgit* and *Niamh* are both participating, along with the groom's wife, a large, muscular woman named *Fiadh*, but I am shocked when I see my sister-in-law enter the arena as well. I look to Declan, who doesn't seem quite as shocked as I. *"Did you know about this?"* I ask.

His calm expression doesn't change. *"Aye, Love. I knew. 'Tis a wise Lord who makes it his business ta' know what gossip floats among the staff."*

"And it never crossed your husbandly mind that perhaps you should have told me in advance?" I complain.

"And what good would that have accomplished, Lass? You would have only had more time ta' fret over it." A set jaw is the only outwardly sign of my mate's annoyance. That's irri-

tating in itself, since I should be the only annoyed party here.

"Did it even cross your mind that I might not enjoy this nasty surprise, Tax Man?" I keep my eyes straight ahead though I have no doubt my frosty temperance is being received loud and clear.

"What wad' ya' have me do, Rosie? Order her locked in har' room? Forbid har' participation in today's competition? She is no here at Dun Siorai as a prisoner. Herself has granted ma' sibling a full pardon. Meghan is a blood Nuada with her own magical skill set. Plus, she has The Morrigan's backing. For the time being, we two must play the hand that has been dealt us. At least until I can gather enough intelligence on what Herself truly intends. I am not without my own resources, Love. Besides, we leave for Salem in a few days. Then you will be free of har' distressin' presence for several weeks until Samhain."

I'm inclined to ask the Tax Man what stops Menacing Meghan from harassing us in the Mundane world. Though she rarely choses to do so, my sister-in-law is able to cross the Veil and safely live in the human dimension as easily as the rest of us with mixed blood. However, I hold my tongue. Communicating in a public space like this, even telepathically, is a dangerous game to play. I've learned to hold a reasonably strong mental shield over the years, but I'm no *Sidhe* Fae, and my magic is nearly non-existent during daylight hours. Best to keep sensitive conversations for a time and place where we are assured warded privacy. Still, a trickle of guilty annoyance pushes me to add, *"I would guess that despite it being Meghan, you're happy someone in your own family is able and willing to compete in today's games. I know my lack of athletic ability must be an embarrassment for you."*

My Eternal Mate's indignation burns hot within my mental space. *"Feckin' hell, Rosalinda Fitzpatrick! Ya' are perfectly aware that I worship the vera' ground ya' walk upon! Ya' are ma' Eternal Mate...the other half of ma' soul. When ya' say things like that...put forth the belief that I could ever be embarrassed over any part of ya...'tis like a knife ta' ma' par' heart. I donna' understand why ya' say such things ta' me, or why ya' feel the need to hammer away on an old wound, especially on a sabbat."*

My face burns hot and I grab the Tax Man's hand in mine. Even after five years together, I sometimes forget that the Fae mindset doesn't allow for flippant, speak-without-thinking, button-pushing, verbal warfare. Words are powerful to residents of the Otherworld...sacred, in fact...and my casually tossed innuendo comes across as a verbal slap to the face of a man I love more than life itself. *"Oh Declan...Sweetie...I'm sorry. This having your sister here... skulking around like some...some residue nightmare...brings out the worst in me. But it's no excuse to say what I said and I apologize. You're right, in a few days we'll be in Salem and we can take a breather away from the scheming politics of I Idir."*

That's not a hundred percent true statement. *I Idir* will follow us home to the Mundane world whether we like it or not. It's only silly optimism to believe otherwise. As Lord of House *Nuada*, Declan will be forced to live a double life, going back and forth through the Veil to fulfill his multitude of responsibilities in both places. It's difficult life and a possible threat to his health to cross as often as he does, but it's a sacrifice he willingly makes for our children and I, so I vow to do my best in these next few days to make the last hours of our time at *Dun Siorai* as calm and stress free as possible.

When my husband's psycho sister enters the arena for the equestrian challenges, I cheer loudly, waving my maroon and gold banner like a crazed flagman in the Hunger Games, garnishing me a raised eyebrow from Tax Man who apparently finds my antics a tad overblown. My public cheerleading might be play-acting, but Meghan's skill is not. She is good. Very good.

The talented horse part doesn't surprise me. The Fitzpatricks are all superb horsemen and women, their training beginning early in their childhood. At age five, Dylan already has his own pony, *Toirneach* (Thunder), whom he rides and cares for on a daily basis. Liam, who normally is a ball of unscripted energy, is surprisingly calm and confident when allowed time on the back of *Dun Siorai's* gentlest horses. I will guess that when his Da thinks he is ready, Liam will be given the responsibility of a pony as well. Thus, it's no surprise that my sister-in-law sits a horse more comfortably than the other female competitors. It is, however, her obvious talent with the use of weapons while riding said horse that blows me away.

During the first round, she hits the bullseye of the target, not once, but three separate times, all while at a full gallop, earning House *Nuada* a first-place ribbon. In the joust competition, Megan unseats her first opponent, a woman from House *Eadaoin*, who is at least five inches taller and thirty pounds heavier than the Fitzpatrick sibling, then goes on to conquer, in record time, the next two competitors she faces.

"She's very good, isn't she?" I ask Declan.

He frowns, and I can see some level of apprehension in his aurora. "Aye. She has greatly improved since she was banished from *Dun Siorai*. I'd always felt Meghan had more skill than she showed as a teenager if only she had applied herself ta' har' trainin'. I was not aware that she'd continued to work so diligently on her skills while in Avalon."

I understand where his apprehension is coming from. I have a huge batch of my own. And when Meghan Fitzpatrick *Nuada* uses her tip-guarded longsword to easily remove a small silver ring from her opponent's breast plate, I admit to being officially worried over the advanced weapons skill of a young woman who truly hates my guts.

MISSING 10

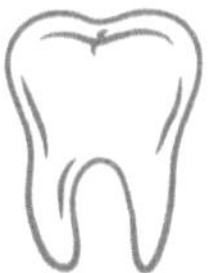

If Looks Could Kill

MEGHAN'S GOLD trophy stands in House *Nuada's* ornate banquet room like a shining beacon to her ability to easily take me completely out of the picture. Permanently. Of course, that's probably not the consensus among the rest of our guests. Within Fae high society, Meghan Fitzpatrick *Nuada's* first place ranking gives her House tremendous bragging rights, and if her stunning good looks weren't enough, this new development makes her a prime "catch" in the handfast market.

The young heirs hover around my husband's sister like moths to flame, reminding me of that famous scene in the film classic, *Gone With the Wind*, in which Scarlett holds court at the Wilkes barbeque. The resemblance to that famous movie scene lies not just in the large crowd of *I Idir's* most elite males scrapping and fawning around her like young bucks during rutting season; there's also the way Megan's eyes keep darting around the room as if she's expecting someone specific in the exact same manner as Scarlett O'Hara searching for her beloved Ashley Wilkes.

I consider mentioning this to Declan, but his purplish-gray aurora is testament to his high level of simmering anxiety and I don't relish adding to it. Meghan would have to be an idiot to "try something" during this celebration. There is far too much security at *Dun Siorai* tonight, both magical and traditional, for anyone to consider creating chaos or mayhem. With the underlying, but very real tensions between the Mundanes and the residents of the Otherworld, no one takes chances these days.

The evening meal for the *Lughnasadh* celebration is more akin to a Mundane open house than to a formal banquet. Each House will offer its own "event" and the Ruling Council hoity-toities, especially the males, will float from one estate to another, celebrating into the wee hours of the morning. Although people like and respect my Tax Man, his *athair's* traitorous actions have kept House *Nuada* out of the "cool kids" inner social circles, and crowds of Fae in their prime visiting our *Lammas* buffet have always been on the smallish side. If this has ever embarrassed his Lordship, he's never made a big deal about it. Declan never seems to care much for the snobbishness and social climbing antics of his counterparts, and he lets their snubbing of him roll off his shoulders without any angst. This year, however, when news that the exiled Lady Meghan *Nuada* would return home to *Dun Siorai* became common knowledge, our expected number of guests swelled to almost double what we had originally planned for. This, coupled with the woman's sterling performance at this afternoon's games, means every eligible, titled bachelor is here for their own "look-see." Thank goodness Cook insists on keeping a very generous larder. We needed everything she has in reserve to meet the growing demands for refreshments.

Playing the role of House *Nuada's* hostess, I don't have much down time to keep track of Maniac Meghan, but when I do finally notice her again, she is on a settee in the corner of the room sharing conversation and dessert with Lord Cillian *Mac Badh,* the Queen's second cousin. The entourage of interested suitors have dispersed in obvious deference to the young heir's high-ranking position. The couple is talking low and laughing between bites, their body language relaxed and easy-going, and my woman's intuition (or perhaps it's magically related; it is after sundown, after all) is suddenly on high alert. They look far too comfortable together for a twosome who haven't seen each other in a number of years, and something about the whole scenario sets off warning bells in my head.

This time, I decide it's imperative that I voice my concerns to my husband. I track him down to the small "gentlemen's parlor" that is adjacent to the banquet room where he is deep in discussion with the Black Knight and his cousin, Duncan, who also happens to be my BFF, Mel's, mate. The space is heavily spell-warded and they stop talking when I enter the room, clueing me in that whatever they were discussing was for their ears only. Declan sees me and waves his hand, releasing the vacuum like bubble that engulfed the three men. "You are in need of me, ma' Lady?" he asks.

"Only for a minute or two, my Lord. A short conversation is all," I reply.

Declan excuses himself and walks with me to the hallway between the gentlemen's parlor and the banquet room. He waves his hand again and I find the two of us in the same magical bubble. All this cloak and dagger shit makes me tense. "What troubles ya', Lass? I ken' sense yar' concern clear as day," he asks.

"It might be nothing so I apologize for taking you away from your discussion. It looked important," I note.

"There is not a thing in this world or the other mar' important than you, Love. What has ya' bothered?"

"I just saw your sister and *Cillian Mac Badh* canoodling in a corner of the banquet room. I wasn't aware they knew each other. It seemed...well...odd." The heir of House *Badh* and my husband have a complicated relationship going back years. It was brought to a truce five years ago when *Mac Badh* stood for Declan on the day he was made Lord of House *Nuada*, but there is no way anyone could call the two men "friends." By nature, Cillian is even more competitive than my husband, which is saying a lot about the young man's constant desire to "best" those around him. His joining forces with Declan's psycho sister, as he did with the late Marcy Kilcrabtree, would not be a good thing.

"Canoodling? What in Lugh's name does that even mean, Lass? Are ya' sayin' the man is attempin' ta' seduce ma' sister right there on the settee? In front of everyone?"

"Oh, hell no, Tax Man! That's not what I'm saying. They weren't even touching...not really," I try to explain.

"Then just what in feckin' hell do ya' mean, Rosie?" he asks, cranky Declan out in full force.

"They just seem…well…too friendly. Like confidantes. I don't know about you, but Cillian has a history of backing the wrong horse, especially when it comes to beautiful women. Even though she's your sister and totally off her nut, you have to admit she's a very attractive female, and *Mac Badh* has already proven he's easily led by his dick, Sweetie."

My *Mo Shiorghra* frowns and I'm not sure if it's over the idea of his sister and *Mac Badh* as a couple, or my mentioning another man's dick. Either way, he's not a happy camper. "I need ta' finish ma' conversation in the parlor and then I will have a little discussion of ma' own with the heir of House *Badh*."

"Good plan, Tax Man. But do it…tactfully. We don't need to be starting something contentious with Cillian, or House *Badh*. Maybe you could just clue him in a little about Meghan's…uhm…personality disorder.

In return, I get another "cranky Declan" look as he turns and heads back to the parlor while I return to the banquet room. On the way, I am stopped by the House's sommelier who asks permission to open yet another case of Declan's best Cabernet, and by the time I enter the room, the settee is empty and the gruesome twosome are nowhere to be seen.

I thread through the room, thinking that perhaps I've somehow missed them in the crowd, but there is no sight of either party. By the time his Lordship joins me, I am in a full panic mood, my imagination running wild, convinced that the two of them are off somewhere plotting my impending demise. *"It's like they've just up and disappeared,"* I mentally relate to my husband. *"I'd feel a lot better off knowing that the two of them just snuck off to do the nasty somewhere instead of joining forces to kill me."* In return, I get an exasperated look, but I'm too agitated to care. *"Don't give me that look, Tax Man. They're both healthy, consenting adults and it's a high sabbat. You're the one always going on about how, unlike the prudish Mundane population, the Fae treat sex as the natural order of the Universe."*

I can tell I'm not winning any points. Hubby's reply is more than a tad frosty. *"That does not mean I want that particular...visual in ma' head, Lass. Meghan may have a selfish, murderous heart, and I don't hold any trust in har', but, like it or not, she is my youngest sister. Plus, as House Nuada's Lord, I ken no act like I don' respect her birthright. But yar' right about knowin' far' sure what the two of them are up ta'."* He puts his hand out for me to take. "Come. We will make a general sweep of the estate together. Just to put our minds at ease."

The fact that he's taking me with him and not leaving me here alone is a measure of how actually concerned he is about the situation. I'd be lying if I didn't say I'm glad of it. I'm not crazy about the idea of being a sitting duck. We head first toward Meghan's quarters, but it's obvious the suite is empty. The security detail on that side of the estate assures his Lordship that no one has passed this way, and no magic has been detected.

We do a sweep of the other guest rooms but find them empty as well. Before we can move to the other side of the estate, Declan's attention shifts to something outside the tall arched windows of the hallway. Without explaining, he tugs me along as we traipse down the wide staircase to the first floor and out through the south service exit on the ground floor. "Where are we going? Did you see them?" I ask.

"There is the glow of Fae light in the pole barn. Someone capable of magically producing such a thing is in there. It's worth checking out," Declan explains, practically dragging me behind me.

Magical skill and ability among the Fae population is very diverse depending on race and bloodline. Everyone with any Fae genetic markers has some degree of magical energy. For example, I inherited my mother's tooth fairy bloodline. Like all of our kind, my magic is limited to the hours without the light of the sun, which overpowers our limited magical energy. I can change size and move myself over long distances in the Mundane world, something other Fae can't do because of the physics of gravity. It's why tooth fairies have the job of collecting children's teeth. Unfortunately, that's about all we can do.

Sidhe Fae, especially those with *Tuatha de Danann* bloodlines like my husband, *Cillian*, and undoubtedly, Meghan, have a much wider range of magical ability that varies from House to House and person to person. Declan's own abilities were tampered with five years ago by the North Koreans while he was held prisoner, and his Lordship is still in the process of determining all the new increased skills he's gained or lost since then. However, producing "Fae light," which is actually a physical ball of glowing pure energy, is a phenomenon that is relegated to the hoity-toity Fae with ancient bloodlines.

Declan signals me to silence as we enter the pole barn.

Unlike the multiple animal barns belonging to the estate, the pole barn is solely used for tool storage along with extra hay and animal feed. Having no livestock makes the odor of the place much more palatable than the other outbuildings. I know this on a personal level because my Tax Man and I have spent many a pleasant afternoon or evening in its cozy, hay-filled loft. Apparently, ours was not an original idea if the sounds coming from up there are any indication. With a flick of his wrist, Declan sets all the lights in the place ablaze. The sounds of a very "busy" couple abruptly ends, replaced by shuffling and urgent whispers. It's Cillian's head and bare shoulders that emerge around a towering pile of hay that hides the rest of the space. "It appears ya' have me at an embarrassin' disadvantage, Lord *Nuada*," the young man says with no sign that he is in the least bit sheepish about being caught *in flagrante delicto*.

"So, it would seem," my husband replies. "By any chance is it ma' Lady Sister that ya' have up there with ya?"

Lord *Mac Nuada* doesn't bother to answer, as Meghan Fitzpatrick, wearing only her paramour's shirt and a smirk the size of Manhattan, reveals herself from behind the hay pile. "And a pleasant *Lughnasad* evening to you, ma' Lord," she says.

Declan ignores his sister and addresses the younger man. "This is a breach of proper thanks towards ma' House's generous hospitality, *Mac Badh*. 'Tis low even for you ta' take yar' pleasure with ma' youngest sister in the pole barn as if she war' nothin' more than a common *stri-*

apach (trollop/strumpet) and not a blooded daughter of House *Nuada*."

I have to look down at my feet at this point, holding the strongest shield I can possibly muster. The Tax Man is being a genuine hypocrite in his scolding of the young couple knowing darn well the two of us have used the loft for the very same purpose. Still, I hold my piece of mind.

Mac Badh's carefree expression drops and his face suddenly registers anger in its place. "I would use caution when ya' refer ta' ma' Lady in such foul terms, Lord *Nuada.* You will surely regret yar' disrespect toward yar' Lady Sister."

"And why is that?" Declan questions, his own expression stony.

"Because in its wisdom, the Universe has finally provided me with my perfect *Mo Shiorghra*...my darling One and Only," *Mac Badh* says, reaching out to grab Megan's hand.

Both Declan and I stand in utter shock as my husband's youngest sister raises the hem of the shirt she's wearing to reveal the center design of *Cillian's* Ritual ink on her upper left thigh, a warrior shield featuring a three headed raven, the sigil for House *Bahd.*

MISSING 11

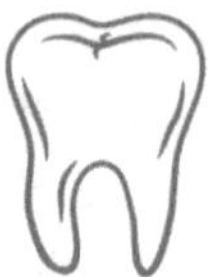

Back at Home in Fitzpatrick's Folly

WE LEAVE for Salem the next afternoon, two days earlier than we'd originally planned and without the normal staff fanfare that usually precedes our late summer return to the Mundane world. Declan explains our hurried departure as necessary due to a rescheduled shareholder's meeting he needs to attend in Boston on August 6th, expressing his desire to "see us all settled in Salem" before that date. I know this quick exit has nothing to do with a supposed business meeting and everything to do with being left out of the loop regarding his sister Meghan's sudden appearance in our life and her apparently not-so-new relationship with *Cillian Mac Badh*.

The conversation in the pole barn on the night of *Lughnasadh* between my Tax Man and the heir of House *Badh* was both heated and in rapid fire Fae Gaelic. Although I've gotten a better understanding of the ancient language in the past five years, when the parties involved have spoken the native tongue from birth and barely take a half breath in between words, I still struggle to understand the entire gist of the conversation. From what I could decipher, *Cillian* and Meghan were not newly matched that very night in the barn, as we originally believed, but rather six weeks beforehand.

According to the young heir, Meghan had been offered, by The Morrigan, Herself, the chance to commute her exile if she consented to becoming part of the Black Knight's secret intelligence team, the very same group of elite Fae my husband, his mother, and yours truly were also part of. Related to the Queen by blood as he was, *Cillian* was sent in secret by Her Highness to Avalon to attend to Meghan's intense training. Although the two had known of each other before the girl's exile, Meghan was a few months past her sixteenth birthday when she'd attempted to murder me and was thus exiled. At that time, she was not part of *Mac Badh's* inner social circle, he being four years older than she. The two of them had previously spent little time together, and her immature, girlish behavior wasn't attractive to then twenty-year old *Cillian.* As it sometimes happens with fated mates, upon meeting each other again, their attraction to each other was instant, and Lady Meghan *Nuada* was wearing House *Badh's* ink within three days of his arrival in Avalon.

None of this explained why his Lordship and I weren't told any of this in advance of last night, and who, in fact, did know and hadn't bothered to share the information with us. In answer to this question, Declan was told he needed to speak to either the Black Knight, or, if he dared,

The Morrigan, Herself, as the young couple had been ordered to keep their silence.

Had I'd been in my husband's position I would have marched my indignant self over to *Crann Bethadh* that very night to demand answers. However, Lord Declan Phineas Fitzpatrick *Nuada* has been raised from toddlerhood to put the welfare of his House and its constituents before any fleeting personal emotions. The Tax Man was cool and collected in his acceptance of *Mac Badh's* explanation and half-ass apology despite the glass blowing out of all six windows in the pole barn, a throwback to the brain tinkering Declan suffered at the hands of the North Koreans. Ignoring my suggestion to just sit down and talk to the Black Knight, someone my mate considered a good friend, the rest of the evening and the following morning were taken up with frantic last-minute packing and pre-travel chores before crossing the Veil back to Salem.

Thus, we arrived home to Fitzpatrick's Folly, as Declan has so aptly named our extensively remodeled Mundane home, at 6:00 AM Salem time, amidst a torrential late summer rain storm that caused all kinds of extra magical energy to be tossed around, leaving all of us, Baby Ronin included, edgy and cranky.

My husband isn't being altogether humorous regarding his choice of monikers for our Mundane residence. My tiny New England style cottage was never meant to shelter a family as large as ours. Before our handfasting, the Tax Man had strongly suggested we both sell our existing homes and buy a larger abode together. At the time, I'd been completely overwhelmed with all of the fast-moving changes in my life and hadn't wanted to part with the last trace of the familiar. My loving *Mo Shiorghra* accepted my need to stay put, sold his luxurious townhouse, and moved in with me instead. When we found out Dylan was on the way, I should have conceded that the Tax Man was correct in his assessment that my home, cozy as it was, did not meet the needs of a growing family. Still, my hormonal personality begged and pleaded to remain put, so we went forward with a large remodel that put my house way over value when compared to all the homes surrounding it. As the Universe would have it, two small children later, plus a teen-age uncle and two *scathach* live-in nannies, made the expanded home still too small. When the house next door went on the market, my husband didn't even blink; he bought it at full-asking price, knocked it down, and expanded our home once more to better accommodate our family's needs. We now own the largest home in all of our Mill Hill neighborhood, one that we will never be able to sell at its full value. I imagine this sticks in my Number Guy's financial craw, but it also stands testament to his love and devotion to me and our children and his ongoing commitment to make me happy.

It takes the better part of the day to air out the house, unpack the necessary "stuff," and move everyone into their respective spaces. The latest addition provides for a huge nursery suite for our sons and their nannies, though Ronin will remain in the cradle in our room for a few months until he no longer needs night time feedings. *Oisin* has his own room in the new addition, to which he has currently isolated himself with the door closed, in full disagreeable pout mode because our unexpected departure did not leave the amorous Fae adolescent with time enough for an appropriate "farewell" to his "Lady Love." His Lordship followed suit, closing himself in his expansive office suite off the main entry. This is not a bad thing. My mates's mood is not much better than his half-brother's, and though he doesn't wear a pout or slam his door like *Oisin*, everyone is made keenly aware they should stay out of his Lordship's way.

For as long as I've known Declan Fitzpatrick, he's been what you would call "a rule follower." He likes his schedules, he likes things tidy and organized, and he adheres to whatever rules govern whatever dimension or place he finds himself in. He is the most loyal, most honorable man I know, which among the snake pit atmosphere of both *I Idir* and Mundane world politics, is a rarity. This secret "betrayal" over Megan by his superiors, people he trusts with his very life, cuts deep, and I imagine he is more hurt than angry. From experience, I've learned to just give him "space" and not take his "crankiness" personally. Most of all, I don't try to console him. The Tax Man has a hard time accepting anything he considers "senseless pity."

Except for Ronin's ongoing colic and Liam peeling off an entire section of the dining room wallpaper, the day goes relatively smoothly. I am far too busy "moving in" to pay attention to the male moodiness of either of the Fitzpatrick men. Lunch is a magically produced fare of bread, fruit and cheese, courtesy of *Birgit*, but for dinner I want good ole' fashion Mundane comfort food; Boston style pizza and creamy clam chowder. Sure. It's an odd combination, but one the Tax Man and I have favored since we first met. I'm too tired to face Salem's rush hour traffic, I place separate orders from a local food delivery network. When the doorbell rings, I just assume it's our dinner, so I go to answer it without bothering to check the security camera on my phone. Before I reach the door, the Tax Man stops me and makes a face. I immediately realize why he's frowning. "Sorry. I'm out of practice at being paranoid," I admit. "I just take it for granted that we're safe at *Dun Siorai.*" Which is a very ironic statement considering that Meghan Fitzpatrick now resides there and I no longer feel safe in the Otherworld.

Declan just shakes his head and says, "Never mind. I'll get it. It's for me anyway."

Curiosity gets the best of me and I finally check my phone. The grainy images show two men on our stoop; the Black Knight, Ted Beckett, and his royal brother-in-law, Fr. Kevin O'Kenney, Prince of *I Idir*. This causes me to mutter under my breath. I definitely didn't order enough food for two more guests, the house isn't "company ready," my husband is in no mood for Otherworldly visitors, and I'm dead on my feet. This is not the night to play "hostess with the most-est."

Declan opens the wooden door, but leaves the storm door firmly closed. Through it, he blandly says, "Lord Knight. Lord *Caoihmin.* What ken' I do far' ya'?"

"We come bearing a gift. A "Welcome home to Salem" token," the priest says as he raises a gift bag for Declan to notice.

"'Tis totally unnecessary," my Lord Husband responds.

"Aren't you going to invite us in?" The Black Knight asks, not hiding his annoyance at being kept on the other side of the storm door.

"I'm afraid this isn't a good time, Lord Knight. Perhaps another night," my husband answers. "We are all vera' tired from the crossover. We need ta' feed the children and get them inta' bed far' the night."

Truthfully, I'm shocked at the borderline disrespectful way Declan is treating our important guests. If the Tax Man is anything, he's a huge proponent of Otherworld courtesy and protocol. Keeping these two highly-placed gentlemen, men he considers good friends, on the other side of the storm door, is unlike him, and shows me just how pissed the Tax Man really is over not being included in the discussion regarding Meghan becoming a member of the Queen's Intelligence Network, her subsequent return to *Dun Siorai*, or her relationship with Lord *Mac Badh*.

"Don't be a dick, Fritz. Let us in," Beck replies with a bluntness all his own. "I know you have your balls all in a knot over a perceived slight. But you don't have all the facts. At least give me the courtesy of bringing you up to date. Not because I am your superior officer, but because we're comrades and long-time friends."

It's a typical Black Knight style comment; an air of casual friendliness and camaraderie, but always with a thinly veiled reminder of who is actually in charge. In the five years I've known both the Princess of *I Idir* and her wizard-born husband, I've yet to uncover the "real" Ted Beckett. Sometimes I wonder if anyone has, even his fated mate.

Fr. Kevin, who one can't help but like because he's genuinely a nice person, adds, "We understand that you rightfully feel disrespected, Fitz. The two of us would feel the same in your position. All we're asking is a few moments of your time to explain the truth of the matter."

There's an awkward few moments of silence before the Tax Man opens the storm door. "Welcome to our home," he says in accordance with the Fae mandate that Otherworldly visitors must be "invited" inside, though it's obvious to all of us his greeting holds little warmth or sincerity. As on cue, both of the delivery workers pull up at the curb within seconds of each other, and in my head, I mentally try to determine how I can divide up the orders to accommodate two more diners. Apparently, my husband has somehow already noted this problem and has taken care of that dilemma. The order now contains two extra pizzas and two additional quarts of soup I know I didn't originally order, courtesy, I'm sure, of the Tax Man's magic. Since Declan's experience in North Korea, I'm still finding the extent of his "abilities" a mystery. What I do know is that my beloved husband returned home after his kidnapping with far more magical prowess than he left with, in addition to a boat load of PTSD that both of us are still trying to deal with.

Birgit observes me trying to balance the multiple pizza boxes and plastic bags and comes to my rescue, while Dylan and Liam peek at our guests from the safety of the kitchen doorway. Noticing the arrival of the food, The Black Knight says, "I'm sorry to disturb your family meal, Lady *Nuada*. I suppose Kevin and I could come back a bit later. We certainly don't wish to cause you any kind of imposition."

"I'd rather you just said what ya' came ta' say, Lord Knight. 'Tis not as if concern for the welfare of ma' family is at the heart of any of the decisions you make," Lord *Nuada* states.

The Black Knight of *I Idir* twists his expression into a grimace. "I suppose I deserved that."

Even I am shocked at the blatant anger my *Mo Shiorghra* is throwing at The Morrigan's representatives. I knew he was disgruntled over this turn of events, but apparently, I hadn't realized just how deep his discontent really went. Lord Declan Fitzpatrick *Nuada* has always been the poster child for proper Fae protocol. This is a stronger prickly side of him that I'm more familiar with seeing in the formidable Lady *Siobhan*.

Brigit and *Niahm* must sense the tension in the room as well. The younger nanny gathers up some soup and a pizza to take to the kitchen for the children. "Do ya' wish for me ta' take Master Ronin as well, ma' Lady?" *Birgit* asks. I look over to where my youngest son is peacefully sleeping in his infant seat despite all the noise and chaos. He seems to be the most chill of all three of our children. "No, he's fine for now. You can come for him after dinner," I reply.

"As ya' wish. Once we have finished eating, we will see ta' Dylan and Liam's bath and night time routine, ma' Lady. Unless you wish otherwise?"

"No. That would be perfect, *Birgit*. His Lordship and I will join you in the nursery as soon as we are finished here," I answer.

I decide to end this awkward pissing match between my husband and his comrades by taking charge. "Gentlemen, please join us for some refreshments," I say as I usher them towards the dining room.

"We didn't mean to intrude on your meal, Lady *Nuada*," the *Prionsa* (Prince) apologizes.

"Nonsense, my Lord. It's no intrusion. I would be honored for you to share our humble meal," I reply.

"Then far be it for me to turn down such a gracious invitation," Fr. Kevin says with a polite bow as he follows me into the dining room.

When Declan and the Black Knight stay rooted to their spots, still glaring at each other, I send the Tax Man a mental scolding. *"You and I have never ignored proper protocol, Declan Phineas Fitzpatrick, and I'm not about to let you start now. You are House Nuada's Lord, not some posturing teenager. And don't give me that 'look.' You know I'm right."*

MISSING 12

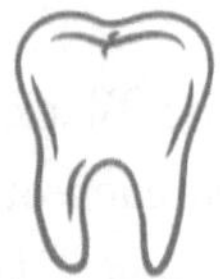

Dealing With a Lord Who's Far From Jolly

"Please join us, Lord Knight. I insist," Lord *Nuada* says without emotion, and I have no doubt I will be privy to "Cranky Declan" for the next few hours until he finally admits I was right all along.

I Idir's Hand of Justice acquiesces with a slight nod of his head, then the two men take seats at our large dining room table. I continue with my hostess duties; laying out plates, bowls and silverware, fetching our crystal stemware for the expensive bottle of whatever I'm sure is inside that gift bag Lord *Caoimhin* has placed on the table, all the while trying to keep the conversation light and drama free. It takes the completion of one whole pizza and the entire bottle of The Morrigan's best Cabernet before we get down to the real reason our *Crann Bethadh* visitors are here.

The Black Knight pushes away his plate and swallows the last mouthful of his wine, then leans back in his chair.

"Look Fitz, I'm just going to lay it all out there. Keeping you out of the loop regarding your sister's return to *I Idir* was a necessity. None of us liked having to do it, but this mission is too damn important to worry about stepping on anyone's toes."

My husband swirls the ruby colored wine in his glass, then sets it back on the table. "Am I to understand then, that despite being actively involved in your network for the past seven years, at great personal sacrifice, I might add, that I am suddenly deemed 'untrustworthy?' Because if that is the case, then let me tender my resignation immediately."

"That's not it at all, and you fucking know that, Fitz! I can't believe you of all people are taking this so personally," Beckett argued. "By now you should understand that everything is decided by Herself and information as to the how and why is always on a 'need to know' basis. Hell, I can't tell you how many times she's played me simply to 'test' my resolve or my loyalty. This particular decision wasn't meant to cast any doubt on your loyalty to The Throne"

"The feckin' hell it wasn't," the Tax Man replied. "I am the son of a traitor. I donna' believe far' one moment that The Morrigan doesn't have doubts about what lingers in ma' soul. A man's bloodline runs deep."

The Black Knight swears under his breath, something in the old language that runs along the lines of my husband having his head shoved too far up his ass to hear correctly. He pulls a faded, folded parchment from his back pocket and tosses it across the table towards Declan. "Herself asked me to give this to you as a sign of her gratitude for the loyalty and strength of character exhibited by both you and your Lady Mate, as well as that of your House."

Lord *Nuada* stares at the yellowed square, but doesn't reach for it. "My loyalty was never far' sale. I give it far' the good of *I Idir* and the integrity of ma' House," Declan says with just the tiniest bit of bitterness woven into the words.

Fr. Kevin took the last bite of his pizza, then dabbed at the corner of his mouth with a napkin. "We're all aware that your character is gold, Fitz, my Grandmother included. She's offering this to you not as some sort of... payment, but rather as a sign of how much she's come to admire you and yours, Lord *Nuada*. Taking on the role of your House's Lord after the shame your father brought to it was no easy task. You've done a remarkable job in building up House *Nuada's* holdings after they were stripped from you, and yours has been a logical and calm voice among the heated members of *I Idir's* Ruling Council during these troubled times. Herself just wants to let you know that she is aware of all this."

Declan still didn't pick up the parchment. "If Her Majesty feels this way, then she should have proven it by including me in this so-called 'mission' regardin' my youngest sister. I deserved ta' know," my husband states.

The two men of *Crann Bethadh* looked at each other, then the Black Knight said, "Herself guessed you'd say that. If I vet you in, understand that your life will become entirely more complicated. You know what they say about ignorance being bliss."

"I understand," Lord *Nuada* replied. "I deserve to know."

I stood up to excuse myself, believing this conversation to be just for my husband's ears, but Lord *Caoihmin* stopped me. "You should hear this as well, Lady *Nuada,* as this affects you and your children as much as it does your husband."

His words instantly cause me a great deal of anxiety. All of us had just finally gotten used to not looking over our shoulder for the "Daddy Boogie Man." To hear that we were right back to where we started was greatly upsetting. My children didn't deserve this type of constant upheaval in their lives.

Declan reached over to take my hand, still avoiding the Queen's "gift" parchment in front of him. "Ma' Lady and I will handle whatever awaits us together."

Beckett nods and leans forward, his hands clasped in front of him on the table. "Callum Fitzpatrick reached out to your sister, Meghan, about ten months ago. He railed on about how she'd been treated unjustly at the hands of her brother's mate. He promised her that she could have her revenge against the two of you...even become Lady of House *Nuada*...if she only would join with him against The Throne. Your father wanted Meghan to do her best to convince her mother that her youngest daughter needed to come home or she would never find a mate. Once that had been accomplished, he wanted his daughter to...finish what she had started before your handfasting. To murder Lady Rosalinda."

"Well, Shit!" I curse. "I knew she felt the same way about me. However, Callum must have known that

Declan would instantly take his revenge. How is my being dead going to help him take back House *Nuada?* If anything, Declan would be even more rage-filled and set on vengeance."

The *Crann Bethadh* pair remained silent, looking towards the Tax Man to answer my question. This, of course, set off a whole symphony of warning bells in my head. The Tax Man turned around to look at me directly. "As you are my Eternal Mate, Lass, if something were ta' happen ta' ya' befar' the time the Universe has destined far' ma' own end', I would have no choice but ta' take on the role of *Bás Beo*. I would be unable ta' properly…function…within either world, leavin' ma' sire free reign ta' attempt to take over leadership of House *Nuada* with the additional hope of furthering its line."

"*Bás Beo?* What the hell is that?" For a few seconds, Declan's words don't make any sense to me. Then I recall the old language I've been struggling with for five years. "Wait…doesn't that mean 'living death' in ancient Gaelic? Just what in *Dubnos* are we talking about here?"

Held captive by politeness and rank, the Black Knight and Fr. Kevin look down-right uncomfortable about being part of this awkward conversation, testifying to the fact that I'm really not going to like what my fated mate is about to tell me. Declan sighs before launching into his explanation, ramping up my anxiety. "Under the magic of the bonded ink making us *cúpláilte go síoraí* (eternally mated), if ma' true *Mo Shiorghra* were to die during the 'fruitful' years of our union, thus ending the possibility of furthering House *Nuada's* bloodline, I would be forced by sacred law ta' abdicate my position as its Lord and thus 'disappear' ta' live on ma' own as a *taibhse* (ghost) until the Universe allowed me ta' join ya' in Eternity. If that were ta' happen, ma' heir, our Dylan, would become Lord of House *Nuada*, and someday further the bloodline with offspring of his own."

The absurdity of the whole concept makes my voice sound whiningly shrill, even to my own ears. "That's the most ridiculous thing I've ever heard. I know you would be grief-stricken if something happened to me...rage filled, for sure, if I were to be murdered...but there's no logical reason for you to be forced to 'step out' of your life! Who the feckin' hell would take care of our children?" The pitch of my voice is high now I'm pretty sure every dog all-over the neighborhood can hear and react to it. "And Dylan is still a child. There's no way he's capable of taking over as Lord! Are you *Tuatha de Danann* types all crazy? Is insanity part of your biological make-up?"

By now I'm up from the table and pacing the dining room. I look at the three men, none of whom can meet my gaze. "Please Declan...tell me you're not truly serious about any of this."

"Please Rosie...sit down and let me finish," the Tax Man pleads.

I know my outburst in front of his comrades must embarrass him. There is no greater "rule follower" than Lord Declan Phineas Fitzpatrick *Nuada*, and my current behavior obviously doesn't follow feckin' *I Idir* protocol. But only because I love the guy beyond all reason, and not because I agree with any of this hocus-pocus bullshit, I work to reign in my outrage. I swallow a sarcastic retort, pull out my chair, and finish the contents of my glass in one gulp. "I'm listening," I say through clenched teeth.

"Everything I just said is part of the contract we signed when we added the "eternal" contingency to our hand-fasting ink. It is the reason many fated mates donna' add this extra magic to their bond. Not while there may be a chance of conceiving any children together. 'Tis a big gamble to take on whether the Universe will not seek to interrupt a happy life between two Eternally Bonded *Mo Shiorghras*. When ya' asked for the extra magical ink ta' be applied I'd assumed ya' had read through the entire contract. So lost was I in the notion that ya' wanted to be with ma' soul in the Afterlife, that I never checked that ya' fully understood everything that would be involved, and far' that, Love, I take full responsibility."

The words hit their mark and I realize that if anyone should be embarrassed, it's me. "Oh Declan...I'm so sorry for calling you out. If anyone's to blame, it's me. I was just so determined to prove to you and the world...in that very instant...that what happened in North Korea didn't change my love for you in any way, I wasn't as careful as I should have been. I should have realized that Fae sacred law has all these different caveats..." The words are a lump in my throat and I find it hard to continue.

The Tax Man leans over and kisses my cheek. "I could never hold you in fault, Sweet Rosie Lass, far' lovin' me the way ya' do. I consider ma'self a vera' blessed man and I dare ta' hope that the Universe won't call in its markers, but if it does, we need ta' be ready. Besides, once ya' are beyond yar' child bearin' years, that part of the contract is null and void."

"Whoa. Hold On! Is that supposed to make me feel better, Declan? The notion that when I can no longer produce "offspring" my value as an Eternal Mate is reduced in importance? What kind of patriarchal bullshit is that?" I complain.

"'Tis an old law, Love, one I donna' completely understand ma'self, but I'm sure had somethin' ta' do with rightful heirs. It has nothin' ta' do with what I feel far ya' nor with the purity of ma' bloodline. We have three fine sons. According to the Old Ways, I have completed ma' commitment ta' ma' House."

My face must be a mask of anguished confusion, because he puts his hand over mine and matter- of-factly continues his explanation. "There is only one thing we need ta' be concerned about regarding this clause in the Eternal Contract. There be no doubt that ma' sire is aware that we have taken the Eternal Bond and knows exactly how the contract reads. 'Tis the weight behind his whole plan. Should ya' move on into the Afterlife by the hand of ma' sister, it is she who will be held accountable, not him. I have no doubt that he would easily sacrifice his flesh and blood daughter for his own personal gain. Then, when I step out of ma' life as the law requires, Dylan would be in need a Guardian to speak for him until he reached the age of manhood and could take The Ritual ink on his own. Undoubtedly, his paternal grandfather would lay claim to that right, as his next of blood kin."

The thought of Callum Fitzpatrick near our son makes me ill. I don't even consider that if we've gotten to this point, I've already been murdered. "What about your *mathair*? Couldn't she take guardianship of Dylan instead of your father?"

Declan shakes his head in the negative. "No, Lass. My Lady *Mathair* carries no trace of *Nuada* blood. Callum Fitzpatrick would have first rights."

"But he's a wanted man!" I argue. "He's sure to be sentenced to death by the Ruling Council for murder and treason. How can the law allow him to take over guardianship of Dylan? That makes no sense," I question.

"House leadership and the guardianship of an underage heir falls under the tenets of Sacred Otherworld Law, not the Civil Laws of *I Idir*. House *Nuada* must be led by someone with the ancient blood of the King with the Silver Arm," its current Lord explains. "Any charges against ma' sire would be delayed until Dylan became of age…and who knows what the man might do in the interim. I believe in ma' soul that his evil and greed knows no bounds."

"Unless, of course, the man in question somehow ends up dead before that," the Black Knight interjects, his first comment since warning us about the dangers that being included in this "mission" would cause us.

"Aye," my husband agrees. "There is that possibility."

The idea that murder is being casually discussed at my dining room, in a home I consider my safe space, is more than my psyche and stomach can handle. I quickly stand and mumble, "Please excuse me for a moment, gentlemen," then head straight for the guest bathroom off the kitchen doorway. I manage to hold my swirling stomach contents down, though the pepperoni pizza and wine are doing the tango in my gut. I splash cold water over my face then return to the dining room with shaking hands.

The wine glasses are gone, replaced with our Irish crystal tumblers and my husband's best Scotch, three of them already used. That alone tells me that decisions have been made while I've been hiding out in the restroom. Declan Fitzpatrick is no drinker, so if he's partaken in some joint toast, I am pretty sure clandestine plans have been made in my absence. Frankly, I'm glad not to be part of their "spy shet" games of murder and mayhem, though truthfully, I wouldn't be at all sad if news came to me that Callum Fitzpatrick was no longer our problem.

Lord *Nuada* takes the folded parchment in his hand, which also signals that whatever has been discussed is agreeable to my fated mate. He unfolds the document and I see his eyebrows raise in surprise. "This is vera' generous of Her Majesty," he says.

"As I said, earlier, Fitz, my grandmother wants you to understand how much she truly appreciates your House's loyalty. This is her way of showing you," said the Prince of *I Idir*. "Herself never does anything in a small way," he adds with a smile.

"What is it?" I ask my husband.

Declan slides the parchment over to me. It's a deed of some kind, with an illustrated map and the ancient text penned in a heavily ornate script. I pick out the words I know and ask, "Is this what I think it is?

"Aye. 'Tis the deed for *Tir na Fathach* (The Land of the Giants)," my mate replies.

"Didn't House *Nuada* already own that land," I question.

"We were its caretakers for hundreds of years, my Lady, but ownership belonged to the Throne of *I Idir*. According to this document, Her Majesty has given the land to House *Nuada* as its own. It makes my House the largest landowner in all of *I Idir*," Declan explains.

"Herself knows that the property is special to you and your Lady," the Black Knight says. "She said she hopes it can always be a place of retreat for the two of you."

The Raven Queen is right on that account. That mountain range holds a lot of wonderful memories for my *Mo Shiorghra* and I, including our "first date," the night of our handfasting, along with multiple "romantic" picnics enjoyed in the past five years. I'm pretty sure Liam was conceived there, and I'd always wanted to build a charming, get-away cottage on that spot, just for the two of us.

"Aye, ma' Rose. Now that the land officially belongs to us, we can build that little love nest ya' always wanted," my *Mo Shiorghra* says to my mind.

And, for the first time in several days, my heart feels just a tad bit lighter.

MISSING 13

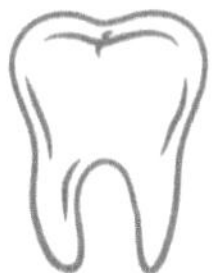

School Bells

THE TEN DAYS leading up to the start of the new school year are too frantically busy to dwell on the political espionage that encircles the Throne of *I Idir*. Thus, we are given a short reprieve from worrying exclusively over the plotting of Declan's traitorous father and where his murderous sister might fit into all of this mayhem. Both Declan and I return to our Mundane livelihoods within days of our arrival, leaving *Birgit* and *Niamh* to hold down the fort, caring for the four young charges under their rule until the new school year begins. Through a personal recommendation from the *Banphrionsa* of *I Idir*, we were fortunate to hire a great cleaning service that caters to Otherworldly clientele. Because of the size of our house, and the large number of people living in it, "Local Lassies Domestic Services," led by the very capable, Mary Francis McCarthy, has a team that visits twice a week to handle the general housekeeping chores, as well as the ever-growing pile of laundry for our family unit of eight. I totally realize that all this extra help makes me the envy of my fellow working moms, and I don't take my gratitude for this gift lightly. Without the benefit of all these privileges, it's doubtful our life in the Mundane world would be as efficient as it's become.

Still, the weeks spent preparing for the new semester prove extra busy this year, due to the addition of another full-time, school-age child. Dylan's growth spurt over the summer months requires a whole new set of Mundane style clothes, and though the private Fae-centered school he will attend mandates the wearing of a uniform, there is still a necessary wardrobe of everyday attire to fill, along with proper Mundane shoes, pajamas and underwear that's part of a normal life here. Being as he is his father's "mini-me," and despite being only five-years old, Dylan is terribly picky about the cut, color and fit of his clothes, so much so, that after a few extremely frustrating trips to the mall with his mother, the completion of the job of outfitting young *Mac Nuada* is eventually turned over to his Lord *Athair*.

Our teenager is another story completely. He and I take one solitary trip to a popular department store where upon *Oisin* selects six pairs of the same pants in the same dark color, a stack of black cotton t-shirts with breast pocket, and one additional white polo shirt, but only because I insist he needs something with a collar that isn't black. Despite plenty of subtle suggestions from yours truly about what might be fashionable among the Mundane high school crowd, *Oisin* refuses to add anything more to his wardrobe, grumpily explaining to me that he "has no need ta' catch the attention of any Mundane ladies, since his true love remains locked away from him in *I Idir.*" As you can tell from that comment, someone hasn't quite come to terms with his elder brother's orders that he live with his family in the Mundane world during the coming school year.

Truthfully, I am more than likely the happiest member of our little family regarding the fall return to Salem. I always miss my dentistry work during the summer months we spend in the Otherworld, and this year, I'm especially anxious to introduce a brand-new incentive I've developed for the Tooth Fairy Cadets under my Corp leadership. Though there is a gaggle of responsibilities within the walls of *Dun Siorai* in my role as Lady *Nuada*, life in Salem fulfills me in a way I'd be hard pressed to explain to my Otherworld-loving husband. Plus, being back home in "Fitzpatrick's Folly" always fills me with a deep sense of comfort.

The first day of the new school is accompanied by scorching heat, not unusual for August on the east coast of the United States. In his *Cerridwen Prep* school uniform, with its knee length khaki pants and monogrammed polo shirt, our Dylan looks far too "grown-up" for my liking, and I have to work not to shed a few tears as I help him slip on his new backpack. I look over at the Tax Man and note the wistful expression on his face, and I guess he's feeling the same thing about our eldest son beginning Mundane kindergarten. I remember the two of us being excited and worried a few years ago when we dropped *Oisin* off at the school for the first time, but my husband's half-brother was already a strapping, worldly-wise ten-year-old on his own first day at *Cerridwen.* In addition, despite our genuine love and concern for the boy we consider a member of the family, there's a different tug at the heartstrings when it's your own baby leaving the safety of your arms.

It gives us some peace of mind that, being a school for children with Fae heritage, *Cerridwen Prep* has over-the-top security, both the traditional type as well as the magical. The school and its grounds are heavily warded with top level magic, and blessed with top-notch Mundane security protocol personally designed by the Black Knight of *I Idir*, whose own daughter, the Princess *Mairead*, will also begin her education at *Cerridwen* this year. The Tax Man and I have both arranged for late starts this morning so that we may accompany the two boys to school, this being their first day. Only one of them is excited by this prospect.

On the drive over to the Mundane public high school *Oisin* will attend, my husband's brother begs to be dropped off two blocks away and allowed to walk the rest of the distance on his own. His Lordship frowns, a crease forming between his dark ginger brows. He doesn't immediately reply, which to those of us who know Declan Fitzpatrick well enough, means you haven't a snowball's chance in Hell of getting your own way. The teenager looks to me with a pleading expression, mentally imploring me to intercede on his behalf. I feel for the kid. At his age, being driven to the door as "the new kid," in a hoity-toity car, one that costs over a hundred grand, isn't the best way to "fit in."

Sitting next to him in the front seat, I lay a hand on my

husband's arm. "Declan…perhaps *Oisin* is right. He might adapt better to this new experience if we let him arrive in a…less conspicuous manner."

Even from behind his favorite Ray-Bans, I see that damn eyebrow rise in what I know is a sign of annoyance. "Is that how you truly feel, brother?" he asks the boy, not keeping the "lordship tone" from his voice. "You are embarrassed by this mode of transportation?"

"No, ma' Lord. I think it is a vera' fine vehicle. For ya' ta' drive, that is. But not far' a student who is only a lowly 'freshman.' I donna' wish far' the others ta' think that I am puttin' on airs, Sir," the boy explains.

"A man of House *Nuada* shud' never apologize for who he is, *Oisin*, or what he has, as long as ya' always remember that those things are fleeting. 'Tis one's character and sense of confidence that matters most," my husband lectures, but then concedes to the boy's request and pulls up along the curb a few blocks from the school.

"Thank you, ma' Lord," the boy says as he gets out of the car with more than a little relief in his voice. "I will do ma' best ta' make our House proud."

"Of that I have no doubt, *dearthair nios oige* (younger brother). Now off with ya'. Have a productive first day," Declan replies. "Unfortunately, your Lady Sister and I are unable to pick you up when the day is over because of our schedule. I will send Duncan instead."

"Aye, my Lord. I will look far' him." *Oisin* leans into my side of the car and kisses my cheek. "Thank you, Rosie."

I pat his cheek in return. "Have a wonderful first day, *Oisin*. I know you'll do great. Make lots of friends," I advise.

"I will try, Lady Sister," he answers as he walks off down the block, stopping a second and then waving us off.

The Tax Man pulls away and says to our son left alone in the back seat. "I hope ya' do not wish ta' be dropped off two blocks away as well, Dylan."

"Oh no, Da," our son says, using Declan's preferred informal title. "I want ya' ta' come see ma' new school and meet all the friends I will surely make. 'Tis no doubt I will be chosen as class leader."

His father laughs at this comment, but I mentally chide him. *"Don't encourage him, Declan. He already has enough of that Fitzpatrick-Nuada competitiveness. You know that Cerridwen Prep insists on toning down all that Otherworld hoity-toity shit. The use of titles and rank pulling is strictly prohibited. There's no reason to get Dylan all riled up."*

"I am doin' no such thing, Lass. It is good far' the lad ta' have a strong level of confidence. It is in his blood and ken' not be helped."

"He does have two parents, you know," I reply with a bit of frostiness.

"Aye, and his gorgeous mathair is no shrinkin' violet herself," the Tax Man adds with a smile. *" 'Tis easier ta' sway a majority of the Rulin' Council than my own mate when she has har' mind made up.* He pauses, and then adds, *"And if I haven't told ya yet today, ya' look especially fetchin' in that green frock, Love. It draws the eyes ta' every delicious curve. 'Tis a great shame that we both have pressin' morning appointments. I'd most enjoy takin' it off ya."*

And that's the way it rolls with the Tax Man. If a subject comes up between us on a topic he'd rather not debate, he moves on to seduction. It's been this way from the very beginning, and even when the logical, adult woman in me calls him out about it, the other half of me falls right under his spell. You would think after five years and four children, some of the "lustful pull" of the bond would have eased up. Nope. Not in the least. Whatever magic is behind the connection between *Mo Shiorghras*, it's incredibly strong. I used to wonder how my husband's parents had managed to produce six living children given that they absolutely despise each other. Now I fully understand and am thus eternally grateful that my fated mate turned out to be honorable, compassionate, and loving. It apparently doesn't always work out that way.

"Nice counter distraction, Tax Man. I'm gonna have to take a 'raincheck' on that offer. Mel already had to do some heavy schedule juggling just so I could be here this morning." Our conversational "dance" is interrupted by our son's excitement as we pull into the drop-off parking area of the school.

"There it is! Ma' new school! Hurry, Da! I don' wanna' be late far' the first day," Dylan scolds from the back seat. My husband parks the car and I go around to help our son out of his car seat, but he pushes me away. "Thank you, *Mhamai* (Mommy), but I ken' do it ma'self. I'm no wee *bairn* anymore, ya' know."

Part of me dies inside. Dylan is our first born, mine and Declan's, dreamed of and hoped for before he even came to be. Our sweet little "Pay-not." I knew this day would come. I thought I would be ready for it. It seems I was wrong. I look at Declan who has joined me outside the car, and I can feel his warring emotions as well; a deep sense of loving pride and the reluctance of his father's heart to "let go" of his first-born child and heir. So, it is with parents. It takes every bit of self-control not to weep, as both the men in my life, big and little, would find it monumentally distressing. Thankfully, Dylan exits the car and takes each of our hands for the walk to his classroom. I breathe a sigh of relief as I'm not sure I could have gracefully accepted another rejection.

The manicured courtyard of the prep school's entrance is filled with nervous parents and excited children, some of the younger ones anxiously hiding behind the skirts and pant legs of their *mathairs* and *athairs*. A petite woman with tiny, pointed features marking her pixie heritage, waves us over. I recognize Orla Dell, mate to Declan's friend and fellow team member, Connor Dell, and one of *Cerridwen's* three kindergarten teachers. When enrolling Dylan last spring, the Tax Man and I had requested that Dylan be placed in Orla's class, and though the Head Master had casually insisted that "such requests couldn't always be fulfilled," being a well-liked, Ruling Council Lord does have its perks even when the philosophy of *Cerridwen Prep* is supposedly "social-hierarchy free."

Try not to judge me. Rosie Parker has never been a fan of nepotism. But with all the chaos surrounding the tentative truce agreement between the governments of the Mundane world and *I Idir*, any extra layer of security I can add to my son's environment is a top priority. Because Orla's mate, like mine, works for the Black Knight, she's been encouraged to undergo the same self-defense training that was also offered to me. Unlike me, however,

Orla Dell is naturally fierce. According to Declan, she can put down a human man faster than most of her male counterparts. And because students are not allowed to have *scathachs* (nanny bodyguards) with them at school (the belief that such a thing would be considered "elitist" and "a distraction to the learning environment"), the knowledge that Dylan's teacher would be worthy adversary against any "bad actors" helps relieve my mother's anxiety.

"Mrs. Dell," Orla's title in this "protocol-free" zone, greets me with a hug. Adult Fae types usually avoid physical contact lest there is an unwitting transfer of magical energy, but it's no secret that I'm a tooth fairy and magically free after sunrise. Plus, Orla and I have been friends since the Tax Man first came into my life. "Big day, huh Rosie? How are we holding up, Mama? These 'first days' are heart-crushing. I cried for a week when our Pippa started kindergarten."

"I'm trying really hard not to make a spectacle of myself," I admit. "I can't believe Dylan is starting school already. It seems like only yesterday he was still toddling around in diapers. Where the hell did all the time go?" I know. It's a lame statement. One I'm sure the teacher has heard hundreds of times before. As Orla chats with my husband, I watch our son leave the safety of our hands to interact with a small group of other children. Suddenly, I watch as heads turn to observe the arrival of another family. No surprise there. The *Banphrionsa* of *I Idir* and the Black Knight tend to cause notice wherever they go. Today, they are joined by their oldest daughter, *Mairead*, also a princess of *I Idir*, as well as The Morrigan's named heiress. Upon seeing the two of us, the little *banphrionsa's* eyes dart around the courtyard crowd, no doubt looking for our son.

Since before Dylan was born, the littlest Raven has seemed oddly fascinated by our Dylan. I can still clearly recall a Solstice gathering I attended at the home of her parents when I was about six months pregnant with him. *Mairead*, who is about five months older than our son, was in the arms of her royal grandmother and had insisted on being allowed to touch my rounded belly. According to The Morrigan, the baby told the Queen that she and Dylan "would be great friends someday." At the time I thought it was just a silly sentiment. After all, the princess herself was only an infant. However, after now having three *Sidhe* children of my own and seeing first-hand how their development greatly differs from Mundane babies, perhaps there was something to *Mairead's* prediction.

There's no doubt that the little princess is quite taken with our son, although I wouldn't say it's a "friendship" in the truest meaning of the word; more like a "nemesis competition" in which the two of them are constantly trying to "one-up" each other, be it in horsemanship, competitive games, or general play. It's been this way since they both could barely toddle, and to this day, I believe our first born walked as early as he did simply because *Mairead* had already mastered that skill several weeks before him.

I can tell the exact moment when Dylan is aware that *Mairead* is near. His child-like aurora goes from a confident veil of yellow to a swirling mix of red and teal, signaling his inner emotions towards the little girl that include intense feelings, both positive and negative, along with confused uncertainty about why he feels the way he does. The littlest Raven, on the other hand, is The Morrigan's own, and her aurora is unreadable to someone without a similar strength of magic. To the outward eye, *Mairead* exudes the same calm confidence of her parents. One has to wonder what lies behind such an unnaturally assured facade of a five-year-old. She shakes away the hand of her beaming father and heads straight toward us.

"Good Morn, Dylan *Mac Nuada*. 'Tis finally the first day of school. Does it not feel as if we have waited an entire century for this day?"

"Aye, Princess," my son replies. I pretend I don't notice the blush coloring his cheeks. "I am glad to begin this new adventure."

The little girl smiles and I'm relieved when her face doesn't mirror that of her imposing *athair*, who always reminds me of a smirking shark when he graces you with that same expression. "You musn't call me 'Princess' when we are at school, *Mac Nuada*. 'Tis against the rules. No titles are allowed at *Cerridwen*," she explains. The heir to the Throne of *I Idir* reaches out her tiny hand with its long graceful fingers, testament to her *Sidhe* blood, for my son to grasp. "When we are at school, you must call me *'Mairead,'* and I shall call you 'my dearest friend and companion, Dylan.' Is not that the best solution, *comrádaí mo chroí* (comrade of my heart).

MISSING 14

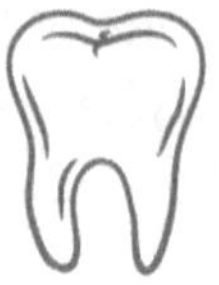

Handfast Hell

LIKE MOST MUNDANE families at the start of a new school year, our little clan falls into the chaotic state of everyday routine. Declan often spends a good portion of his Mundane evening hours handling House and Ruling Council business in *I Idir*, which is mid-afternoon of the following day in the Otherworld. It's a grueling schedule, but husband and father tries his best to have dinner with the family before leaving. This has required me to give up my own evening hours at my practice, which then forces me to take on the dreaded Saturday shift instead. Truthfully, I hate losing a day of a weekend at home with my children and husband, but I don't complain, as it is my sacrifice towards making this dual Mundane-Otherworld lifestyle work.

I know how much it saddens my Tax Man that many nights he returns home after the younger kids have gone to sleep for the night, thus missing his beloved story time ritual. In reaction to that, he goes above and beyond in his fatherly duties during the hours he is at home in Salem; coaching Dylan's pee-wee soccer league, monitoring *Liam's* swimming lessons at the community center, taking Ronin to an infant Gymboree class, and sitting on the fund-raising committee of *Oisin's* high school, which is as much "participation" as our resident teenager will allow him.

It's a crazy, hectic schedule, but one we've tried hard to make work so that everyone's needs can be met on some level. That's why when the damn raven appears at our bedroom window early on an overcast Saturday morning, while I'm still dressing for work, I inwardly groan. Okay, maybe I actually outwardly groaned. Loudly. Those blasted birds never bring good news.

This delivery is no different. I make Declan take care of retrieving the scroll from the beady- eyed, winged demon, and I can tell by my mate's face that the message is not the one announcing that we had won the annual *Lammas* Sweepstakes. "What the hell is it this time?" I ask, not bothering to hide my annoyance.

My husband rolls the scroll back up and sends the raven off without a response before answering my question. "It is an invitation for my *deirfuir's* (sister's) handfast to *Cillian Mac Badh*," he says with no emotion whatsoever.

"You're not really planning on attending, are you? I question, already knowing the answer.

Declan doesn't respond. Instead, he flops into my nursing chair, then pulls out his phone to check the detailed calendar I know he keeps on the device. "I ken' move around a few clients, though Dylan will have to miss his Saturday game. He will not be happy about it, but it ken' no be helped. You will have to make arrangements for coverage at yar' practice. I assume Mel will be needin' the time off as well. No doubt she and Duncan received the same invite."

There's no assumption on my husband's part that I will ultimately refuse to attend. He understands me well enough to know that I am keenly aware of his duties and commitments as Lord of House *Nuada*, and fully convinced that I love him enough to support him, even as the thought of celebrating this union makes me want to scream until I turn various shades of purple. "What dates are we talking about?" I ask. "I also have a Tooth Fairy Corps training seminar coming up this month. Changing dates this late in the game would be difficult for attendees coming in from out of town."

"The handfast isn't until next month. October 12th, ta' be exact, though I am surprised the parties involved would plan for such an extravagant celebration so close to *Samhain*. 'Tis no secret House *Mac Badh* likes to entertain in the most lavish of ways. Two events so close ta' gether would be a challenge, both physically and financially, far' any House."

I think to myself how relieved I am that House *Nuada* is not hosting this handfast from hell. At one time, Declan's mother had her own inheritance set aside in anticipation of the handfasting costs of her youngest daughter's union, but that little nest egg was stolen by his father, along with most of the House's treasury. Although my husband has managed to rebuild House *Nuada's* wealth over the past five years, the cost of a lavish affair between two social and politically prominent families would have cost us a hefty chunk of change. I apparently am not shielding very well, as my Tax Man replies out loud to the musings in my head. "I am relieved as well, Lass. As political equals, *Mac Badh* would have been in his right ta' ask that House *Nuada* host this celebration of their union. Whatever their reasonin', I am glad House *Badh* has taken on the responsibility. I would not have enjoyed bearin' the costs."

Another realization comes to mind. "Are you still planning on returning to *Dun Siorai* for *Samhain* as well? That would mean two trips through the Veil in the same month, Sweetie. Two visits would require a tremendous amount of planning, not to mention the disruption to the kid's schedule."

The Tax Man makes a sour face. "I realize this a large burden ta' place on yar' shoulders, Rosie Lass. But there is little I ken do ta' change the circumstances. As Lord and Lady of House *Nuada*, there is the expectation that we will attend both gatherings, though thankfully we will only be required to play host ta' one. I will lay most of the plannin' for the *Samhain* meal on Tuck and Cook, and the sacred ceremonies at the discretion of the House Mages. The other events will take place elsewhere, so all we need ta' do is show up for those. There is no need ta' arrive any earlier than a day or two for either event, and ya' have ma' word that we will return back ta' Salem as soon as the last blessing is given and the last glass raised."

I let out a big, dramatic sigh of self-suffering, surely worthy of an Oscar. My stalwart mate doesn't react, instead calmly asking, "What else would ya' have me do, Rosie? I am open ta' reasonable suggestions?"

I hate when he appears so calm. It always works to take the fire out of my belly. Still, I'm not one hundred percent ready to roll over and be a wifely doormat. "I suppose you wouldn't consider going to the handfasting by yourself, would you?" I suggest. "I get that we can't miss *Samhain*, it being a *sabbat* and all, but it would be so much easier if just you crossed over for the handfast and the rest of us stayed here in Salem. We could explain to people that we didn't wish to interrupt the children's education so early in the school year."

In reply to my suggested compromise, I get "the look." You know the one; when your significant other thinks the words leaving your mouth are total nonsense and is debating how to best tell you without causing a full-blown argument. The truth is, the Tax Man is…well…the Tax Man. Even after five years of bonded matrimony, he can still be as filter-less and blunt as he was that first time I met him in my office. "I was lookin' for 'responsible' suggestions, Rosie. Not emotional reactions." I open my mouth to speak, but he holds up a hand to stop me. "Hear me out, Lass. Even if I were to put us through the speculation and gossip that would follow my attendin' an important House handfast without my *Mo Shiorghra* and family, there is no chance in feckin' *Dubnos* I would leave you and the children alone here in the Mundane world for days at a time. The wards I place when I go back and forth have set time limits and I am careful to always be back befar' the spell evaporates. I know of nothing that would last for longer time periods. I donna' care what the Throne is sayin' about any treaties, nor how talented and devoted *Birgit* and *Niamh* are as *scathachs*. I have met this enemy on a personal level and learned ma' lesson the hard way. I will never let ma' guard down again, nor will I ever gamble with the safety of my own."

I can see the intensity of Declan's words in his aura and I feel them deeply in every fiber of my soul. Trouble is, when my mate speaks of "the enemy," I'm not sure if he means the brutal North Koreans who once kidnapped him, or the man behind the whole tragedy...his own father.

MISSING 15

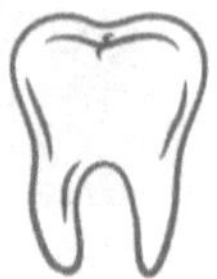

Oisin Reasons

SOMEDAYS, I can't believe that our family life is…well…as normal as it appears. Despite our dual roles in both worlds, we Fitzpatricks spend our days and nights in what most folks would call "boring" routine. Considering what has happened in the past, and what could happen in the future, I am one hundred percent grateful to the Universe for each blessedly monotonous, dull day.

That isn't to say that we don't have our share of typical Mundane modern family problems. Often the children's out of school activities are re-scheduled, causing us to scramble and switch everything up at the last minute. Plus, since the frosty Eleanor Pitch, Declan's Mundane PA, left his employment two years ago, there's been a revolving door of new hires, wisely this time, all of the Fae persuasion. Unfortunately, the Tax Man is a rather demanding boss who expects his employees to have the same drive for work and perfection that he does. This trait, plus the gossip about what happened to Rory Dell, makes finding and keeping loyal and responsible office help difficult.

There's also parenting dilemmas within our little clan that at times leave both Declan and I frustrated. Since we've returned to the Mundane world, *Liam* has taken to shucking all his clothes and walking around naked. I understand that this is a perfectly normal sign of growing independence in toddler development, but his propensity for doing so in public venues, i.e. the supermarket, the playground, and his Mommy and Me class, makes for a multitude of embarrassing moments. In addition, Dylan, who, like his father, is usually a poster child for rule following, has now decided to protest his nightly bath, throwing a fit nearly every night. And my wee Ronin, who I always claimed to be the most "scheduled" of my babies, has decided to prove me a liar, changing his routine daily.

Then, of course, there's our resident teenager. When it comes to adolescent *Sidhe* males, I am a complete novice. Declan claims that *Oisin's* rebellious nature is to be expected as he moves closer toward the Fae age of manhood. Still, I notice even the staid Tax Man is losing patience with the boy's boldness, which, on some occasions, has bordered on blatant disrespect. Of course, his Lordship blames the influence of Mundane culture for his brother's lack of decorum. I suppose I'd rather believe that than what I'm really thinking; that *Oisin* has inherited some of his own awful father's sense of entitlement.

This evening, the discussion at the dinner table is centered on our teenager's current set curfew. Though we are relieved that *Oisin* has made an abundance of school friends here in the Mundane plane, his preference for spending time with them over everything and everyone else is less than optimal. The current issue tonight is in regards to us demanding that he be home by 10:00 pm on a school night, and 11:00 pm on weekends. My young brother-in-law is arguing for 11:00 pm on school nights, and midnight on Fridays and Saturdays.

"'Tis what all of ma' *cairde* (friends) are allowed, ma' Lord. I donna' think 'tis too much ta' ask that I be allowed the same liberties," the boy argues. "I am no wee tot. In *I Idir* I am allowed ta' be ma' own man."

So far, *Oisin* has delivered his request only to Declan, which, if I am to be honest, I find a tad annoying. In the last few months, I've noticed a change in his general attitude toward females; a level of patronizing I'd found disheartening for a male with one foot in both of the worlds. Up until now, I hadn't mentioned this to my mate, but in witnessing how I am being left totally out of the conversation, perhaps it needs to be discussed.

It's also obvious that his Lordship is tired of being questioned. Groomed his entire life for a position as Lord of House *Nuada*, as well as a member of *I Idir's* Ruling Council, being harangued over a decision he's already made doesn't sit well with the Tax Man. "I must confess ta' growin' impatient with yar' need ta' keep beatin' a dead harse, *deartháir* (brother). I have already given ya' ma' answer. Ma' Lady and I feel that we have been mar' than generous in allowin' ya' the extra freedoms ya' already possess, especially when yar' attention shad' be entirely focused on yar' studies so that ya' will have top options far' college. Ya' need not be out runnin' the streets of

Salem any later than what I have determined to be satisfactory."

"But ma' Lord, 'twas ma' Lady Sister who was adamant that I shud' make friends here in the Mundane world," the kid argues, throwing me under the bus. "'Tis hard to keep friends when yar' rules make me look like a wee *glóhach* (gelding/castrated male horse)."

His Lordship puts down his fork and levels his teenage brother with a look that signals he's done being polite. "Yar' Lady Sister wants only ta' see ya' happy and content. I, on the other hand, am yar' elder brother and your Liege Lord. Ma' responsibility is to see that ya' become the man that House *Nuada,* and the people of *Idir*, need. Yar' personal 'happiness,' and yar' busy social life is a far second ta' what really matters. Am I makin' myself clear, *Oisin* Fitzpatrick *Nuada*?"

I'll go ahead and admit that the kid deserves to be taken down a notch, but even I realize that my *Mo Shiorghra* is being rather harsh. Those thoughts earn me a quick reply. *"I ken' no give the boy a long rope of freedom, Lass. His bloodline will someday make him a magical force to be reckoned with. I must do all I ken' ta' keep him on the straight and narrow; to guide him to an adulthood that won't cause him far mar' pain than ya' ken' imagine. I no want ta' became the parent my athair was, but it does no good to let him wander his formative adolescence without a firm hand."*

MISSING 16

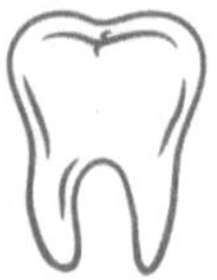

That Halloween Season

FOR A FEW MINUTES AFTERWARD, the table is silent except for Liam, who is banging his plastic Sippee cup in a definite rhythm. (It is looking more and more to me that our middle child has inherited his father's music talent, the gift my Tax Man seemed to lose when the North Koreans tinkered with his brain.) Everyone tucks into their food, no one wanting to throw out another neutral topic while the old one hangs in the air like over-powering, dollar store cologne.

And because all that male testosterone and magical chutzpah is forever racing through his adolescent self, it's *Oisin* who unwisely brings up yet another controversial subject to discuss over dinner. "Ma' Lord, when ya' were a boy studyin' in the Mundane world, did ya' ever participate in the human custom of 'trick or treatin'' as part of their Halla'wen' festivities?" he casually asks as he sticks a bite of pork chop into his mouth.

There's no way the kid doesn't know about his older brother's disdain of human holidays, that to Declan's mind, "mock the vera' essence of the 'Old Ways." My husband has always made his views about the "pillagin' of Fae customs," especially by the commercially-centered United States, extremely clear. Out of affection for my Mundane childhood, our Salem home dresses for the Christmas season, but we spend the "holidays," the Fae ones, in *I Idir*, surrounded by the traditions and customs of a culture that is over five thousand years old. *Oisin* bringing up "trick or treating," which I've heard the Tax Man refer to as "organized beggin'," is no doubt meant to antagonize his elder brother, though I'm not sure as to how the kid thinks this will help his chances of any extended freedoms.

Apparently, the Tax Man is very aware that the topic is meant to register a reaction. My hubby calmly butters a slice of sourdough bread before answering, letting the boy hang for a bit. "Nay, brother. When I was of the age far' such foolery, we spent the Mundane school year at our home in Ballydonnelly, Ireland. Although there were a few youngsters who took up the American tradition, 'twas not vera' popular...especially far' males so close ta' the age of manhood," my husband explains in that slightly sarcastic tone of his, getting his own subtle dig in, and making me worry if I'll be privy to these *Sidhe* pissing matches for the next twenty years as each of my sons hits adolescence.

Unfortunately, His Lordship's snarky remark about *Oisin's* lack of maturity doesn't have the desired effect Declan was hoping for. The kid shrugs and replies, "That was a long time ago, ma' Lord. 'Tis vera' different in Salem now. The Mundanes in the United States celebrate *Samhain* almost as much as the Fae."

It must be in the blood, because the teen-ager knows exactly which buttons to push to get a rise out of his elder brother. My mate puts down the slice of bread and gives *Oisin* yet another stink eye; the one he's perfected since becoming a Lord of *I Idir's* Ruling Council. "The Mundanes have no idea of the meanin' of *Samhain, Oisin.* They have turned the sacred *sabbat* inta' a ghoulish, silly parody of our reverence towards the 'Old Ways.' 'Tis The Morrigan's own sabbat, Her Majesty's name day. To demean it with such nonsense is unbecomin' of someone with a *Nuada* bloodline."

There are times I feel my *Mo Shiorghra* is too tough on the poor kid, especially considering his rough start in life. We've had this discussion enough times over the past five years that I know better than to come to *Oisin's* defense. Neither male will appreciate my interference, so I bite my tongue, vowing to have this discussion later in private. The teenager's cheeks pinken, but he doesn't back down in the same inbred stubbornness also held by his much older half-brother. "I apologize, ma Lord, if ya' believed I was makin' light of our sacred traditions. It just be that ma' friends at school make the celebration sound full of such merriment, and I truly donna' understand what is so wrong with colletin' as much free *milseán* (candy/sweets) as a body ken' carry."

At the word "*milsean,*" Dylan, who up until now has ignored the conversation in favor of his favorite dinner, comes to attention. "Candy, *Uncail Oisin*? As much as I ken' carry?"

"Aye, Nephew. 'Tis free for the askin'. Truthfully, the Mundanes encourage it." Catching my disapproving eye, the teenager adds, "Of course, I have never taken part myself, but 'tis what I am told."

Dylan looks at his father, eyes bright with excitement. "Ken' I get free *milseán* as well, Da? I want ta' try 'track an' tradin'" too!"

My husband flashes me a "cranky Declan" look which I think is totally unfair since I'm not the one who brought this whole Halloween thing up in the first place. I don't react, instead busying myself with stacking some of the empty plates. Without missing a beat, *Birgit* and *Niamh* gather up *Liam* and Ronin to start them on their baths, politely leaving yours truly to deal with what will undoubtedly be a contentious family discussion. As seriously as my mate wears his mantle as Lord of House *Nuada*, when it comes to his offspring, of which he includes *Oisin*, it is difficult for Himself to find middle ground between being the indulgent, doting, father-figure he adores and holding to the responsibilities regarding sacred tradition in his role as a member of the Ruling Council. Tonight, it appears that the Universe is testing him on a level I haven't seen before.

Watching him steeple his fingertips while leaning back in his chair, I guess that in this situation, Declan has once again decided upon the Lordship role. I've seen that same body language a hundred times when he's conducting House business. "I'm afraid we won't be in Salem on the day the Mundanes partake in thar' customary beggin',

Dylan. We will need ta' be at *Dun Siorai*. Surely ya' don' wan' ta' miss yar' first chance ta' represent House *Nuada* in the *Samhain Comortas Capall* (Horse Tournament). Ya' have been tainin' with *Toirneach* (Thunder) all summer far' the opportunity to compete."

Wiping the grease from his mouth and speaking as Declan's "mini me," Dylan shakes his head in the negative. "You are right, Da. I would not wanta' miss out on the competition. Me and *Toirneach* plan on takin' home the cup in the Junior Division. I will have ta' try 'track an' tradin,' another time, lest I allow the Princess *Mairead* ta' win ma' prize by default."

The Tax Man leans across the table and ruffles his son's hair. "That a boy, Dylan. I've no doubts you and *Toirneach* will make our House proud." Changing his attention, he questions *Oisin*. "And you brother, will you not enter the competition as well? With yar' birthday only a month away I am sure the guild will allow ya' to compete as a young adult rather than a Junior."

"Aye, ma' Lord. I have already spoken to Master McPhearson at the guild. I will be registerin' in the Young Adult division. But may I ra'mind ya' of somethin' ya' seem ta' have forgotten, brother?"

By the expression painted on my husband's face, I'm pretty sure he will not appreciate being "reminded" of anything. However, Declan is forever the pillar of rationality, so he calmly asks, "What is that, *Oisin*?"

Unwilling to back down now, the teenager explains. "You have not taken into consideration the time change between the Otherworld and the Mundane, ma' Lord. If we leave *I Idir* directly after the tournament, we can return to the Mundane world just in time for the Halla'wen celebration." Placing the cherry on top of his argument, *Oisin* innocently adds, "I would still have time to try some 'trick or treatin', and I'd no mind takin' Dylan with me."

"I could go with you, *Oisin*?" Dylan asks, his eyes shining with excitement. "Ta' get the free *milsean*?" Our son dives from his chair and crawls into his father's lap. "Oh please, Da...can we? Can we go back ta' Salem in time far' the candy beggin'? Please?"

Later that evening, still entwined and out of breath, I ask the Tax Man why he agreed to even "think" about allowing *Oisin* and Dylan to go trick or treating. My *Mo Shiorghra* opens one green eye to look at me and then quickly shuts it. "I must be losin' ma' touch if that's what's on yar mind at this particular moment, Lass."

I run my hands across the muscles in his back and plant them on the cheeks of his perfect ass. "No worries about that, Tax Man. I'm pretty sure my toes still haven't uncurled. It's just...well...not like you to be so... indecisive."

He rolls off of me and onto his back, throwing an arm across his forehead, and because the connection between us is still so strong, I can feel that my words hurt his feelings. "Oh Declan, I didn't mean to upset you. I'm just surprised, is all. You're always so self-assured about your decisions. Knowing how you feel about Mundane celebrations, especially Halloween, I honestly expected you to straight up tell both boys that their focus needed to be on *Samhain* and not Halloween, and that any Mundane 'trick or treating' was out of the question. Especially after *Oisin* was so belligerent about his curfew."

He flips to his side to speak directly to me. "As I have said, I don' want ta' be the same kind of father as ma' own, Rosie. The man made no secret of ignorin' the feelins' or opinions of his offspring, not even when I was older and could be of use ta' him. I don' think he even once acknowledged the fact that our Mundane holdins' were financially prosperous because of the decisions I made about them."

Truthfully, if you ask me, not taking advice from his heir was the least of Callum Fitzpatrick's faults. The man was a certifiable murderer, an evil, narcissistic ego-manic. However, this wasn't the time to bring that up. This wasn't the first time I'd heard Declan voice concern over his parental skills, a fear I personally think is ludicrous. "Oh, Sweetie, you're nothing like your father. You are the kindest, most loving husband and father any family could have. I just know how the boys are, especially *Oisin*. Once an idea gets into his head, he's like a dog with a bone. He'll never give up on it. And our son is no slouch in the stubborn category either." I politely don't add that it's obviously a family trait. None of the Fitzpatricks could be called "shrinking violets' when it came to getting their way.

"Aye, Love. Yar' right on that count, but I am hopin' that the distractions offered by the *Samhain* sabbat in *I Idir* will chase these silly demands about Halloween away. Not ta' mention the allure of the girl *Oisin* professes ta' love waitin' far him." Tucking a few stray hairs behind my ear, he explains. "This will be Dylan's first *Comortas Capall* and he will be one of the youngest competitors in his division. I have no doubt that after a day full of excitement plus hours in the saddle, our boy will fight to keep his eyes open during the picnic. By the time the bonfire activities are over, he will have both feet in *Tir Aisling* (Dream Land)."

The Tax Man isn't wrong in his assessment. Dylan, like his father, has always been a morning person, often joining his younger brothers in their earlier bedtimes. I could see how my mate's plan might work with Dylan, but *Oisin* was a completely different story. "I agree that our son might sleep through Mundane Halloween, but that's not going to be the case with your younger brother. He's got his *Nuada* obstinance up on these two topics; his curfew and Halloween. And if his friends have something planned for the evening, I believe the kid will do all he can to join them."

Smiling, Declan says, "There are different techniques far' handlin' muleheaded *Sidhes*, my Love. Because he has nearly reached the age of Fae manhood, and has been granted placement in the Young Adult division for the tournament, *Oisin* will undoubtedly be invited to the *Oiche Fiain* (Wilding Night) afterwards. Being that this will be his vera' first one, I don' think he will trade that away to go beggin' in the Mundane world "

Though I've never participated in *Oiche Fiain*, I know perfectly well what goes on during those waning hours of *Samhain*. The tradition supposedly has its roots in ancient fertility rites practiced by the early Druids, but over the generations, it has become an accepted night of sanctioned debauchery. Children conceived during the *Oiche Fiain* are considered especially blessed by The Morrigan. Maternal instincts, wrought by my Mundane upbringing, kick in. "Hell, no, Tax Man! I'm not letting that child take part in a booze and magic infused orgy! It's...well... wrong! He's still a kid, for goddesses' sake. I can't believe you'd approve of *Oisin* being out all night doing who knows what!"

"He's *Sidhe*, Lass. And Elven. The blood of his people runs through his veins. This is the Otherworld, and according to our sacred traditions, *Oisin* is on the brink of manhood. Our *Sidhe* ways are not shaped by the morality of Mundane religions. I promise ya, Love, it is no like he will be scarred for life by the experience. In fact, it may be a highlight in his memories far' years ta' come. When I was his age, I remember my..."

I instantly put a hand up to stop him. "Hold it right there, Bucko! I absolutely don't need to hear how my then teenage husband spent the whole night 'entertaining' nubile young things in the woods. I get that things are different here in the Otherworld, but the Eternal Mate, as well as the 'mom' in me, has major concerns."

My *Mo Shiorghra* pulls me into an embrace and kisses me before answering. "Ya' are a fabulous *mathair*, Rosie Fitzpatrick, and as my Eternal Mate, ya' own me body and soul. I would have it no other way. Trust me, Lass, when I swear that ma' "Wilding" days are long over and I wouldn't trade what I have with ya' for any chance at relivin' them. But these are sacred celebrations in *I Idir* that have been in place for a millennium. 'Tis not our place to judge or change them. Still, if it will make ya' feel better, I will have some of the younger men I trust keep an eye out far' the lad. As I was gonna' say befar' ya' interrupted me, durin' ma' first *Oiche Fiain*, ma' *athair's* men got me so stinkin' drunk, I could barely stand. There was no way I was gonna' fulfil any romantic fantasies in that condition. I curled up in some corner and passed out in a stupor. Woke up the next mornin' with a doozy of a hangover that kept me away from ale for nearly a year. 'Tis how the younger males are kept in line, Lass. Ya' will see. It will all work out exactly as the Universe sees fit."

Me? I have my doubts where ever and whenever the Universe is concerned.

MISSING 17

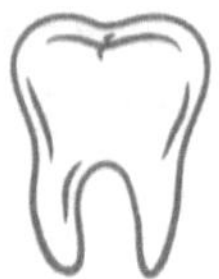

The Tax Man Gets It Wrong

THOUGH I DON'T ALWAYS TRUST its design, I will admit that the Universe does has a sense of humor. If Declan truly thought that *Oisin* and Dylan would move-on and give-up their Halloween planning, the Powers That Be let him know he was dead wrong. Halloween was all the two boys could talk about in the weeks leading up to the kid-centered holiday, bonding over talk of costumes and decorations and the weight of the candy they'd collect. Frankly, it was near impossible to get them interested in anything else.

Because of the infamous history centered around the awful witch trials, Salem celebrates the spooky tradition of Halloween like no other place on Earth. As children, my older sister, Claire, and I partook of the festivities on a grand scale, with my dad always making sure our front porch was creepily ready for a steady stream of trick or treaters. If my mom was disappointed that her youngest daughter, the who inherited her Fae heritage, showed no interest in learning more about *Samhain*, she never complained. Instead, Annie (*Aine*) Parker attacked the celebration of Mundane Halloween with the same gusto and creativity in which she did everything else. Claire and I were spoiled with homemade caramel apples, crunchy, made-from-scratch popcorn balls, and original, hand sewn costumes.

As a young girl, I'd always envisioned someday doing these same things for my own children. However, the Universe, in its mysterious wisdom, had other plans. Since I began sharing my life with Declan, a true believer in the Old Ways, I've traded the elaborately carved pumpkins and dancing skeletons of my youth for boughs of Hawthorn and Rowan, set among bowls of the best apples the fall harvest offered. For the Fae of the Otherworld, October 31st and November 1st are sacred days of one year ending and another beginning. It is a serious sabbat, filled with spiritual meditation and the petitioning of one's ancestors for blessings in the coming year, especially those having to do with fertility, success, and new growth. Although masks and simple costumes are sometimes worn by the mages and druids during the spiritual services, they are nothing like the menagerie of disguises worn by children and adults alike in the Mundane world.

All this comes to mind as the Tax Man and I find ourselves fighting the crowds at "Sal's Carnival of Costumes," trying to keep *Oisin* and Dylan in sight among the horde of kids and parents spending their precious Sunday hours shopping for the perfect Halloween attire. I thought the plan of letting them buy costumes for the holiday was a bad idea. A very bad idea, setting the wrong expectation. To my mind, it reinforced the notion that their father and brother was in agreement, when I knew the man in question wholly expected the kids would never make it back from *I Idir* in time to participate. My opinions fell on deaf husband ears. In the five years he'd spent serving as a Ruling Council Lord, Declan had built up an even stronger stubborn resolve about "knowin' what's best far' the parties involved," and, if anything, had grown more stubborn in holding on to a decision if he thought he was doing it for all the right reasons.

When the kids actively began whining to shop for their Halloween disguises, I had planned to slip out and go it alone with just the two boys, knowing full well that his Lordship would hate every moment of the experience. I wasn't up for a constant stream of mental lectures on how "the Mundanes had gotten it all wrong," and "why the garish costumes depicting Otherworld folk were a form of racial and religious discrimination." Nor was I up for the alternative tirade on "the ridiculously inflated prices for poor quality workmanship." It appeared, however, that the Tax Man was determined not be left out of the outing for reasons of which I'm not completely sure.

As expected, the costume mega-store was mobbed. Because of his Fae bloodline, *Oisin* was unusually tall and broad shouldered for a boy the age of thirteen, making child-sized costumes a no-go for him. Not wanting to lose our five-year-old in the crowd, we send the impatient teenager off alone to the aisles with adult costumes, while we helped Dylan select something my husband found "appropriate for a small child of *Tuatha de Danann* heritage." Our little boy seemed overwhelmed by the multitude of choices, and thoroughly confused by the "mythological and story book" sections. Because it's that kind of day, Dylan immediately points out a bubblegum pink, tulle costume with a tooth-tipped wand, silver crown, and iridescent wings that attach to the back with metal snaps. It's boldly labeled in block letters as a "Tooth Fairy" costume.

"Mama, that outfit says it's for a tooth fairy. I have never seen you with wings. Do you really have a pair such as these? Can you fly with them like a *fabht* (bug)?" our first-born asks a tad too loudly for such a public venue. Several people in the vicinity look at him and smile at what they believe is a child's imagination.

We have already had "the talk" with Dylan about keeping our heritage a secret while in the Mundane world. He's usually very conscientious about keeping Otherworldly conversation to a minimum when we are out in public, but as excited as he is over this costume business, his boundaries are unfiltered. I bend down and silently whisper in his ear, "Dylan, honey, remember what Da and I told you about keeping that kind of information to yourself when we are out in public places."

Embarrassed, the child clamps a hand over his mouth, before whispering, "Sorry, Mama. I forgot."

"It's okay, baby," I reply. "I know you're very excited to be here. And to answer your question, no, Mommy doesn't have wings. That's just how our Mundane friends believe fairies look."

"All Fae?" he whispers to me. "Even boys like me?"

I shrug. "Yes. I suppose even boys like you. They don't know any better, Honey."

Dylan shakes his head in disgust, reminding me so much of his father when he does it. "'Tis vera' silly of them ta' think that." He walks past a troll mask, a silly grin painted on its cave-man-like face. and points it out to me, rolling his eyes and shaking his head while tugging on my sleeve so I might bend down to hear him. "The trolls at *Crann Bethadh* are fierce warriors. They no look a thing like this," he states. Disgusted, he focuses his attention on a rack of animal costumes instead, and I breathe a sigh of relief. Tigers and bears I can handle.

I turn to the Tax Man, who until this moment, has remained oddly silent. "Thanks for all the help back there, Dad. I was worried about what our boy would think about such outlandish portrayals of our kind."

"Ya' were doin' an excellent job of handlin' his questions, Rosie. There was no reason far' me ta' be stickin' ma' two cents in."

"Hmmm," I answer. "Seems like a cop out to me. Thankfully, Dylan seemed to handle the preconceived Mundane ideas without much of a struggle. That, I'm sure, he gets from you. I've always grappled with the ridiculous notions humans have about the Fae."

"There's no use gettin' yourself all worked up about it, Lass. Folks are gonna' go right on believing what they want, even when the truth is starin' them straight in the eye. I donna' give a *asal francach* ("rat's ass") what the Mundanes think of us, as long as they stay on their side of the Veil when they're thinkin' it."

* * *

After what seemed like five hours of indecision and whining, but was actually only forty-five minutes, the four of us walk out of Sam's Carnival of Costumes with Halloween disguises for both boys. Despite the multiple x-rated mental images the Tax Man kept sending me about a certain desired purchase, I had to insist that he NOT buy the woman's "sexy tooth fairy" costume he found in the adult sized section. The one with the short tutu, gartered stockings, and slip on "fairy" wings. Well... at least not when the children were with us.

Dylan had chosen a dinosaur costume, a cute T-Rex one piece zip-up that would fit over his fall jacket, while *Oisin* selected an all-black ninja outfit, which, truthfully, wasn't all that different from the clothes he usually wore. Both were choices his Lordship begrudgingly approved of, as neither of them represented disrespectful caricatures of Otherworldly folk.

Once we returned home, a fashion show was held for the rest of the family. I was worried that *Liam* would be unhappy that he had no costume, but my motherly concern was for naught. My middle child was happy enough to climb into the large, plastic shopping bag the costumes came home in and hop around the room, bumping into furniture and eventually knocking over a lamp.

Afterwards, the costumes were neatly put back on the hangers and placed in the front hall closet in anticipation of "the big day," with all the store tags left on, of course. Just in case.

MISSING 18

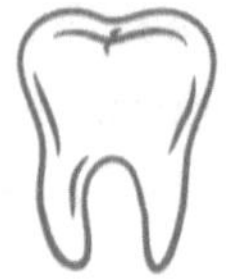

Two Days is Still Too Long

A MAN OF HIS WORD, Declan keeps any hassles regarding our mandated attendance at his sister's handfasting to a bare minimum. We arrange to leave Salem on October 10th, a Friday in the Mundane World, as soon as the two oldest children return home from school, thus missing the least amount of classroom time. Our late afternoon departure puts us in the Otherworld in the early evening hours of Saturday, October 11th, keeping everyone on the same circadian rhythm, even if we do lose an entire day by passing through the two dimensions. At this time of the year, so close to *Samhain*, the Veil is naturally thin so the magical travel of the eight of us is easy and smooth, free of the metaphysical friction that sometimes results from the transfer of magical energy. In addition, we're able to travel light, with almost no luggage, as everything we'll need for the next few days is available at *Dun Siorai*. This will allow us one good night's sleep and a few leisurely hours before joining other family members and guests at *Cuach an Fhithich* (Raven's Hollow).

Like every public spectacle in the Otherworld, hand-fast celebrations are explicitly family affairs. This is in contrast to the current social philosophy of many Mundane weddings in the US, one in which children are not readily welcome at the wholly adult affair. In contrast, Fae couples are strongly encouraged to trot out the kids in the same way one might "dress to impress. Offspring are the "jewels" of the *Sidhe* people, especially for those within the elite Fae hierarchy and graced with fancy pedigrees. The ability to procreate is an envied gift among people who can trace their genetic bloodline back over at least a thousand years, and in the blunt truth of the matter, children represent the survival of a rapidly shrinking race of proud people.

Alarmingly, the birth rate for every kingdom and race of people living in the Otherworld has dropped by nearly 78% over the past four hundred years, with no signs of this decline slowing. It doesn't help that many Otherworldly women enter into the menopausal stage far sooner than their human counterparts, thus significantly shortening their biological clocks. No one, not even The Morrigan, Herself, or our leading man of science, Dr. Robyn Brannigan, can pinpoint with any certainty the cause for this continuing rate of infertility among not only the Fae, but all races of folk on the other side of the Veil. The implications are staggering. If this anomaly continues at the same rate without any intervention, whole species of preternatural peoples will eventually cease to exist. While unions between mixed blood

Mundane and Otherworldly couples have produced some children, the rate of growth has been too slow to make a huge difference in the possibility of looming extinction. Thus, procreation has become a rally call to preternatural patriotism among all the Otherworldly races.

I share this anthropological discourse with you only so you will understand why I am currently wrestling my wailing infant into formal *Sidhe* apparel when he should be having his evening bottle and settling down to sleep. Over Ronin's yowling, I can hear Dylan and Liam bickering in the parlor, both boys over-tired and whiny. It's not lost on me that before I found myself in this maternal role, I found the tradition of late evening handfast celebrations under a star-filled sky to be wildly romantic. Now, I wonder how I will possibly keep two small boys and a colicky infant calm and quiet during the long ceremony and extravagant gala that will follow, all the while hiding my own yawns in a polite manner. I have my fingers crossed that once everyone in attendance has duly cooed and fussed over the *Nuada* progeny, I can send at least the three younger children back to *Dun Siora* in the care of *Birgit* and *Niamh*.

Declan joins me in the nursery just as I am finishing tying the teeny-tiny laces on Ronin's booties. "Are ya' about ready ta' leave, Lass? 'Tis gettin' late, ya' know," he announces, like a man who has only had himself to dress.

In response, I hand over our youngest son. "I need to grab my wool cape, and then we can head out."

"Yar' not wearin' the fox?" he asks with a not-so-well-hidden frown.

I understand why Declan is disappointed. The silver

fox caplet was a birthday gift from my Tax Man and comes with a dramatic story he never tires of retelling. Repeatedly. Although the cape is beautiful and luxurious, it's much too warm for such an early autumn evening, especially at this stage of my life. Since Ronin's birth, I've been plagued with bouts of nighttime hot flashes, which could just be a normal postpartum symptom or a sign that I've entered the perimenopause stage of Fae womanhood. Either way, I know I'd prefer not to be sweating my ass off in that heavy fur. "I'm sorry, Sweetie, I know the fox is the nicest piece of outer wear I own, but it's really too mild for it tonight. I'd be way too warm."

Either my expression or my aura gives me away because, despite looking as if he wants to debate the decision, my *Mo Shiorghra* takes the baby from me. "As ya' wish, ma' Love, though we do need ta' move with some speed lest we arrive late and listen ta' my *mathair* accuse us of purposely embarassin' Meghan."

He's not wrong in that warning. Dragon Mama is a natural born scolder. I swear that woman could strip skin with her words alone. I sigh, then pull my light-weight wool cape from the armoire and follow my husband toward the parlor where we gather up the rest of the family to join the thrre-ring circus this handfast will most certainly be.

* * *

In an effort to be an impartial observer, I will be the first one to admit that *Cuach an Fhithich* (Raven's Hollow) is definitely a larger and grander estate than House *Nuada's*

Dun Siorai. I don't share this opinion with my *Mo Shiorghra.* I already have three cranky children in tow. I don't wish to add a cranky husband to my plate. Truthfully, the only member of our entourage who seems pleased to be present at this celebration is *Oisin,* and that itself is worrisome. Like most teenagers, my husband's half-brother runs on full adolescent angst; House and family obligations are usually met with perfected eye rolling, dramatic sighs, and thoroughly disgruntled expressions. Tonight, he's nearly bouncing on his toes with excitement, and if I'd had to guess, he's even using a bit of *Sidhe* glamour magic to make himself appear taller and older than his biological age. I could swear the face I saw across the breakfast table this morning was baby-faced and free of any sort of facial hair, and surely not covered in that manly five o'clock shadow that has suddenly appeared in the past twelve hours. Even with the fast-growing hair anomaly of the Otherworld, *Oisin's* new "beard" is a bit over the top.

No doubt a female is somehow at the root of his sudden "maturity," so I turn to share this fact with Declan. Unfortunately, he's already wandered off to converse with a group of cronies within the Ruling Council, leaving me and the *scathachs* to gather up the children and take our seats on Meghan's side of House *Badh's* sacred grove. As beautiful as this setting is, I also hold to the opinion that the grove at *Dun Siorai* is far prettier than the one here tonight. It's true that I might harbor some prejudice on the topic since it's where the Tax Man and I exchanged our vows. However, the way the branches of the ancient oaks at *Dun Siorai* have been pruned to grow together to form a natural canopy is…well…the stuff of fairy tales, and although the landscaping here is expensive and top notch, it lacks that special "magical vibe" of our own Otherworld home.

As the attending guests settle themselves down, the tempo of the music changes as Meghan's entourage enters the space. As Lord of House *Nuada*, Declan escorts his sister to her spot within the sacred grove before he will join our own little clan. The family resemblance between the two of them has always been obvious, but seeing them stand side by side, dressed in House colors, with their warrior-souled *mathair* behind them, I can understand how Callum Fitzpatrick might have felt a tad uneasy regarding the loyalty of some of his own off-spring. The three of them together like this exude a powerful sense of magical destiny that is no doubt felt throughout the crowd. Even my low-skilled tooth fairy senses can feel the ripple of energy beneath my feet.

This "tuned in," I am also fully aware of when Meghan's *Mo Shiorghra* enters into the sacred space even before I can actually see him with my eyes. *Cillian Mac Badh's* personal energy can be likened to the electrical charge one can sometimes feel during a violent thunderstorm. Unlike my husband's magical force, which always reminds me of swift, rushing waters, the young bridegroom's power crackles with violent intensity, most likely in response to the ceremony about to take place and his part in it, not to mention the overwhelming lust that surrounds fated mates. There's no surprise *Cillian's* aura is as strong as it is; House *Badh* traces its lineage to the ancient triad of warrior goddesses, of which our own

Queen is part of. The three sisters of war and destruction, Morrigan, *Macha* and *Badh* once belonged to a single House, but as it sometimes goes with powerful families, greed, treachery and deceit caused a separation that went on to have far-reaching consequences.

The rise of The Morrigan's power and the eventual execution of her sister, *Macha,* for treason against the Throne, is a tale most residents of *I Idir* are only too willing to share. Before I met my husband, I knew only the vaguest bits and pieces of *I Idirian* history, with most of that knowledge not coming until well into my adulthood. Since the time Declan and I joined our lives together, I've made a conscientious effort to learn more about the narrative of the Kingdom's past along with the ongoing philosophy and hierarchy that currently holds it together. It came as no surprise that the execution of *Macha* was tied to her traitorous partnership with certain countries within the Mundane world. The defeat of *Macha's* wretched grandson, Owen, by our current Black Knight, is a tale still celebrated by royalty and common folk alike. Having been raised in the political awareness of the Mundane existence, I personally take the "official" transcript of those events with a grain of salt. I'm savvy enough to understand that every form of government has its own set agenda when it comes to what "the people" are allowed to know. In deference to my role as Lady *Nuada,* I've also keenly learned to keep my Mundane opinions to myself despite the lingering presence of The Morrigan in my head.

I'm obviously not shielding as well as I should because my hubby gives me a questioning look over the thoughts circling in my mind. I shake my head and turn my attention back to the couple in the center of the circle. In spite of my less than warm and fuzzy feelings towards Meghan and *Cillian*, I can't help but note that they make a very attractive couple, and their auras give testament to their strong feelings for one another. "Like to like," I suppose, as to my mind, neither of them have very strong moral boundaries. The reaction to that particular thought is instant. *"Feckin' hell, Rosie! Ken ya' not save those incendiary thoughts until we are safely home? 'Tis not the time nor place ta' be leakin' such opinions, as true as they might be."*

I've never liked being scolded, ever, and in my annoyance, I try to pull my hand away from his, but he just squeezes tighter. I suppose the Tax Man is not wrong. These are troubling times for both sides of the Veil, and in the same manner "loose lips sink ships" was true during past Mundane history, "leaking views fuel news" is the new reality here in the present.

Callum Fitzpatrick's shadow hangs over the Kingdom of *I Idir* like early morning fog that refuses to burn off with the rising of the sun. Despite all efforts to locate and capture the Fae Lord turned traitor, the powerful *Jotun* sorcerer has eluded the vengeful hands of the Throne. Even here, in the sacred grove where arms are usually forbidden, both House *Nuada* and House *Badh* have heavy security personnel in attendance. And because the Queen and the Royal Circle are guests, this being a "family" handfast, a whole retinue of fierce troll warriors circle the tented row of seats where The Morrigan has taken her place.

As expected in a Ruling Council joining of this importance, the 26th Merlin himself is the officiant. I never tire of the sacred beauty behind a *Sidhe* handfast, but for some odd reason, this evening I find myself unable to concentrate on the ceremony in front of me. Something dark pokes at my sub-conscience, a strange feeling of being watched. I hang on to Baby Ronin a little lighter, and pull *Liam* out from under my chair where he's crawled and place him onto my knee where I can keep a better eye on him. I'm glad to see that Dylan is safely ensconced in his father's lap, but when I check on *Oisin* sitting on Declan's left, I notice the concerned expression on his face as he turns his head around to look behind him. Catching me watching him, his eyes go wide, and then he suddenly turns his full attention back to the ceremony and ignores me all together.

MISSING 19

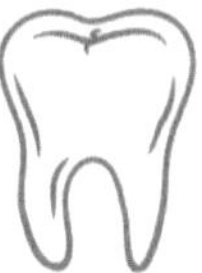

When You Party With The Fae

SAY what you want about the moral ambiguity of the Raven Houses, but hot damn, these elite *Sidhe* types really know how to party. From the delicious array of rich banquet offerings, to the generous pour of *I Idir's* finest wine and ale, awash in non-stop music and dancing, the celebratory trimmings offered by House *Badh* make for a near perfect gala. If Meghan's less than enthusiastic response to my best wishes were a bit off-putting, I now find myself having a wonderful time despite her bad attitude.

I think the same thing can be said for the Tax Man. I look over to watch Declan, his handsome face flushed from laughing, obviously enjoying the conversation and company of the Black Knight, the Prince of *I Idir*, who greatly prefers to be called just "Kevin," and my husband's favorite cousin, Duncan. "Looks like our gentleman friends are having a good time," I comment to the ladies at my table.

"And I'm thrilled for that," adds the *Banphrionsa* of *I Idir*. "Ted almost never lets his guard down. It's good seeing him so relaxed."

Even after five years, Maureen Beckett's casual informality in the midst of such structured Otherworldly protocol shocks me. Somehow, I don't believe the Black Knight of *I Idir* ever forgets who he is or what the purpose of his role requires in either world. Still, I understand the *Banphrionsa's* desire to see her mate enjoying an event that undoubtedly registers as a social obligation. In my five years as Lady *Nuada,* Declan and I had weathered through more protocol heavy, Ruling Class functions than I care to remember. It's always a bonus when they're fun as well.

We are joined at the table by Dr. Robyn Brannigan and his new bride, the stunning Lady Roxanne Spinelli, who is a ward of Her Majesty. It's always strange seeing the Doc in his Otherworldly apparel, especially knowing that he prefers his white lab coat to anything else. Nonetheless, he cuts a very handsome figure with the sash across his chest noting his rank as a Prince of Avalon. The couple is red-faced and sweaty, coming as they are from a vigorous, lengthy reel, causing Lady Roxanne to flop into her chair. "Phew," she exhales. "That was quite a work-out."

"'Tis the honest truth," her husband agrees. "The *Rince Na Cosa Sona* (Dance of the Happy Feet) is not for the weak of heart, though I will admit that I recovered from its pace a lot quicker when I was a lad." From the next table comes the sound of raucous male laughter. Kissing his wife on the cheek, he adds, "I think I will join my gentlemen friends and discover what has them so joyously engaged. If you ladies will please excuse me," the doctor says as he gives a short bow before taking his leave.

When the man is out of ear shot, Maureen teases her good friend, "Don't you look like the cat who swallowed the canary."

Roxanne's already-red face pinkens even more, but the huge grin gracing her face gives her true feelings away. "I'll be the first to admit. I never dreamed I'd be so gloriously happy. Robyn is…" she pauses and looks around the table at the rest of us, "well…you all know him…he's the kindest, sweetest, most honorable man I know. There isn't anything he wouldn't do for someone in need. Despite our…rough start…we're gloriously happy and I consider myself Universe blessed."

Lady Roxanne isn't kidding about their romance having a rough start. It was like something out of that "Runaway Bride" movie starring Julia Roberts. However, before the new bride can confess anything more, my *Mo Shiorghra* joins us at the table. "I was hopin' my lovely Lady would give me the honor of this next dance. 'Tis our favorite," he says, putting out his hand to reach for mine.

I look across the dance floor to where the House's Dance Master is holding up a placard with a hand over a heart, the symbol for *"La Volta,"* a dance requiring a more intimate touch between partners. Not as blatantly erotic as the Spanish tango, the Fae style of *La Volta* calls for focused, direct eye contact between the participants to accomplish exact mirrored movements, while requiring the gentleman to place his hands firmly on his partner's waist and hips in order to lift her in time with the music. The two of us have often joked about it being the dance form of tantric sex, but there's a grain of truth in that statement, as when done correctly, even the couple's breathing will match each other.

Though I will never be called "light on my feet," and I surely wouldn't make the finals on "Dancing with the Stars," the Tax Man and I dance *La Volta* vera,' vera' well. No doubt it has something to do with our Eternal Bond and the physical and spiritual connection we share. Tonight, protocol inhibitions lowered by an abundance of good wine, the dance we share leaves us breathless and flushed, and as we return to our tables, I hear a fellow dancer remark that he wouldn't be surprised if Lord *Nuada* didn't add yet another son to his line this evening.

The guy isn't kidding. If there were a way for us to escape notice and wander off somewhere to be alone, we'd probably do so. Unfortunately, two of our children are impatiently waiting for us at the "lady's table," causing us to slip out of "lovers" mode and back into our parental roles.

I was able to send our two youngest children back to *Dun Siorai* with *Birgit* and *Niamh* after dinner, but Dylan had begged to remain, abandoning his father's false notion that his son tired easily when faced with a day of excitement. I'm sure part of the child's resolve to stay at the handfast celebration was the continued presence of Her Royal Highness, *Mairead* Morrigan Mrydynn Beckett. The two kindergartners had been inseparable since the completion of the ceremony, with Dylan gobbling down his dinner in a mad rush to rejoin his royal buddy as quickly as possible. Though only a few weeks short of her 6th birthday, there was little doubt the heir of *I Idir* would one day be a stunning beauty. How could she be anything else, given her weighted genetic pool? It seemed poor Dylan had already lost his little boy's heart to the youngest Raven.

Dylan was flanked by his young *uncail* (uncle), who, despite dropping a whole litany of complaints over the protocol required for an evening such as this one, seemed to be having a very enjoyable time. His glassy eyes and silly expression meant one of two things; either he was totally soused on the free-flowing ale and wine, or there was a certain lady in attendance that was causing his lustful stupor. Not surprisingly, it was our son who spoke his petition first with the confidence that came with childlike abandon.

"Lord *Athair* and Lady *Mathair*," he asks, using our formal titles in public as he'd been taught, may I escort the *Banphrionsa* to the barn? She would like to visit with ma' amazin' *Toirneach* (Thunder)."

Toirneach was Dylan's pony, a breed similar in appearance and temperament to the Irish Connemara. As *Sidhe* tradition dictated, the pony was gifted to Dylan on his fifth birthday as a way for the child to build confidence in his horsemanship skills in anticipation of him one day owning a Fae stallion. Our son adored the animal he'd named "Thunder," and had begged to be allowed to ride to the handfasting celebration alongside his father and uncle, rather than travel in the carriage with the ladies and smaller children. When we left *Dun Sorai*, it had already been the beginning of twilight and I held serious concerns over our five-year-old riding horseback on darkening roads. But Declan had promised me that he and *Oisin* would be extra vigilant and that the early evening ride would be good practice for the boy. I agreed, but only with the caveat that Dylan would leave the pony to shelter at *Cuach an Fhitichor* for the night and travel home with me in the carriage. Thus, it was for this reason that Thunder was currently sheltered in House *Badh's* barn and close enough for a nocturnal visit by his young Master.

Before either Declan or I could answer, *Oisin* jumped into the conversation. "I would be pleased to provide a watchful eye, ma' Lord...so no harm befalls the *Banphrionsa* or ma' bonnie nephew."

In the state he was in, I'm wasn't sure *Oisin* was the man for the job, but my mate apparently had made his decision. "I will allow it, but I must have yar' word, *Mac Nuada*," he states, using our son's birthright title, "that neither of you will enter the pony's stall. Take a few *ciúbanna siúcra* (sugar cubes) with ya' and give *Toirneach* a treat. I am sure he would enjoy that." Then addressing *Oisin*, he adds, "I am entrustin' the *leanaí* (children) ta' yar care, *deartháir* (brother). Mind them well."

MISSING 20

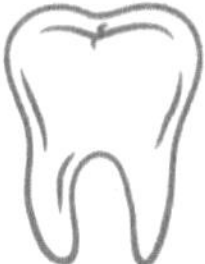

Oh Unhappy Day

THE BRIDE and groom finally make their triumphant escape, *Mac Badh* outwitting and outplaying his young comrades in the silly "Bride Stealing" game. Our jolly little band of friends grew increasingly mellow, while the jokes and stories circulating the joined table of males and females got more and more off color despite the inclusion of the Catholic priest doubling as the Prince of *I Idir.* Our raucous laughter draws the attention of other guests, who look over at us with a combination of longing and envy over being a part of the inner "Royal Circle." It's shallow of me, I know, to get a kick out of being part of "the cool kids club," especially here in *I Idir* where social hierarchy is everything. It's a new feeling, this being on the inside rather than outside looking in.

Sadly, I don't have much time to enjoy the exhilaration of the moment. As if to slap me in the back of the head for my ridiculous vanity, I suddenly look up and see *Oisin* step through the banquet room door, the Princess *Mairead* in his arms, blood soaking through a tear in the right sleeve of her chemise and her left foot turned at an abnormal angle. Our Dylan is two steps behind them, his round, frightened eyes set in a paler than usual complexion.

We all instantly rush at the kids, all nine of us at once, causing *Oisin* and Dylan to take a hesitant step backwards. "Give her to me," the doctor orders.

The teenager slides the bleeding princess into Robyn's arms, and the doc lays her gently down on one of the small settees lining the banquet room walls, with the Black Knight and Lady Dear Heart right behind him. For a few seconds, we all hold our breath waiting for the physician's assessment. I once again feel eyes upon me, but this time, when I look up, I see The Morrigan staring at me from her ornate chair on the other side of the room. The logical person in me assumes that because the Queen is not hovering over her youngest offspring, the Princess *Mairead* is in no real danger.

Doc Brannigan verifies my conjecture. "The *Banphri-onsa's* injuries are not serious. She has a nasty gash in her upper right arm, and her left ankle is badly sprained, but she can heal these on her own before morning. There's also a growing bump on the back of her head. We will have to be watchful of a possible concussion over the next few hours. I suggest the princess return to *Crann Bethadh*. I can continue to monitor her there."

While Lady Dear Heart makes plans to take her daughter home, the Black Knight turns to my husband. Although there is a touch of anger in his expression, out of friendship and respect for Declan, he lets Lord *Nuada* interrogate his younger brother about the events that led to this outcome. "Explain yourself, *Nuada*. How did this happen," my *Mo Shiorghra* asks. His physical voice is calm, but I feel his mixed emotions swirling in my own mind; annoyance, anger, embarrassment all covered in a blanket of real fear over what the consequences might be over the *Banphrionsa's* injuries. *Mairead* is The Raven's stated heir. There are laws about her safety.

The teenager is deathly pale, and he works to force himself to face the two men. "'Twas an accident, ma' Lord. The *Banphrionsa*…she fell."

"Fell from where?" his Lordship questions.

Oisin looks down at his feet. "*Toirneach*, ma' Lord."

I can see Declan's jaw tighten. This was bad. Very bad. "Are ya' tellin' me, *Nuada*, that Princess *Mairead* was atop the pony when she fell?"

"Aye, ma' Lord," the boy mumbled.

"Did I not give ya' orders to mind the behavior of the two children? Why in the wisdom of the Universe would ya' allow a young girl ta' sit a strange pony she has no training' with?"

Stammering, *Oisin* admits, "I was…no there when it happened, Lord Brother."

"And why not, *Nuada*? Whatever excuse could ya' give for disobeyin' a direct order from yar' Liege Lord."

At this challenge, his younger brother holds his chin up. "I offer no excuses for ma' poor judgement, ma' Lord. I am willin' to accept all consequences ma' Lord feels necessary far' ma' disobedient and reckless behavior."

Oisin's response is the absolute only correct way to

answer his Lordship's accusations. Making excuses, whining, and not accepting responsibility when one is undoubtedly guilty is a sign of poor moral character and a blemish on one's bloodline. Trust me, House *Nuada* had enough of such behavior in its recent history. It didn't need yet another member giving the Ruling Council something more to gossip about. I hear the Tax Man sigh his relief in my head.

At the same time, I catch a glimpse of a female head poking around the corner of the ballroom door. I recognize the girl as being the infamous *Laoise, Oisin's* love interest. Right there and then, all the pieces begin to fit and I know exactly why the teenage boy was not in attendance when *Mairead* fell off that pony. I must not be shielding very well because both my husband and the Black Knight look in the same direction, and, noting that she'd been discovered, the feminine head of curls disappears from the doorway.

Declan raises that one eyebrow, obviously having the same epiphany as my own. Clasping his hands behind his back he says, "Ya' speak the truth in that, young *Nuada,* and there will be, without doubt, serious consequences for yar' dereliction of duty this evening. I hope ya' are prepared to face them." Then, my husband turns his attention to our son. Dylan looks as if he's going to be sick at any moment, and I pray to all the maternal goddesses that our little boy doesn't up-chuck his entire dinner onto the shoes of the two men in front of him. "What have ya' got to say about this evening's disaster, *Mac Nuada?* Did I not directly tell you not to go inside *Toirneach's* stall?" his father asks.

"Aya, ma' Lord *Athair*. Ya' told me that exact thing," Dylan answers.

"Then explain, son, how the *Banphrionsa* came ta' fall off yar' pony's back and injure herself if you were told not ta' go inta' the pony's stall?"

Dylan looks over to where the Princess *Mairead* is being lifted up by the stretcher bearers sent to help get her into the Royal carriage for her trip back to *Crann Bethadh*. Our son stares directly at her, and she stares right back at him. I would bet all the gold in *I Idir* that something is going on between the two of them. Following his uncle's lead, Dylan holds up his chin, albeit a trembling one, and says, "It was all ma' fault, ma' Lord. I challenged the *Banphrionsa* ta' sit ma' *Toirneach*. She did not wish ta' do so, but I teased her until she gave in. 'Twas all me."

I want to clue my mate into the probability that something is not one hundred percent true about our son's story, but surrounded by as much magical energy as I am, I don't risk sending any telepathic messages. Any probing into Dylan's less than truthful story and *Oisin's* bad choice can wait until we return to the security of *Dun Siorai's* walls and wards.

MISSING 21

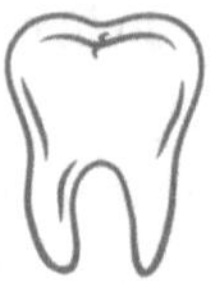

Dylan Spills the Beans

AND RETURN to *Dun Siorai* is exactly what we do. At Declan's request, Dylan and I are asked to immediately take our House carriage home while he and *Oisin* plan on riding their horses back. But not before his Lordship insists on personally apologizing to all the affected parties, beginning with the Black Knight and Lady Dear Heart, followed by Her Majesty, Lord and Lady *Badh*, and their circle of personal friends whose pleasant evening has been disappointingly cut short. No doubt, Lord and Lady *Mac Badh* will receive a carefully worded message of contrition and an expensive token from House *Nuada* upon their return to Raven's Hollow.

I am privy to none of my Tax Man's eloquent communications of regret, as I have been assigned an altogether different task by my Eternal Mate: One that takes a mother's skill in getting her child to speak on a topic he'd rather not discuss. Dylan has been completely withdrawn and silent since professing his guilt to his father regarding Princess *Mairead's* accident. Although the little girl's injuries are not serious, a blessing for which I am most grateful, the social and political fallout of tonight's misstep causes me a thread of concern.

I realize it sounds silly. Afterall, this was simply an unfortunate accident: Some bad choices made by a handful of children. (And yes. I do consider *Oisin* a child even though in *Sidhe* culture he's considered nearly a man. However, as someone who has been working with kids for the past fifteen years, I can firmly attest to the fact that thirteen-year-old boys are often incapable of making adult-like decisions. Hell. I know some thirty-year-old men who still regularly make bad choices.) Still, as my darling Tax Man often pontificates, every decision, bad or good, has its consequences. He's not wrong. One just needs to note the number of lawsuits filed in the Mundane world along with the sea of personal injury lawyers they produce. It's no different in the Otherworld. Missteps, mistakes and mayhem by one House is often considered a golden opportunity for another. It was imperative for House *Nuada* to handle this fiasco with all the facts uncovered.

Getting Dylan to tell me what really happened in the horse barn will be no easy feat. Even at his young age, our *Sidhe child* shows the predilection of the Fae for keeping secrets. It's a trait that seems embedded in their DNA, though I suppose if you spend several generations needing to hide who and what you are, the Universe might offer you the skill set to do so. Right at this moment, my beloved child is sitting on the carriage bench across from me, sniffling into his sleeve. "Dylan, Baby, why don't you come sit in mommy's lap," I offer.

At first, he just looks up at me with red-rimmed eyes, but then the temptation for comfort is too great, and he slides off his seat and into my lap. The two of us sit quietly as the carriage rolls home to *Dun Siorai*. At some point, I give my best "mama technique" a try. "I'm sorry the evening turned out this way, Honey. It seemed like you were having lots of fun with the *Banphrionsa*." I hear a sniffle or two, but the child doesn't answer. I try again. "I know you didn't mean for *Mairead* to get hurt, Dylan. You and she have been good friends since you were babies. You just let your need to be better than she get the best of you. It happens."

As I figured, my blaming him for someone else's possible mistake gets his *Nuada* dander up. Like his competitive father, Dylan will fully admit when he is at fault for a "loss." It's in their *Tuatha de Danann* nature. But neither father or son is very good about shouldering someone else's errors, never wanting to appear to be someone's "patsy." "But Mama, ya' don' understand!" he wails. "'Twas no my fault!"

Bingo! It's just as Declan and I both thought. There's more to this story than what was spoken at House *Badh's* estate. "But, Dylan, Honey, you told me, and Da and the Black Knight that you teased the *Banphrionsa* into getting on *Toirneach*. Are you telling me that's not what really happened?" Realizing he'd just spilled the beans, my son buries his head under my arm and resumes his wailing. I can tell from the twisting and curving of the road under the carriage wheels that we are almost home. If I don't get answers before we arrive, the opportunity for honest clarification will undoubtedly be lost. I coax my child a wee bit harder to come clean. "You will be *Mac Nuada* someday, Dylan. Honesty is the trademark of a good Lord."

As soon as the words leave my mouth, I want to swallow them back. How hypocritical of me, trading on a cultural philosophy that I profess to thoroughly disdain. Using this *Sidhe* style coercion on my own child! It's living proof that spending so much time in the Otherworld has changed Dr. Rosie Parker, and perhaps not for the better. My comment, however, hits the right button. Dylan untucks his head and looks up at me with his father's genes written across his handsome, little face. "You are right, Mama. I must be honest of nature if I am to lead my House like ma' Da someday. I would not want the people to think their Lord is a *bréagadóir salach* (dirty liar)."

I hate myself for this whole conversation. "No one could ever think that of you, Dylan Edmund Fitzpatrick. Da and I love you to the moon and back and we know you are a most courageous and honest boy."

With a trembling lip, Dylan tells his story. "The *Banphrionsa* and I went ta' the horse barn ta' say goodnight to *Toirneach*. The Princess *Mairead* was sad because her Da would no let her ride her pony *Gaoth Dorcha* (Dark Wind) to the handfast celebration. We gave *Toirneach* the sugar cubes we brought and ma' pony boy was vera' happy ta' see us and have his treats. But then the Princess said that her *chapaillíní* (pony) was much taller than mine. 'Tis not true, Mama! I have seen *Gaoth Dorcha* in the training ring many times. *Toirneah* is a head taller than her filly, but the *Banphrionsa* would no believe me! She said I must prove it by sittin' on his back and matchin' our height ta'gether against the stall door. I tol' her that ma' Lord *Athair* said we shad' not go in the stall, but she laughed at me and said I was no more than a wee *bairn* if I always did what ma' Da told me. Then, she opened the latch and went inta' the pony's stall. Usin' his upturned feed bucket, the Princess mounted him bareback. At first, *Toirneach* was as gentle as a wee lamb. But then she went and pulled on his mane ta' get him to move closer ta' the stall door so she could measure their height. Ya' know, yar'self, Mama, that ma' pony boy does no like havin' his mane pulled. 'Tis the one thing that riles him up like a wet *iora* (squirrel) in a bucket! Ma' poor boy bucked and threw her off his back. The princess caught her sleeve on a nail in the wall. 'Tis how she cut her arm."

My heart stands completely still in my chest at the realization of how badly this could have ended up. In the tight confines of the stall, the little girl could have gotten kicked or trampled. It is only by some divine protection from the Universe that this scenario hadn't ended in true tragedy. Thinking back to the silent communication between the two children, I question him further "But Dylan, why didn't you tell us all this when we first asked? Why did you tell your father and the Black Knight that it was you who convinced the *Banphrionsa* to sit *Toirneach*?"

With a furled brow and averted gaze, the boy explains, his tone matter-of-fact and strangely serious for one of such a tender age. "She is ma' Princess, Lady *Mathair,* and I am har' brave and loyal Knight. 'Tis ma' duty to protect her in any way I ken', even if it is only from a *pionós* (punishment) handed down by her *athair.*

Though I've achieved my directive in finding out what really happened tonight, this intimate conversation with my oldest child leaves me troubled and anxious. Is this whole "Princess and her brave Knight" thing just childish play-acting? A way for the children to mirror the actions of the adults around them? Or is there…something deeper in play here? The *Banphrionsa Mairead* is the Raven's own, her heir apparent, and prophecy is a Morrigan trademark. This thought causes all the hair on my arm to stand straight up and now, more than ever, I long for the Mundane "normalcy" of Salem, Massachusetts.

MISSING 22

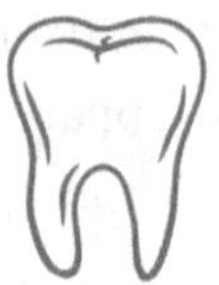

What Does it Mean?

I'T'S LATE when we all finally return home. I leave Dylan in the loving hands of *Birgit* and nurse Ronin before retiring, but there is still no sign of my husband or *Oisin.* It's not until I finish my night time routine that Declan finally joins me in our bedroom suite. His rigid body language and the sour expression give evidence that the ride back to *Dun Siorai* was not a pleasant experience. "That bad, huh?" I ask as I pull on my robe against the evening chill in the room. Immediately, without me asking, flames begin to blaze in the fireplace across the room. "Thank you," I added. "It's rather damp in our room. Definitely a touch of autumn in the air tonight."

My *Mo Shiorghra* kisses me in greeting. "I am glad ta' be home, Love. The ride from *Cuach an Fhithich* felt twice as long coming back then it did goin', though perhaps it was just the boy's dreary silence that made it seem so. I hope yar' little chat with Dylan was mar' productive than the one I dinna' have with *Oisin*."

"As a matter of fact, your sneaky *Mo Shiorghra* Mata Hara was able to get the "scoop," as they say. And…as we both guessed, …"

The Tax Man holds up a hand to stop me. "Hold that thought, Lass. I need to get out of these clothes and rinse the road dust from ma'self befar' I can begin ta' tackle all that has happened."

My mate goes off to wash up and I fight to keep my eyes open. The warmth and the sounds of the crackling fire lull me into a drowsy stupor, so I'm a bit startled when Declan returns to the bedroom, toweling his dry his ginger hair. Thank the goddesses he's wearing running shorts. A naked Tax Man is far too much of a distraction to a useful conversation. "I fixed us a night cap," I say, pointing to the crystal decanter and two snifters. "It's the honeyed brandy you like from Avalon."

"'Tis just the thing. Thank ya, Love." He lowers himself into the chair on the other side of the table between us, pours a finger of brandy in each glass, then pats his lap, inviting me to take a seat there. I settle myself into my favorite spot and for a few moments, the two of us sip our brandy and enjoy the quiet comfort of being together. Eventually, his Lordship puts his glass down and sighs. "I suppose we need ta' talk about the fiasco that befell us this evening. I have no doubt it will come back ta' haunt us in so manner or another."

"I get that the *Banphrionsa* was injured, Sweetie, and on '*Nuada* watch,' so to speak. But clearly, it was an accident. And, as I discovered on the way home, it really wasn't

Dylan's fault." I relate the story our son told me in the carriage; how it was actually the little princess who decided to enter *Toirneach's* stall against Dylan's warnings, and thus got thrown when she pulled on the pony's mane.

When I get to that part, Declan lets loose a stream of colorful obscenities over what might have happened but thankfully didn't. "I had a feelin' the story Dylan told was not the whole truth. He is not a mean-spirited boy, and though he and the littlest Raven have always had a … complicated friendship, one layered in competitiveness, I do not see our son bullyin' another child. 'Tis not in his nature."

"Complicated friendship" is only the half of it, I think to myself, recalling that whole crazy "knight" part of the conversation. For the time being, I keep that little nugget of weirdness to myself, checking that I have a reasonably secure mental shield in place. Let's deal with one problem at a time. "Will you say something to the Black Knight about his daughter's role in all this?" I ask, expecting my husband to be aghast at the notion of tattling on the Queen's great granddaughter.

Instead, Declan shrugs. "Perhaps. If the topic arises in the correct form, or if there are calls for retribution over the *Banphrionsa's* injuries."

It's my turn to be shocked. "Retribution? Are you serious? Over a silly accident? It's not like the princess won't be one hundred percent herself tomorrow. I can't believe Lady Dear Heart or the Black Knight would hold Dylan responsible for something their own child was behind.

Something that has no long-lasting effects and will be forgotten in a few days."

"Don' be gettin' yourself ina' a *stoirm tine* (firestorm), Love. I dinna' say that retribution was a foregone conclusion. In fact, Beck told me privately befar' I left for home that he was suspicious that his daughter had mar' ta' do with the accident than she was lettin' on. As har' father, he said that he doubted anyone could talk his *Mairead* into doin' anything that didn't suit her fancy. He flat-out told me the girl was a mini version of Herself, the Queen. I' am guessin' ya' understand what he meant by that statement."

If *Mairead* Beckett was truly a younger version of The Morrigan, then our friends were in store for a rough road getting their beloved daughter to mature adulthood. However, the fact that her father rationally understood this about his darling child was a relief. "It's good to know he feels that way. Maybe this whole thing will blow over without a lot of fuss."

"Far' Dylan? Probably. But yar' missin' an entirely different part of the story, Lass. The fact remains that *Oisin* was given the responsibility of keepin' watch over the two younger children. He was technically ordered ta' do so by his Liege Lord. Everyone at the table, includin' the Black Knight, heard me tell him this. Though the boy has refused to discuss the details of the incident with me, repeatedly statin' he will willingly accept the consequences of his actions, he has thus far not spoken the truth about where he was or what he was doin' while the wee tots were busy in the harse' barn. I don' suppose Dylan had any insight on where his *uncail* was when *Mairead* went into the stall?"

I shake my head in the negative, and take another sip of the brandy. I can taste the sweet layer of summer clover honey while the heat of the brandy warms my insides. "No. Unfortunately, he didn't mention *Oisin* at all except to say his uncle wasn't in attendance when this all went down. However, I did notice a young teenage girl standing in the doorway when your brother carried *Mairead* into the banquet room. When she saw me looking at her, she disappeared from sight. I guessed *Oisin* was off with her instead of minding Dylan. The call of 'young love,' if you get my drift."

"Aye. I saw her as well," Declan concurs. "As did Beck. I assumed the same scenario as you, though the lad's aura was 'off' far' someone so recently engaged in passion. The whole thing is disconcerting, and I will have to talk to both boys myself and try to get ta' the bottom of all this." My husband holds up the decanter to ascertain if I'd like a second shot of brandy."

"No thanks," I responded. "I think I've had enough 'happy juice' for one day". A yawn escapes me, and I add, "Maybe we can pick this discussion up tomorrow. I'm starting to fade. It's been a long day."

"That it has, ma' Love, though I'd be lyin' if I said I wasn't hopin' ta' finish the La Volta we started earlier in the evening," he says with a grin.

And just like that sleep is no longer the number one thing on my mind. I stand up and put out my hand for my *Mo Shiorghra* to take. "Come, ma' Lord. Let us finish our dance."

MISSING 23

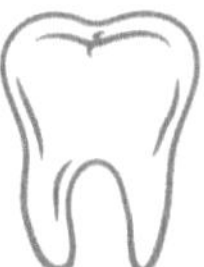

Acting the Part When Duty Calls

WE LEAVE for our return to the Mundane world directly after breakfast. I had expected Declan to meet with *Oisin* and Dylan before leaving *Dun Siorai,* but I am incorrect, his reasoning being that neither boy will like what he is planning on telling them, and he doesn't wish for their negative energy to hinder a comfortable crossing of the Veil. This time of the year, so close to *Samhain,* the Veil between the Mundane dimension and the Otherworld is moving toward its thinnest point, so if anything, our travel should be easier. Plus, I don't believe either boy has the bravado to try and disrupt his Lordship's magic. Practical me believes that my mate would prefer not to have this particular discussion in a place that always seems to have unseen ears and eyes to carry tales.

I feel I know my Tax Man well enough to be confident that he won't treat either beloved child overly harshly, though it's no secret that the Fae, especially the titled

Sidhe, don't believe in coddling their children when it comes to the matters of expected behavior and responsibility. Therefore, I'm more than curious when instead of calling for a *"cruinniú teaghlaigh"* (informal family/clan gathering) around the dining room table which is his usual practice regarding Fitzpatrick family matters, Declan instructs them to promptly unpack their things and join him in his office in one hour. As it's yesterday afternoon here in Salem, I'm lacking the magical energy to read the children's auras, but my tooth fairy skills aren't necessary to note by maternal observation that their anxiety levels have risen substantially over my mate's directive. His Lordship's personal space, here in Salem, as well as at *Dun Siorai,* is traditionally "off-limits" to the children. To be commanded there causes Dylan to grow wide-eyed and ball up the hem of the tunic he was wearing when he crossed over, while *Oisin's* usually ruddy complexion goes a shade lighter, and his eyes stay glued to his feet.

"Do ya' both understand ma' instructions?" the Tax Man asks.

"Aye, ma' Lord," the teenager mumbles, still unable to meet his elder brother's eyes.

When Dylan doesn't answer, his father asks him again. "And you, *Mac Nuada?* Do ya' understand what I'm requirin'?"

The little boy shakes his head in the affirmative. "Aye, Da," he replies, his nervousness causing Dylan to use his father's informal moniker instead of the protocol designated one. "I understand."

"Very well. Then off with you. I will see you both in

one hour," his Lordship commands before abruptly turning around and walking toward his office.

Properly trained for their work among the titled Fae, neither *Birgit* or *Niamh* comment on the little family drama going on within their hearing. Like the pros they are, the *scathachs* take their younger charges off to the nursery with a plan of changing their Otherworldly clothes then heading off to the park down the street, leaving the rest of us precious privacy. I'm glad I had the foresight to feed Ronin before we crossed, thus allowing me to give whatever is going on with my husband and our older boys all the attention it deserves.

I follow Declan to his office. The door is closed so I knock rather than just barging in, not wishing to add any additional emotion to the situation by barging in. The door swings open of its own accord allowing me entrance. "I was expectin' ya'd want me ta' explain ma'self, Love," my Eternal Mate says.

I join him on the small leather loveseat. "Lots of unnecessary theatrics, don't you think, Tax Man? I question. "You had our son shaking in his little boy boots."

My husband sighs and throws an arm around me. "As I have confessed on mar' than one occasion, Rosie Lass, I do not wish ta' be the same kind of domineering, bullying parent ma' own *athair* was, but I need ta' make both boys realize that everythin' they do, even as *daioine óga* (youngsters) will be doubly scrutinized and judged by the people of *I Idir*, especially those who hold power. Because of ma' sire's traitorous actions, a cloud of conspiracy will hang around House *Nuada* until the man is caught and brought ta' justice. Even then, when he has faced the consequences of his actions and is gone from this existence, I fear the stain of his legacy will undoubtedly continue to tarnish the good name of *Nuada.* I must make *Oisin* and Dylan understand this, as well as *Liam* and Ronin someday in the future, even if they view me as harsh and unloving."

I know my Eternal Mate is hurting, and I want nothing more than to be able to throw my arms around him and soothe him, but I learned my lesson about that very thing early on in our relationship: The Tax Man does not appreciate being "comforted" if it comes across as pity, and, in fact, becomes down right snarky over it being offered. Because of that, I reach for his hand instead and lace his fingers through mine. "Oh Sweetie, the children love you deeply. All of them. I realize *Oisin* is at an awkward age, but that boy worships the ground you walk on. None of them would ever think poorly of you, no matter what happens. Trust me on that."

"I love ya' for saying that, "*Stór Mo Chroí* (Treasure of My Heart)," my husband replies, "but I hold great concern for ma' young brother. I hear the mumblins' and side talk of the *Sidhe* elite over the boy's Elven heritage and the magical potential he may hold. It was one thing when he was a child and easily managed, but as he moves toward manhood, I fear some of the other Lords now look upon him with suspicious eyes. The *Sidhe* have always held a deep prejudice against the *Seior* magic of our *Nordboerne* neighbors, though truly its energy is no different than our own. Otherworld Fae especially look upon the ancient *Jotun* magic of the *Dökkálfar* with much hostility and dread, believin' it ta' be evil in nature. I owe it ta' the boy, as his elder brother and guardian, ta' make sure he understands and accepts this reality of his life. Far' his own good, I must keep ma' brother walkin' the straight and narrow path of righteous behavior. Dylan along with him, and Liam and Ronin as well when the time comes, lest it appear I show favoritism ta' ma' own."

Everything my husband has just explained makes perfect sense. Both of us were fully aware that when we accepted *Oisin* as part of our family, the unusual circumstances of his birth would rest on our shoulders as well. It changed nothing about the deep love we had for the child. I lean over and kiss my Eternal Mate. "Whatever decisions you make will be the right ones for our family, ma' Lord. I have no doubt about it." Still, as much as I mean every syllable of them, as the words leave my mouth, I can't help the little shiver of apprehension that tickles down my spine along with them.

MISSING 24

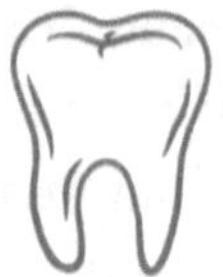

It's Time for His Lordship to Lay Down the Law

I BARELY FINISH TELLING Declan the odd details regarding Dylan's covering for the Princess *Mairead* when there is a knock at the door, which is no doubt the two older Fitzpatrick boys. "It is *Mac Nuada* and I, ma' Lord. As you have ordered." *Oisin's* adolescent voice cracks midsentence, and I see the Tax Man grimace. Despite all this playing at Ruling Council bullshit, *Oisin* and Dylan are just children.

"Do you want me to leave? I ask."

"No. Best ya' stay, Love. Ya' will be a sweet motherly presence ta' counter the words they will hear from me." Truthfully, his statement doesn't instill a great deal of hope in me that this little "chat" will go easily and my own anxiety level rises. Lord *Nuada* grimaces and then stands up. "Enter," he tells them.

Both boys step inside Declan's impressive home office, a two story space that includes not only his business paraphernalia, but his beloved baby grand piano (which sits untouched since North Korea), a state-of-the-art, sound system, an extensive collection of vinyl covering all types of music, an array of carefully mounted medieval swords, and a complete wall of leather bound and paperback books, fiction and non-fiction alike. As they are not often invited into his Lordship's "inner sanctum," the kids stop to take in their surroundings in wide-eyed admiration. Having *Sidhe* blood running through their veins, both pairs of eyes go directly to the sword collection on the east wall. As I've probably mentioned before, the Fae have a predilection for sharp, pointy things.

My Tax Man takes a seat behind his desk, a beautiful antique piece we found while vacationing last summer on Cape Cod, and signals the two boys to come forward. Dylan, with the confidence of a five-year-old, matter-of-factly plops his dinosaur-shirted self in one of the leather chairs in front of his father, but *Oisin* nudges him and shakes his head in the negative, and our son slides himself off and stands next to his uncle, following the teenagers lead and clasping his little hands behind his back in tradi-tional protocol pose.

It's all I can do not to giggle at the sight, and thus get a warning from my Eternal Mate. *"Please, Rosie. Don' make this any harder for me than it already is."*

I put on my most somber expression while the boys try not to fidget in the nervous tension of the deafening silence. His Lordship folds his hands on his desk. "I assume ya' both know why I have called ya' here?"

"Aye, ma' Lord. 'Tis in regards ta'ma' poor decision on the night of the handfast. I would like ta' say far' the ears of yar' Lordship and ma' dear Lady Sister, that wee *Mac Nuada* is no ta' blame for the events of that evening and shad' therefore bear none of the consequences," *Oisin* explained.

"Though I appreciate yar' candor, Master Fitzpatrick, I donna' think it's yar decision as to who shad' and shad' not accept responsibility. Am I wrong?" his Lordship questioned, the tone of his voice allowing for no disagreement

Any trace of bravado the teenager might have come in with, evaporated under his elder brother's cold, expressionless facade. "No, ma' Lord," the boy answered.

"I am glad we ken' agree on something, Brother. 'Tis obvious ya' did not follow through in watching the younger children after I directly ordered ya' to do so. Please explain ta' yar' Lady Sister and ma'self what ya' were doin' instead," Declan said.

The boy looked away before answering. "I was with *Laoise*, ma' Lord. In the pole barn. We war'... enjoyin' each other's company. As I have said, I take complete responsibility far' my decision ta' disregard yar' Lordship's orders. I shad be whipped like the ruffian I am."

I'm shocked at *Oisin's* belief that my husband is capable of having anyone whipped, especially his own brother. I open my mouth to say just that, but the Tax Man cuts me off. "As I already have said, Master Fitzpatrick, it is I, Lord of House *Nuada*, who will decide what punishment yar' deservin' of. Not you." Then, my Eternal Mate turns his attention to our son. "And you, *Mac Nuada*...ya' told both yar' *athair* and the Black Knight, as well as everyone gathered, that you were the cause behind the Princess *Mairead* going into the stall and getting on yar' pony's back. But that isn't true, is it, *Mac Nuada?*"

Dylan shifts his weight from foot to foot, then replies, "No, ma' Lord. It was not the truth."

"So, you are admitting you lied to everyone, including yar' own *athair* and beloved *mathair.*"

It's too much for my baby. I can see his lower lip trembling and I have to physically stop myself from picking him up into my lap and telling him it will all be okay. "*Tread lightly here, Tax Man,*" I mentally warn. *He's still a baby.*"

"*Do ya' think I would treat ma' own son...ma' first born child ...with anything but a father's love and guidance, Mo Shiorghra? It pains me ta' no end to have ya' believe that about me, Rosalinda, but I will not let Dylan believe that falsehood is the best way ta' handle one's problems. Our son will be Lord someday. There is enough dishonesty and negative energy in the Ruling Council. I will not raise my own bloodline to follow that philosophy.*"

I hold back an angry retort that goes along the lines of not giving a rat's ass about Ruling Council policies where my children are concerned. Nor do I approve of his nonchalant disregard of Dylan's odd loyalty to *Mairead* Beckett. But this is not the time nor place for any of that argument. I bite my lip and bring up my mental shield, closing my husband off to my raging thoughts.

His Lordship leans back in his chair, perfectly calm and without a hint of anger. "I would like ta' think that ya' both regret the poor decisions that led ta' the events at the handfasting? Am I correct in my belief?"

"Aye, ma' Lord," both boys reply in unison.

"That is good to hear. It takes a great weight off ma' shoulders that ma' own understand the importance of responsibility. However, as ya' are aware, all actions have consequences. It is the great law of the Universe. Thus, I have decided on what I believe ta' be an appropriate consequence."

"I am ready for whatever yar' Lordship deems fair, ma' Lord," *Oisin* states, his back ramrod straight with that touch of *Nuada* confidence I've seen in his elder brother on multiple occasions.

"I am vera' glad ta' hear that, *Dearthár* (Brother). It proves ya' have principle and courage. That bein' said, as of today, and for the next twenty-one days, a total of three Mundane weeks, you and Dylan are hereby... as the Mundanes strangely call it...'grounded.'"

Dylan scrunches up his forehead. "I donna' know what that means, Da."

His uncle answers, the confidence of a few seconds ago now turning to teenage snarky-ness. "It means, *Mac Nuada*, that we no longer have personal freedom. We are like birds in a cage, with his Lordship holding our keys."

I can tell by the narrowed eyes that Declan doesn't care much for *Oisin's* sarcasm. I, on the other hand, have been on the receiving end of the same type of acerbity by the Tax Man himself, so it's hard for me not to mentally retort a comment about apples not falling from the same tree. Then Dylan, with blinking, terrified eyes, "You are locking me in a cage, Da?" making me ready to lose my shit over this whole "meeting."

At least my husband has the decency to look completely mortified at his son's question. "Of course not,

Dylan. I love ya' ta' the moon and back, son. I'd never put ya' in a cage or do anything ta' harm ya. Yar' uncle is just being vera' dramatic. Bein' grounded just means that ya' ken' no do the outside things ya' enjoy after school…no ridin' yar bike, or goin' to the park with *Birgit* and *Niamh*, no playdates with yar' friend, Sam."

"What about soccer, Da? No soccer either?" our son asks. "Ma' team needs me. I am ta' be goalie this month."

"'Twould not be fair to punish yar' teammates far' yar' poor decisions, Dylan. Ya' may attend soccer practice and games, but there will be no trips for treats afterwards," his Lordship explains. "And when the twenty-one days are up, ya' will gain all yar' privileges back and hopefully understand that lying is never a good choice."

Dylan turns to his uncle. "See, *Uncail Oisin*, I told ya' it would no be so bad. At least there are no whippins'"

"I would prefer the whipping to this unjust long imprisonment, *Mac Nuada*," the older boy replies.

"That is a silly thought, *Uncail*. Why wad' ya' want to be beaten instead," our son asks, a lack of understanding painted on his little face. "That would hurt somethin' awful."

"Ya' don' understand, wee boy. This 'groundin' means no Halloween either…no trick or treatin' with ar' friends on the feast of Mundane *Samhain*," *Oisin* reveals.

Apparently, this little caveat regarding the rules of "grounding" was one our eldest son didn't count on. His little head swivels towards his father. "This is true, *Athair*? No Halloween?"

I can tell by the way Declan is jiggling his right leg that he's having trouble being the "bad guy" in his son's eyes, but he calmly answers, "Aye, son. No outside activities. That includes Halloween."

Our little boy then looks at me. "Mama, I am ta' no have Halloween," the full weight of his disappointment evident in his dejected expression and the sadness in his voice.

It tears me up inside to have my beautiful boy so heartbroken, but I am unwilling to throw my Eternal Mate under the bus. We are a team in this parenting game and I don't want to jeopardize our united front after Declan has worked so tirelessly to try to balance our dual lives. I answer my eldest son. "Aye, wee boy. Not this year. There will be other Halloweens in the future for you to enjoy."

I've gone and said what needed to be said, and every word stabs at me. As I look away, I see *Oisin* across the room, staring out the window with staid indifference. In that moment, I forge an uneasy feeling that the adolescent boy is working towards distancing himself from not only this difficult conversation, but from our family altogether, and in the quiet of my head, I hear the cawing of birds.

MISSING 25

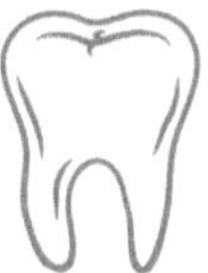

From Bad to Worse

FOR THE MOST PART, the aftermath of Declan's "consequences" presents a scenario of what is to be expected when children are faced with discipline, even Fae ones. For the first few days after his "meeting" with his father, Dylan is quiet and withdrawn, keeping to himself and going out of his way to ignore his younger brother, who sadly doesn't understand why his big brother is shunning him. Eventually, in the hopeful optimism of a nearly six-year-old boy, our son focuses his attention on other exciting factors in his life to change his dreary mood; a class field trip to a local historical candy shop to see how their famous Gibralter and Blackjack treats are made, the paper-mache *sionnach* (fox) mask he is creating for his part in the school *Samhain* pageant, and his successful role as the soccer team's new goalie.

As for my young brother-in-law, his reaction to the "grounding" is perfectly normal for the pinnacle of adolescence. Upon his return from school each afternoon, *Oisin* holes himself up in his bedroom, venturing out for dinner only because it is a house rule that we eat the meal as a family. He speaks only when he is directly asked a question, and even then, he is miserly with his words. I know the boy's public sulking annoys the Tax Man who himself is a "stiff-upper-lip-and-make-the -best-of it" kind of guy when faced with problems. But having spent years of my practice dealing with kids of all ages, *Oisin's* behavior is pretty on par with what I have noticed among his Mundane peers.

As important as our family issues are to us, Declan and I are both overwhelmed with responsibilities outside the home as well. Because of the approaching *Samhain* sabbat and the thinning of the Veil between the Mundane world and the Otherworld, tensions have risen at the Veil border closest to *I Idir*. Although there are other kingdoms in the Otherworld with a passageway between the two dimensions, *I Idir's* is the largest and the one most of the Mundane governments seemed to be focused on, primarily due to The Morrigan's resolve to keep them out. The past two months have seen an increase in skirmishes at the border as well as multiple Mundane deaths, including the son of one of the Mundanes' most fervent, Fae-hating leaders. The hours my Eternal Mate spends in *I Idir* have doubled, causing him to miss a handful of Dylan's soccer games while filling his guard rotation duty on the border. In addition, one of my husband's biggest Mundane corporate clients is being audited by the IRS, adding yet another level of stress to his already heavy schedule.

On my end, one of my associates, a young male dentist, just heartbreakingly announced that he is taking a six-month family leave to be with his wife while she undergoes chemo, while at the same time I've also lost two hygienists in just the past week; one to retirement that I knew about, and one to go back to nursing school that I didn't. Normally, my go-to-girl Mel would be at my side handling all these turns of events, but this week, she's taking a handful of personal days with Duncan to travel to Edinburgh, Scotland over a rumor of a young *Sidhe* girl who might be considering placing her unplanned baby up for adoption.

As the House Mages predicted, though Mel and Duncan are gloriously happy together, their union has yet to produce any offspring. She and I are both closing in on forty, and thus, are jointly beginning to experience the early symptoms of female Fae menopause. With the window of them having their own biological children beginning to permanently close for them, Duncan and Mel have decided to seek an alternate route, though a nearly impossible one. I pray that this trip doesn't end with another huge disappointment that, once again, leaves our two dearest friends broken hearted.

Mel not being in the office is the reason I am in the office much earlier than my normal schedule dictates, and am therefore already at my desk and not at home or in the car when the high school calls me to inform me that *Oisin* Fitzpatrick is not in class today and the Dean's office has not been officially notified of his absence.

My heart stops in my chest over this news because I was the one who dropped *Oisin* off in front of the building on my way to work. Our situation being what it is, I lie through my teeth, telling the school that *Oisin* wasn't feeling well and I simply forgot to call him in. If I had been honest about dropping the kid off like I did, the school would be mandated to notify the Sheriff's Office to investigate him as "missing." On the very small chance *Oisin's* disappearance is related to Otherworldly "business," it needs to be handled discreetly by my husband and the Black Knight, who, ironically, also happens to be the "Sheriff" in said "Sheriff's Office."

I dial Declan's cell, and he picks up on the first ring. Because of our unique bond, he immediately asks, "What's wrong, Lass? I ken feel yar' heart racin!"

"*Oisin's* school just called. He didn't show up for class this morning. I dropped him off in front of the building, Declan. Where the hell can he be? If something happened to him, I…I…" The rest of the words stick in my throat, and I feel sick to my stomach.

"Don' jump ta' conclusions, Love. This might just be an angry reaction to ma' punishment. I will find him. I promise," my mate says, trying to reassure me.

"Are you going to call the Black Knight?" I question.

There is a slight pause before he answers. "Aye. Is best I do so. I will be most embarrassed if it turns out the boy is only testin' ma' resolve, but with all that is goin' on at the border, it wouldn't be wise ta' take unnecessary chances. If ya' ken cancel yar' appointments far' today, then do so and head directly home. If *Oisin* shows up there, 'tis best if you are there as well. I will let ya' know the minute I find out anything."

"I need to help look for him, Declan!"

"'Tis a bad plan, Love. At this point, we have no idea where the boy is, or what is involved in his disappearance. Ya' need to be there for the other children. I will let *Birgit* and *Niamh* know what has happened. They are quite capable of securin' the house and everyone in it."

MISSING 26

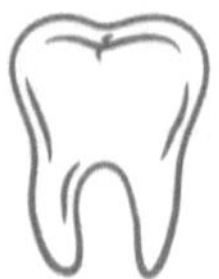

Adolescence is a Curse

I DO what any mother figure would do in a situation like this. I pace, I fret, I send reams of prayers to the Celtic Pantheon, while making outlandish deals with the Universe to keep *Oisin* safe. Our two *scathachs* remain calm, taking Ronin and Liam up to the nursery with a promise of a magical teddy bear picnic, a space I am sure will be heavily warded. Protocol set up in advance will have them immediately taking the kids and jumping to *Dun Siorai* if required, but I don't even let myself think that any of those actions will be necessary.

After two hours, I consider reaching out to my husband despite his explicit instructions for me to wait to hear from him. That's when I spot the non-descript, gray Volvo pulling up to the curb in front of our house. Fr. Kevin O'Kenney, the Prince of *I Idir* and the Black Knight's Second, steps out from the driver's side, clerical collar and all, then goes around to open the door for his passenger. I immediately recognize my husband's brother as the person clambering out of the car, and I almost sink to the floor in relief.

I don't wait for them to knock, instead opening the door and throwing my arms around *Oisin*, who feels stiff and awkward in my arms. "Oh, Honey...I'm so glad you're okay." As I pull away, I feel just the slightest tingle of residual magical energy that still clings to the boy. It's the middle of the day when my own Fae gifts are nearly non-existent, so the fact that I can still feel this electrical charge speaks to its strength.

Obviously, I am naive because I expect some level of relief, or remorse, or, at the very least, embarrassment from the kid. I get none of that. "Of course, I am fine, Lady Sister. It is a silly notion far' ya' ta' think that I am unable of carin' far' myself."

Behind him, Fr. Kevin clears his throat. "You're lucky to have people who care for your well-being, *Oisin*. There are no better people than Lord and Lady *Nuada*."

The kid immediately tones down his snark. It's one thing to sass your sister-in-law, and another thing entirely to "dis" The Morrigan's own. "You are right, ma' Lord. I am far luckier than I deserve." Taking my hands in his own, my brother-in-law apologizes. "I am sorry far' causin' ya' worry, Lady Rosie. It was vera' thoughtless of me ta' disrupt yar' day like this."

Disrupt my frickin' day? Is that he thinks his disappearance meant to me? To Declan? I'm not sure how to react to this less-than-sincere show of remorse, and while I struggle to come up with a sage-like reply, the front door opens and my husband storms in followed by the

Black Knight dressed in his Sheriff's uniform. Declan puts a hand on each of the boy's shoulders, as demonstrative as he will get in such a public setting. "Are ya' free of injury, *Dearthair* (Brother)?" My husband's eye brows raise at the magical residue rolling off the boy.

I notice immediately that *Oisin's* teenage confidence level drops several notches in the presence of three of *I Idir's* most influential men. For all his adolescent male bluster, the boy hero- worships his older brother. Always has. And, as a child of the Fae *Otherworld, Oisin* has certainly heard every tall tale and bogey-man rumor regarding our Queen's Hand of Justice. I am glad, for the kid's sake, that he has the wherewithal to look properly contrite over the fuss he's caused. "I am fine, ma' Lord. I bear no injuries except far' my shame at involvin' Her Majesty's finest."

"Perhaps you could enlighten us, Master *Nuada,* on what prevented you from attending your classes this morning?" the Lord Knight cooly suggests. "Fr. Kevin says he found you walking down Bridge Street, seemingly coming from the direction of the Salem-Beverly Bridge. That's a long way from the high school and the complete opposite direction of your home. How did you come to be there?"

The boy looks away, unable to keep up the stare match with the Queen's Sword Arm. I've been in that same position and I sympathize with *Oisin's* deer-in-the-headlights discomfort. I try to break the tension in the room with a lame offer of hospitality. "Why don't we all sit down. Can I get anyone something to drink? Tea? Coffee?"

Beckett throws an annoyed glance at my husband, but

reluctantly takes a seat on the sofa, pointing *Oisin* towards the arm chair across from him. "Thank you, Lady *Nuada*, but I don't think refreshments are necessary." In my head, I hear the Tax Man say, *"I know yar' tryin' ta' help the lad, Rosie, but ya' need ta' let Beck do his thing. The boy's behavior of late is odd and if anyone ken' get ta' the heart of the matter, it's the Queen's man."*

In my opinion, the Black Knight finds "cloak-and-dagger" shit everywhere he looks. *"Oh hell, Declan, this is probably nothing more than raging testosterone and teenage angst. Mundane kids cut classes all the time. Even 'yours truly' wasn't immune to a few 'ditch days' in my time. I think you gentlemen are making a mountain out of a molehill,"* I suggest.

"No one would be happier than I, Lass, for it ta' be as ya' say. But there is additional information of which yar' not yet aware that makes it necessary ta' get the truth from the lad."

Of course, I am "not yet aware." It's always that way. Let's keep good ole' Rosie out of the loop. I give my beloved Eternal Mate my best wifely stink eye, but then turn my attention back to the conversation at hand. Our resident teenager is jiggling his leg up and down, a physical quirk he must have inherited from his elder brother. "'Twas only bad judgement on ma' part, Lord Knight. I did no mean ta' cause such anxiety far' my family. First period is World History. Mundane world history, that is, which ta' my mind is wholly dull, as is ma' teacher. I did not wish ta' sit through yet another lecture on the culture of Mundane 'Mees-o-potamia.' If you yar'rself are familiar, ma' Lord, 'tis a backward civilization at a time when ma' our own people were creatin' a masterful dynasty. I could no bear the tedium of it, and bein' such a fine *fómhar* (autumn) day, I decided ta' take a hike along the coastal byway. Far' meditation purposes, and all, Lord Merlin," the boy explained, carefully making sure to get in all of Beck's proper titles in a blatant *Sidhe* effort to curry favor. Even I can tell the kid's story reeks of bullshit.

The Queen's Hand of Justice shows not the slightest glimmer of emotion. "I see. And you were alone on this 'walk of meditation,' Master *Nuada*," stressing the boy's not-quite-a-*Sidhe*-adult- title.

For a mere second, like the maternal presence I am, I can see the wheels turning in *Oisin's* head over the decision to build on his lie, or tell the truth, and at this point, I'm not sure whether he is speaking the truth or making it all up as he goes along. "No ma' Lord. I was not alone. I was with a friend."

"A friend?" Beck asks. "Is this a friend from school? A boy your own age?"

"Aye, Lord Knight. I met him at school. He is older than me. A senior, I believe."

"I see. So, this boy was also a truant today."

Aye, ma' Lord," *Oisin* replies, making the Knight work for every nugget of information.

"And what might this young man's name be?" Beck questions.

The kid pauses, and if I had to guess, he's busy trying to come up with a name. "Finbarr, Sir. Finbarr...Lally," *Oisin* reveals.

"I see," the Lord Knight replies. "Is this a *Sidhe* boy?"

"Aye, ma' Lord. But I donna' think ya' would be

knowin' him. His parents are no involved in *I Idir* political doins'. He has never traveled through the Veil."

"Lally, you say?" the knight repeats, as if to commit the name to memory. "And was this boy's idea to skip classes?"

I can tell the kid is weighing his options because Beck's inquiry is a trick question. If *Oisin* admits ditching school was the older boy's idea, then it appears that he is a weak-minded child, easily led to wrongdoing, a notion abhorrent to any *Nuada* male so close to the age of manhood. On the other hand, if the teenager admits it was his idea, then he shoulders all the consequences himself. *Oisin* decides to play it safe somewhere in between. "'Tis hard ta' say exactly, ma' Lord. I do believe we both came upon the idea at the same time, it bein' such a fine day and all."

"Of course. A fine day for quiet meditation," the Black Knight says, not bothering to withhold the measure of sarcasm in his tone. "I suppose with that being the case, I will leave the consequences of your "spiritual walk-about" to your own Lord Brother, Master *Nuada*, as I feel it is a House and family matter, and not one that requires the attention of The Throne." The Queen's Hand of Justice stands, signaling the end of his little interrogation. He does not look in the least bit pleased with the way it had gone, but adds a final statement. "However, before I return to important business, let me state for the record that I never wish to be called out again to track down your sorry ass because you have decided it would be worthwhile to skip school and ponder the fucking meaning of life. Am I making myself clear enough, Master *Nuada?*"

The kid at least has the decency to look pale and queasy over being cursed out by the infamous Black Knight of *I Idir*. "Aye, ma' Lord. I understand," he stuttered. "Completely."

Beck smiled with his shark-like teeth. "Excellent. Because the next time this happens, boy, be assured that it will be me doling out the consequences of your actions and not the brother who holds you dear."

MISSING 27

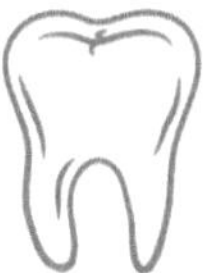

The Fox and the Bunny

IF *OISIN* FELT HIS ORIGINAL "GROUNDING' over the incidents at the handfasting curtailed his "personal freedom," then what came after the truancy episode was surely nothing the boy, who had been on his own since early childhood, had ever experienced. He complained daily to my husband and I that, "he could no even take a *cac* (shit) without someone's *súile* (eyes) upon him."

Truthfully, the kid wasn't wrong. Declan drove him to school every morning and Duncan picked him up and brought him directly home. With the help of the younger Merlin, who might not have the magical prowess his wizard father possessed, but who was undoubtedly the "*sensei* (Master Teacher) of security," the wards on the house had been configured to alert any type of entrance or exit, magical or otherwise. For all intents and purposes, the young *Sidhe* was a "jailbird."

At first, I railed against the Tax Man's heavy-handed tactics to rein in his younger brother. I was convinced it was over-the-top and completely out of line to treat a beloved family member in such a defensive manner while showing a complete lack of trust. That was until my Eternal Mate revealed some additional information that I hadn't been privy to. Despite a detailed search of Fae or Otherworldly mixed families living in the surrounding cities of Salem, Swampscott, Marblehead, and Peabody, the Black Knight and his tech gurus could find no record of anyone by the name "Finbarr Lally." A review of the class lists on the day *Oisin* went missing showed only six other unexcused absences, none of them male and all under classmen. Whoever the teenager was with that day, if he was accompanied by anyone at all, it was not a young man by the unusual name of "Finbarr Lally."

To add weight to their suspicions, Beck also revealed that the Lady Roxanne had done some unofficial chatting with the fair *Laoise*, only to discover that the girl hadn't met with *Oisin* the night of the handfasting, and that her boyfriend had, in fact, stood her up, a situation that had dampened her enthusiasm of him. If the kid hadn't been with the girl the night *Mairead* fell off Dylan's pony, then where in the hell had he been? And why did he lie about it?

Under normal circumstances, I would write off my young brother-in-law's behavior as typical of an adolescent's fight for personal freedom. But *Oisin* wasn't a typical Mundane teen, and the times and situations we all were living in weren't peacefully normal either. After Callum Fitzpatrick's treachery was found to be deeper than originally thought, involving far more of *I Idir's* influential citizens than The Throne had first imagined, retribution had been swift and brutal, and political suspicion ran rampant these days. *Oisin* was already surrounded by a cloud of misgivings and prejudices because of his Elven bloodline. It also didn't help that he was the bastard son of *I Idir's* number one traitor. The poor kid didn't need the spread of any additional gossip about whether he was up to "no good."

Poor Declan tried his very best to get his brother to open up to him on a personal, family level. When the brotherly way didn't work, my husband tried appealing to the boy as his soon-to-be Liege Lord, the man *Oisin* would profess fealty to once he reached the age of manhood. Although the kid was calm and respectful, he resolutely refused to utter one word regarding where he was on those two days in question. With nothing to lose, even I gave it the good ole' maternal try, laced with just a tad of motherly guilt, a conversation that earned me a sweet hug, but no additional revelations. The best we could do was to save the boy from himself by keeping him on a very short leash until whatever this was blew over.

The situation made the two weeks leading up to *Samhain* extremely tense, with everyone walking around on egg shells. Everyone that is, except *Liam*, who had, as I had already mentioned, taken to stripping naked and parading boldly in the nude on personal whim. The Fae don't hold the same moral objections to nudity in the same way the Mundanes did, but both Declan and I found it hugely embarrassing when our middle son decided to go "sans clothes" during a shopping trip to the Mall and later at a retirement party for one of my office hygienists.

As it grew closer to the end of October, with Halloween and *Samhain* both sitting right around the corner, I worried that Dylan would start up again about being allowed to participate in trick or treating. Oddly enough, the little boy never even attempted to bring up the topic. His entire focus seemed directed towards the *Samhain* pageant his school was presenting for parents and staff. He came home daily with updates about the special mask he was creating and how his teacher had let him and *Mairead* "write" the story his class would perform. Curiosity got the best of me, and I even asked Orla Dell for a hint, but the woman said she was sworn to secrecy and reiterated with a grin that she hoped Declan and I both had plans to attend, as she was sure neither of us would want to miss it.

It took some fiddling of the schedules to get us all together in one place, but the excitement in my eldest boy's eyes over his entire family being in the audience was worth every bit of hassle. Even *Oisin*, who had done his best to be non-communitive and disagreeable these past two weeks, put on a cheerful persona for his younger nephew. Declan seemed as much in the dark regarding the topic of Dylan's performance as I, meaning the little boy had even managed to keep the secret from his beloved father, someone he'd shared a unique bond with since birth. I'll admit, this worried mama was offering up prayers that none of the older kids would tease and jeer my little actor and playwright in the way middle school children often do, as I knew my husband would have to keep me from making the ultimate parent mistake by over-reacting to kid nonsense.

Since the pageant was an evening affair, the entertainment began with the school's youngest students. The first class of kindergartners sang two cute songs traditional to the *Samhain* sabbat, while the second class had the teacher reading a story while the students acted it out, a tale centering around the origins of *Samhain* and The Morrigan's role in it, a ploy I thought bordered on worthless toadying, especially since Her Majesty was, of course, not in attendance. Finally, it was Dylan's class's turn. The principal came to the mike and announced, "Tonight we have a special treat. Mrs. Dell's kindergarten class will present an original play written and directed by students Dylan Fitzpatrick and *Mairead* Beckett. All of the students have created their own costume masks with the help of Mrs. Dell and Miss Mavis, the school's art teacher. Let's have a nice round of applause for Kindergarten Class 3-A."

We all clap wildly, and behind me, Fr. Kevin, who is in attendance with the Becketts, whistles loudly through his teeth. An array of small children walk on stage wearing paper-mache face masks depicting all types of different woodland creatures. An older girl, perhaps a fourth or fifth grader, also appeared on stage in street clothes to act as narrator. I search the stage for a sign of Dylan, but don't see him in the crowd. Once the audience settles down, the narrator begins her story:

"Once upon a time, there was a happy clan of animals who lived in the Enchanted Forest. They were ruled by a wise and brave Lord who was called Sionnach Rua (Red Fox)." From

behind the curtains, out stepped our son, Dylan. He was wearing the hand-crafted mask I'd seen in different stages of completion the past few weeks, but the little pants and tunic in the *Nuada* house colors of maroon and gold, along with the white crepe-paper sash across his chest depicting his rank, and the fake bushy tail hanging from the back of his pants was a sight I wasn't expecting. Our son marched across the stage, hand clasped behind his back, chin up, in the manner I'd seen his father do at Council events a million times. I nudge my husband, and smile, though by his expression alone, I can't tell whether Declan's amused by the parody or embarrassed by it. Truthfully, if anything, my Eternal Mate looks...well... concerned, a reaction that makes little sense to me considering the setting we find ourselves in.

The narrator continued. *"Lord Sionnach Rua was a good leader. He made sure the people of his woods were well taken care of and happy. He was honest and trustworthy with all things."* As the older girl read the words, Dylan pulled a parchment from his pocket and a pair of lens-less glasses he put on his long, pointed fox nose, peering over them and pretending to read the document. At this point, anyone in the audience who knew my husband in either the Mundane world or *I Idir*, could easily single Declan out as the boy's role model for *Sionnach Rua*, and throughout the seats surrounding us, I heard whispers and snickers. When I glance at my husband, I see him exchange looks with the Black Knight who is seated to the left in the row behind us. Neither of them appeared amused at Dylan's performance and my level of concern ratchets up several degrees. What the hell is going on now? I can't believe the two of them are getting all worked up over a silly kids show. In my opinion, our son is absolutely adorable.

Up on stage, the Beckett's daughter, the Princess *Mairead*, appeared wearing a rabbit mask and carrying a head of lettuce. The narrator explained that Miss Bunny had been brought before the Lord *Sionnach Rua* for stealing a head of lettuce from her neighbor's garden. Even if I wasn't aware of who the child actor actually was, I'd instantly know she was someone of an almost pure *Sidhe* bloodline by the way she carried herself and the magical energy that surrounded her. There was no missing a Raven amongst a crowd of Fae.

In the sing-song voice of a small child, Miss Bunny begs the Fox Lord for forgiveness of her crime, crying that she hadn't meant to be a thief, but that her family was hungry and needed the lettuce for dinner. For a mere second, I get the eerie feeling that this conversation between my eldest child and the named heir of *I Idir* goes far beyond a child's innocent performance. I shake that thought away as pure nonsense, but there's no denying that the children are play acting the behavior of the adults that share their lives. And in that same spirit of art mimicking life, the foxy version of Lord Declan *Nuada* gratefully forgives the contrite Miss Bunny, declaring the two of them are now the best of friends as they clasp their little hands together, and for reasons I can't begin to explain, I feel tears whelming up in the corners of my eyes.

* * *

After Dylan and *Mairead's* performance, I have a hard time concentrating on the rest of the pageant's presentations, and when the school's principal finally signals the end of the evening, I am more than ready to head to the privacy of our home so I can corner my husband over the multitude questions floating around in my head. Unfortunately, I am foiled in that plan by the Black Knight and his Lady, who invite us back to their home for an impromptu "cast party," complete with *Samhain* inspired apple cake and butter pecan ice cream.

If at all possible, one does not turn down an invite by a member of *I Idir's* Royal Family. Besides, Maureen Beckett is a lovely woman and someone I consider a friend, so the Fitzpatrick clan, all eight of us, head toward the large white Victorian on Oak Street. Although the conversation is light and informal, I feel the shadow of things left unsaid between my husband and his commanding officer, and by the time we finally say our goodbyes, I am a woman on a mission to seek out the truth.

Ronin and *Liam* are both sleeping by the time we arrive home, while Dylan is yawning and drowsy, so putting them to bed is an easy task, with *Birgit* and *Niamh* taking care of most of the pajama wrestling. *Oisin* heads straight for his room without a single word, and I wonder to myself if the younger boys will all be this difficult when they hit adolescence. I make for the bathroom to ready myself for bed, but not without giving my Eternal Mate a not-so-subtle warning. "DO NOT fall asleep before I get out of this bathroom, Tax Man. We need to speak."

"Aye, Love. That we do," he says with enough somberness to ratchet up my anxiety to a whole other level. I rush through my nightly routine, carrying my hairbrush with the plan to brush while we talk. That never happens.

I step into our bedroom suite and come face to face with a very large, red fox, the wholly animal kind, making itself overly comfortable atop my new duvet cover.

MISSING 28

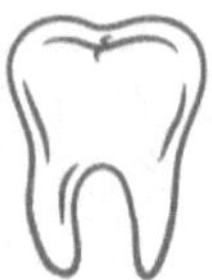

Declan's Prank Isn't Funny

I DO what I've been trained to do when faced with an intruder in close quarters. I drop the hairbrush and reach for anything I can conceivably use as a weapon, which in this case happens to be a lovely antique candlestick lamp Declan brought back from a recent business trip to Paris. With a sharp tug, I rip the cord and plug clear out of the wall and strike a defensive pose, brandishing the lamp as a club. "Stay away," I yell at the animal.

In response, the red fox jumps off the bed and pads towards me. I give the lamp a test swing in front of me and then the damn, frickin' thing says in a voice that sounds decidedly familiar, "Not the lamp, Lass. 'Tis a rare piece and vera' expensive."

For a mere second, my head is confused by what my ears are hearing versus what my eyes are seeing. Then, without warning, the fox shifts and reforms its shape until it's my husband standing in front of me, stark naked, with a peculiar expression gracing his handsome *Sidhe* face. In spite of my shock, I do the only thing I can do in a situation like this one. I calmly put the lamp back on the side table and turn back into the bathroom where I lean over the toilet and vomit.

My *Mo Shiorghra* tries to comfort me but I one-handedly push him away, not wanting any physical contact. With everything going on, my shield is non-existent, so he directly hears what I'm thinking and feeling, and it's… well…not pretty. He pulls his hands away as if I had burned them with a hot iron, then holds them up in the air. "See, Love, 'tis not paws. Just ma' normal hands."

Normal, he says? How can anything be "normal" again after witnessing my spouse, the man I pledged my life eternally to, and the father of my three children, appearing in front of me wearing four legs and a bushy tail? I wipe my sweaty face with a hand towel before I calm down enough to speak to my husband who is standing in the doorway looking a little green himself. "I need for you to go put on some boxers or something before I can talk about this. I can't do it with you standing there naked," I say. Sitting on the edge of the bathtub, I collect my thoughts while I wait for his return. He's back in less than a minute, now wearing a pair of his expensive boxer briefs. In a monotone voice, I ask, "So you can shift now?"

"Aye," is all he says, letting me control the pace of the conversation, a ploy the Tax Man often uses when he knows he is in the wrong.

"Is the fox the only animal form, or are there others I

should know about?" I ask, not really wanting to consider the possibility.

"Currently, it's just the red fox. The Merlin says 'tis more than likely the *sionnach rua* (red fox) is ma' spirit guide and the reason I have been granted this…gift."

By no stretch of the imagination do I believe "shifting" is a gift. Frankly, it's one of the creepier elements of *Sidhe* magic. However, I am relieved by my mate's assurance that he possesses only one animal form, because I'm not much excited by the thought of a whole zoo in my bed. I don't bother to shield my thinking, and in the door way I see Declan cringe at my mental comment about animals in our bed. No doubt it's on the tip of his tongue to reply that he'd never bring his animal form into our bedroom, but then realizes that's exactly what he's just done. Still, there's an even bigger issue with the answer he's just given me. "If the Merlin is offering you counsel on the subject, then I suppose The Morrigan knows as well."

"Aye."

"Anyone else?" I question, knowing full well there are others and I wasn't one of them.

The Tax Man looks away, unable to meet my eye. "The Black Knight and Duncan. But that is all. Herself feels knowledge of my newest gift should remain a tight secret. At least far' the time bein'.'"

Now, not only am I shocked, I also have hurt feelings over the proof that once again I'd been left out of the loop. Me. His Eternal Mate. How many times am I going to have to deal with this bullshit of being the last to know? "And Her Majesty proposed this level of secrecy should extend to your *Mo Shiorghra?*" I ask, not hiding the feeling of betrayal in my tone.

"Oh no, Love. All of them counseled that I shad' tell ya' forthright. Her Majesty warned me that waitin' ta' tell ya' would have consequences I wad' not much like."

Tired of having a life-changing conversation while sitting next to the toilet, I push past my husband and wander over to the chaise in the sitting area of the bedroom. I specifically select this one-person seat because I don't want the physical proximity of him, the pull of the Bond between us, to overshadow the seriousness of this discussion. He notes my choice and thus, with a dramatic Declan sigh, takes a position across from me on the edge of the bed.

I untie, then re-tie the belt to my robe, simply to give me more time to gather my thoughts. When I finally do speak, it's in interrogation style directness. "How long ago did you discover you could do this?"

With hands contritely clasped in front of him, he says, "About a month now. The first time was in the middle of ma' weekly cleansin' meditation. I had gone far' a run that mornin' in the Salem Woods when I saw a large red fox pacin' itself a few feet beside me. We ran the entire trail ta'gether befar' it disappeared inta' the underbrush. I thought perhaps it might be a sign of some sort from the Universe, and later that same day, when I let ma' mind wander free durin' ma' meditation, it just...happened. At first, 'twas a vera' strange feelin', but I ken' no describe the joy of the complete freedom I felt in this different skin. Far' that short time, my mind and body were empty of the weight of ma' responsibilities. I am partly ashamed ta' admit ta' ya', Love, how much I enjoyed that feelin' of liberation, though I will say the switchin' back and forth is not particularly comfortable. Plus, I ruined some of ma' favorite clothes doin' so until I learned to remove them befar' shiftin'. When it happened a fourth time, I struggled for hours afterward ta' completely feel like ma'self again. 'Twas then I knew I needed professional guidance. I first sought out Robyn, who believes this new ability is the result of the North Koreans experimentation on ma' brain. He, however, suggested I consult the Merlin, who took me directly to Herself. They were quite excited over this new gift of mine, callin' it an "unexpected spiritual boon," though everyone concurs that it does offer some... political risks."

Political nonsense was the least of my worries right now, but for the sake of my family, I felt I needed to ask. "What kind of "political risks" are we talking about, Declan?"

He shrugged. "The ability ta' shift physical form is a high level of *Sidhe* magical skill. No other current members of the Ruling Council have this ability. House *Lir* (god of the Sea) and House *Rón* (Seals/Selkies) both have ancient ancestors who possessed the skill ta' shift ta' sea creatures and seals, but no Lords in the past two hundred years have shown ta' be able ta' do such a thing. As ya' are aware, Lass, ma' gainin'a seat on the Council while ma' traitorous sire still roams both worlds unfettered has had its share of naysayers from the vera' beginnin'. They would look upon this recent rise in powerful magic as a threat to their own Houses. There is already mumurin' over our unusually close ties ta' the Royal family. Herself believes 'tis best ta' limit knowledge of ma' gift ta' a select group of trusted few."

Nothing he says is untrue. The Ruling Council of *I Idir* is a bickering group of vain, powerful *Sidhe* males who all put themselves and their Houses above anything else. The knowledge that House *Nuada* was holding something profoundly powerful over their heads would cause ripples of suspicion and jealousy throughout the Council, and would make the Queen's hold on the group even more difficult. Still, Declan's explanation doesn't explain why I'm the last to know despite his being told by reliable sources to come clean to his Eternal Mate. There's no doubt that my Tax Man has used an incredible amount of magical power this past month in shielding this information from me and it breaks my heart to admit how much it wounds me. My voice cracks when I ask, "I get all that, Declan. But I'm not the Ruling Council. I'm your "One and Only." Your Eternal Mate. You should be able to tell me anything, yet you hid this monumental...thing from the person you claim to..." I don't finish the sentence because I feel as if the words are all caught up in my throat and I'm choking on them.

Declan slides off the bed and drops at my feet, grasping both of my hands in his and I fight not to jerk them away while images of furry, long nailed claws slide around in my head. By the horrified expression on his face, I presume my mate is seeing exactly that in his mind, and though he looks, for lack of a better word, shattered, he doesn't let go of my hands, instead lacing his fingers through mine and holding on tighter. The Tax Man looks up at me and I turn my head away. "Look at me, Love.

Please. I am beggin' ya'" he pleads. The Bond is too strong and I don't have the fortitude to fight it, so I let my eyes meet his, trying not to lose myself in their green depths as he continues. "I have wanted ta' tell ya, Sweet Rosie Lass, so many times," Declan explains, "but I was afraid."

"Afraid? That's a ridiculous excuse," I reply, anger seeping through my words while making me able to break eye contact. "What could you possibly have to fear from me? If you love me like you say you do, you should be able to tell me anything. Anything."

"Aye, Love. That is exactly what I feared. That I would tell ya' and with yar' logical brain and lovin' heart ya' would dutifully tell me exactly what I wanted ta' hear... that you can accept this monumental change in ma' person. But because of the Bond we share there is no hidin' yar' true physical response. I have little doubt ya' are repulsed by my animal form." I open my mouth to disagree, but he stops me. "Please don'na lie ta' me, *Mo Shiorghra*. Ya' know I ken' tell. Just this vera' moment, when I took yar' hands in mine, all ya' could see with yar mind's eye was my fox's paws and ya' were profoundly disturbed by them. That ya' could ever find me physically repulsive was a woundin' of my heart that I was not ready to bear."

The sadness and grief rolling off him cuts me to the very core, and, what makes it even worse is the fact that everything he just said is true. I am totally freaked out over the idea that my spouse, my One and Only, has animal...parts. I knew well in advance of our handfast, and later during the undertaking of the Eternal vows, that the man I had permanently attached to myself was more

Fae than human. Not just regular Fae, but the *Sidhe Tuatha de Danann* kind. I had always been aware that Declan's magical elements were far superior to anything I myself could ever imagine, especially after what he'd gone through in North Korea. Still, my *Mo Shiorghra* had always been extremely careful about sharing his magic with me. I know he does this because of my own feelings of inadequacy regarding my limited magical skill; it's him not wanting to make me feel less than he. And because of his compassion, it's made it easy for me to ignore just how gifted he truly is. Until now. These last few shocking minutes of reality had not just creeped up on me. They had come in the form of a red fox who bashed me straight in the head with the truth of it all.

"I don'na think I ken' bear yar' rejection, Rosie, ma' Love. I would not know how ta' begin livin' without yar' touch," he says, his voice hitching on the last three words.

He looks so utterly dejected that I can't keep my own emotions in check. I lean forward and fall into his embrace, weeping in a style that would best be called "ugly crying" with its great breathy sobs, rhythmic hiccups, and a red, running nose. When I finally am able to speak, I get my own truth off my chest. "I'm sorry, Sweetie. I know I should be more understanding. More realistic about how your magic is an important part of who you are. It's just...well... the only other time I witnessed someone shift was on the day you were installed as a Ruling Council Lord. The Morrigan came in through our window as a raven and then just...just suddenly changed back to her normal form. It completely freaked me out, so much so that I ended up backing away in fear and falling over that small footstool in our *Dun Siorai* bedroom. Of course, Herself thought my reaction was quite amusing, but honestly, I had nightmares about it for weeks afterwards" I stood up and grabbed a tissue from the box on my nightstand, blowing my nose and wiping my eyes before continuing. "Perhaps if you had given me a heads up of what was going to happen before I actually saw 'fox Declan,' I might have been better prepared."

"Seein' how much it disturbed ya' I wish I had done it differently as well. But, as I have already admitted, when it comes ta' disappointin' my Sweet Rosie Lass in any manner, I am a weak-hearted coward. I knew I would never have the right words ta' tell ya'," he admitted, "so I thought this was a better option."

Sometimes my beloved husband is a Fae-style, Captain Oblivious. He often misses normal human social cues and boundaries while handling most problems with his Otherworldly point of view. It's led to more than one argument between us in the past five years. "Seriously, Declan? You honestly thought that finding a large, talking red fox on my bed was the best way to go? Out-of-the-blue like that, with no warning whatsoever?"

At least he has the courtesy to admit he was wrong. "Aye. In hindsight, I now believe 'twas a terrible idea."

"No shit, Sherlock," I retort with my usual level of sarcasm. Then, another question comes to mind. "Why tonight, Tax Man? Why bring this up at the very end of a busy day? Surely if you waited this long to tell me, you could have waited until I was a little fresher and clearer of mind?" And that's when the answer hits me. "Damn it!

Does this have something to do with Dylan's little performance tonight? His fascination with making a fox mask?"

Declan runs a hand through his hair several times, a typical Tax Man guilty "tell." "Truthfully, I am not sure, Lass. It ken' no be a coincidence, as neither of us believe in such a thing. 'Tis possible he may have seen me practicin' ma' shiftin' while we were in the Otherworld for Meghan's handfast. 'Tis much easier far' me ta' handle the required magic while at *Dun Siorai* then here in the Mundane world, so I did spend some time shiftin' back and forth in the woods surroundin' the estate befar' the handfast ceremony. I am no sure of what our wee boy might have seen, but I will need ta' speak ta' him about it…and his need far' secrecy. As ya' might imagine, after seein' Dylan's little performance this evening, the Black Knight is…concerned."

"I bet he is, but I don't give a damned wooden nickel about Lord-Know-it-All's 'concern.' I only need to know how YOU intend to handle this discussion with our son. What's your plan, Declan?"

With another deep-shouldered shrug, my One and Only says the words I'm half-heartedly expecting. "I'm not sure, ma' Lady," he replies, "though yar' lovin' husband was hopin' we might tell him together."

MISSING 29

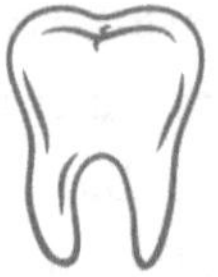

The Parents Have a Chat

THE PRESSING time frame regarding speaking with Dylan over what he might or might not have seen requires me to come to terms with Declan's new "ability" quicker than I might have preferred. Our planned trip through the Veil for the *Samhain* sabbat was less than a week away and there were a multitude of details to organize before we left. Telling our eldest son that his beloved Daddy was sometimes a red fox was not on my original "To Do" list.

After his shocking revelation, Declan had sworn to me that he would do his utmost not to shift in my presence, though he was still in the early stages of learning how to control the magic that caused it. He'd even gone as far as offering to sleep apart from me in fear that the memory of his "furry self" was too troubling for me to deal with. It was true that the possibility of waking up next to a wild fox gave me the heebie-jeebies, and I'd be lying if I said I wasn't half tempted to accept that proposition, but my pride over being the consummate Eternal Mate wouldn't let me concede to that arrangement. Upon discovering what Declan had been through at the hands of the North Koreans, it had been wholly my idea for us to take the *An Banna Siora* (The Eternal Bond) as a public statement of my undying love for my mate no matter what the Universe threw at us. I made a vow that I would accept all aspects of our life together, and damn it to doughnuts, Rosie Parker-Fitzpatrick was no welsher.

So, on a cool October evening, directly after supper, we offer Dylan a chance for a nighttime "walk" with just himself and his parents. Although the little boy seemed apprehensive and slightly confused by this strange suggestion, the fact that *Liam* wasn't coming along was a definite deal closer. I had no doubt Dylan loved his younger brother, but it was a family fact that our second child was generally a "handful," requiring lots of extra attention. Having both of his parent's attention, all to himself, was too big a temptation to ignore.

Declan and I had decided on a plan of action in advance of our discussion. If it appeared, as my husband suspected, that Dylan had seen his father shift, then we would be matter-of-fact about the whole thing, going as far as having his father shift in front of the boy so his Da could answer any questions the child had before we explained the harder part about it being necessary to keep our "family business" a secret.

I had made my Tax Man shift in front of me a few times so that I could practice managing my mental and physical reaction in anticipation of our little family "pow wow," and though it still shocked me every time, I learned to be not quite so obvious in my negative reaction. As it came to be, none of our carefully coordinated efforts were necessary. Upon reaching the darkened wooded trail we'd selected for privacy's sake, Dylan slid out of the car and asked his father if he planned "ta' turn himself inta' Lord *Sionnach Rua*," the main character in the boy's *Samhain* play.

Thus, it became clear to us that Dylan had definitely seen his father shift while at *Dun Siorai* and thought the whole thing was great fun, the event providing the seed for "the best-est pageant play" ever written. Unfortunately, we also learned that *Oisin* had been with our wee boy when they saw Declan shift, and that Dylan had gone on to brag to *Mairead* Beckett about his father's ability, to which the young princess countered that "having a fox shifting Da was 'vera' nice,' but she had seen her maternal grandmother and paternal grandfather shift into 'fiercer animals,' which to her mind, was far more impressive." It was a comment I'd expect from the youngest Raven, so Dylan's story had a definite ring of truth to it.

Because Dylan was Declan's "mini me" in all things, his questions to his father about shifting were logical, concise, and blunt. He wanted to know whether the changing of forms was painful, what happened to his Da's clothes when he became a fox, and whether or not he'd be lucky enough to have any fox-like brothers whom Dylan decided would be more fun than just having *Liam* and Ronin. My Tax Man answered all the boy's concerns with grace and patience, including a tough one regarding whether Dylan himself would someday inherit his sire's ability to shift into fox mode. "I am the *Mac Nuada*, Da. I look just like you. People say that all the time, especially my *Mhaimeo* (Granny). Should I not also be able to shift like you as well?" the little boy pleaded.

"That is a question for a future I ken' no predict, *Fear Beag* (Little Man). Even the Merlin is no sure whether this gift will pass ta' ya'. I suppose we will have ta' wait and see what the Universe has set far' yar' path," his father replied.

"Then I will ask all the goddesses I know ta' make it so, Da. I want ta' someday be the Lord *Sionnach Rua*. Just like you."

Despite my mixed emotions about the whole shifter thing, it was hard not to get all emotional over my son's hero worship of his father. *Oisin* had held Declan in that type of reverence when he was a lad, and I know how disappointed my mate was over the angst between him and his younger brother that had suddenly appeared in the past few months or so. I tried but failed at not recalling the awful curse Callum Fitzpatrick had laid upon his only son the last time we saw him before he went over that cliff, and I knew, without a doubt, I'd be praying to those same goddesses that my boy never broke his father's heart like the evil, old man had predicted.

"Do ya' wish ta' see me shift again? Up closer this time, *mo mhac* (my son)? I want ya' ta' no fear the process," my husband asked.

"Oh yes, Da! That would be awesome!" Dylan said with the special joy of a young child. Our son looked at me, then said with all seriousness, "Ya' will have ta' close yar' eyes, Mama. Da has to take off all his clothes when he shifts and 'tis not far' the eyes of a ladies ta' see his Lordship naked."

I bit my lip and tried not to giggle. "Of course, Dylan. I will surely close my eyes." Not altogether unhappy that I'm not required to witness the magic do its weird-ass thing, I shut my eyes and laugh over the thought that, in truth, my son's father was often more comfortable out of his clothes than in them.

After a few moments, I hear Dylan say, "Okay, Mama. You ken' look now. Lord *Sionnach Rua* is with us."

I open my eyes and see my husband in his red fox form and damned if he's not grinning at me in response to my thoughts of the natural nudist in him. Either the Universe is dropping a bonus on my head, or I'm finally coming around to the idea of having a shifter husband. because there's no denying that the Tax Man makes an exceptionally appealing red fox.

Always polite, Dylan asks his father, "May I pet yar' fur, Da?"

Lord *Sionnach Rua* nods his agreement and our son leans down to run a hand over the fox's ginger fur. "Oh my," Dylan exclaims, "'tis vera' soft! Mama, come pet Da's fur. See how soft and fine it is!"

I hesitate and catch my mate looking at me in the dark with his oval, green fox eyes. Up until this moment, I've never considered actually touching my *Mo Shiorghra* while he was in his shifted form and have no idea whether or not the same intensity of the Bond would still be there. I wasn't even sure I wanted to know. *"It's completely up ta' you, Love. I am not sure how the Bond will react when I am in this form. I did not have the courage ta' ask the Merlin or Herself. I will not be offended if ya' decide touchin' me is too much far' ya' right now. Ya' ken' tell the boy yar' allergic ta' certain kinds of animal fur. He'll understand that."* Though the words sound sincere, I hear the underlying hope and challenge in them

I was never any good about ignoring a dare, thus, I lean down and carefully pat my Tax Man's silky head. Dylan is correct. Lord *Sionnach Rua's* ginger-colored fur is very soft; not unlike the hair on his Fae head that I've braided for him a million times. His foxy Lordship lifts his muzzle up so I can scratch under his chin, and with a giggle, I do just that. He lets out a long purring sound of contentment and without warning the magic of the Bond washes over me, a live wire of energy that flows from my fingertips, up my arm and then heads...elsewhere. Startled, I make an unconscious gasping sound and step backwards, breaking the magical connection.

Dylan notices my actions and mistakes them for fear. Grabbing my hand in his little one, he proclaims, "Don' be afraid, Mama. 'Tis not really a wild fox. It's only our Da. The one we all love."

While I try to slow my racing pulse, I think to myself that there has never been a truer statement. The fox is, without a doubt, the man I love.

MISSING 30

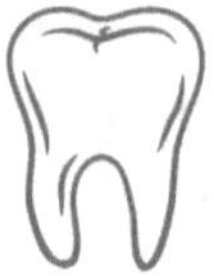

The Family Travels Back

CELEBRATING *Samhain* is a big deal for the Fae. It is one of the two most important spiritual and cultural sabbats in the cyclical calendar of the year, with Beltane, held May1st, being the second. Although the Mundane world has bastardized several aspects of this autumnal celebration, several kingdoms on the other side of the Veil take this end of the seasonal year very seriously, and *I Idir* was no exception, as The Morrigan looked to *Samhain* as her own personal "name day."

With so much to do before we left, there was little time to mull over what Declan's newest magical talent would mean to our family, as well as our intimate relationship. I gladly left my husband with the difficult job of warning *Oisin* about keeping his elder brother's shifting secret to himself. These days, getting more than a handful of words from the teenager was difficult enough, and I distinctly got the impression that the boy I had pretty much raised as my own felt I was a traitor for not taking his side when his Lordship laid out the consequences of the boy's bad choices. I held hope that someday, when he matured, *Oisin* would realize that Declan and I only wanted the very best for him, but until that day came, we were stuck with every facet of *Sidhe* adolescence "attitude."

As Lord and Lady *Nuada*, it was our responsibility to host the silent ancestor dinner for all the House's adults that took place on October 31st, considered the "Eve" of the actual *Samhain* sabbat. This was a monumental task, requiring us to feed nearly a hundred people belonging specifically to House *Nuada*, and even though Cook had handled it superbly for over twenty years, the hostess duties surrounding *Samhain* always gave me the jitters.

The following day, November 1st, always began with the traditional sunrise meditations led by the House Mages, followed by the *Comortas Capall* (Horse Tournament), which usually lasted most of the afternoon. The day was traditionally capped off by a huge bonfire and night time picnic with lots of drinking, music, and dancing. Afterwards, most older folks, handfasted couples, and young children retired to their homes for quiet storytelling and games, as the reminder of the night until dawn was given over to the young, horny and unattached during the hedonistic adventures of *Oiche Fiain* (Wilding Night), which for all intents and purposes, was a no-holds-bar, woodland "rave," of sorts. Our plans had the majority of the Fitzpatricks settled in at *Dun Siorai* for the night, though his Lordship counseled I should not be surprised if *Oisin* chose to partake in everything *Oiche*

Fiain, offered despite my opinions that the boy was still too young for such "adult" entertainment, even if Declan assigned a few men to look after him.

I knew Declan was counting on his younger brother buying into the ancient tradition of celebrating the autumn sabbat, using the promise of the unabandoned "partying" as a bribe. Since neither boy, up to this point, has said a single word about Mundane Halloween or trick or treating, my Tax Man was confident that both *Oisin* and Dylan had grown uninterested in the topic. I personally thought my husband was being extremely unrealistic and when I stated this opinion, I get a cranky look and a jibe that stated his darling Rosie "always looked at the glass half empty." It's on the tip of my tongue to reveal that not only had Dylan not forgotten about Halloween, before leaving for *I Idir* he had asked me if I had returned his dinosaur costume to the store, his little face marked with disappointment. Truthfully, with everything going on, I'd actually forgotten all about taking the costumes back. The disguises were still hanging in the back of the front hall closet where I'd hung them the day we'd brought them home. Thankfully, our conversation was interrupted by *Liam,* who had somehow managed to evade *Niamh* and climb to the top of the china cabinet in the dining room, so I was never required to give my eldest a straight answer. But bringing that topic up to my husband in the hours before we planned on leaving would only work to make the jump through the Veil more contentious and stressful, so, for better or worse, I kept that knowledge to myself.

* * *

If the start of the holiday was any indication of how the rest of the two days would go, we were all in for a very rough time. Upon arrival at *Dun Siorai,* we were met by both Tuck, the Estate Manager, and Cook, who informed us that half the staff has been quarantined by Dr. Brannigan due to a raging case of Fae "*Súile Lofa*"(Rotten Eyes) a type of Otherworldly "Pink Eye," one of the few bacterial infections shared from the Mundane world that the Otherworld folk were susceptible to. This meant that the estate was hugely understaffed for a sabbat that usually required everyone to be on their best game.

There was a discussion about trying to hire outside help from the village to fill in, but being that it was a major holiday, and news of "Rotten Eyes" ravaging *Dun Siorai* was public knowledge, it seemed unlikely there would be a lot of takers despite the promise of extra pay. Tuck also notified us that Lady *Siobhan* Fitzpatrick *Nuada* had sent word that she would be celebrating the sabbat with her youngest daughter at *Cuach an Fhithich* (Raven's Hollow) and would not be joining us until the bonfire the following evening. I was not unhappy over the news, as my mother-in-law adds a whole extra level of tension to the mix, and I was sure *Oisin* was doing the dance of joy over her absence, as Lady *Siobhan* always went out of her way to be rude and mean-spirited to her cheating husband's offspring. On the other hand, Dylan and *Liam* were obviously disappointed. They adored their only grandparent, and for all her faults, Declan's mother appeared to hold my children in special favor even if she'd never used the word "love" to describe her feelings. As for Declan, he viewed his mother's choice of Meghan over him as a personal slight to his role as Lord, a topic he would undoubtedly complain about for the next two days. Which all goes to show you, Fae holidays are not much different from Mundane ones where family is concerned.

On top of everything else, the weather was perfectly lousy; unusually chilly, sleety, and downright gloomy. According to my Tax Man, this would make the competitions of the *Comortas Capall* (Horse Tournament) extra difficult as well as more dangerous because of muddy ground. Thinking of the danger, I questioned out loud whether this was something our boys should still be allowed to participate in and my comment was instantly met with a tirade of tears from Dylan, while *Oisin* gave me an extra nasty death stare from across the room. Are we having fun yet?

Thank all the goddesses that the October 31st dinner was a silent and young-child-free affair in order to keep the solemnity of the occasion. The meal was meant to be a time to reflect on one's ancestors while offering attending adults the chance to keep loving memories of them vibrant in the world of the living. Place settings and platters of food are traditionally set out for wandering spirits, though every year I can't help but hope I don't actually see any ghosts partake of those offerings. Spooky shit like that gives me the willies. Because he was nearing his fourteenth birthday, this was the first year Oisin has been invited to attend, ... Currently, he had his head down as he moved the fork from his plate to his lips in silent rotation and I wondered if he was thinking about the mother he never got to know, who, according to The Morrigan, lies buried somewhere on House *Nuada* land.

I reflect on the memories of my own deceased parents; of my beloved tooth fairy mother who had her young heart badly broken, yet still went on to forge a seemingly happy life with a Mundane husband and family. I think about my devoted father who loved and cherished my mother, a woman from a completely different dimension he couldn't share, and who did all he possibly could to make life happy and sweet for his two adored daughters. Tears slide down my cheeks over the memories, which is perfectly acceptable behavior for participation in *Samhain* Eve's Silent Dinner.

When the meal concludes, my Lord *Nuada* stands to offer the customary toasts; the first in honor of The Morrigan, goddess of war and destruction, and Queen of *I Idir*, the next one lifted for the ancestors of House *Nuada* who built the foundation of the lives we are all now living, and finally a request for blessings in the coming New Year, that the Universe would bless the Fae folk with happiness, fertility, and success.

In the past, the Silent Dinner has always left me retrospective of all that has come to pass in the proceeding twelve months; gratefulness for the good things that offered sweetness to my life, as well as equally grateful for the less than stellar offerings that have made me a stronger person.

Tonight, however, the evening has left me feeling unsettled, as if I were missing some important lesson the Universe desired to teach me.

Later, in our bed at *Dun Siorai*, I toss and turn, unable

to relax, and when I do finally fall asleep, it's in a troubled slumber filled with strange dreams of my parents standing in unrecognizable doorways, frantically waving and calling to me. In those visions, despite their mouths opening and closing as if they were speaking to me, I can't seem to hear a word they're saying.

MISSING 31

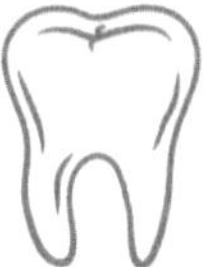

The New Year Dawns Unlucky and Dark

As if to laugh at our feeble attempts at properly celebrating the divine mystique of *Samhain*, the Universe greets us that morning with frost-covered grounds and temperatures well below freezing, unseasonably cold for *I Idir* at this time of the year. His Lordship will get his wish this visit regarding my wearing of the "infamous" silver fox capelet, though the irony of wearing any type of fox fur currently freaks me out. Neither Declan nor I slept very well last night; therefore, when my routine-rigorous Tax Man forgoes his usual morning run, I readily expect the Declan cranky face that greets me as we somberly dress for this early morning's *Samhain* services. Because this day has already begun so poorly, I'm not the least bit shocked when *Niamh* appears at our door with the news that both Liam and Ronin have woken up this morning with red, gooey eyes, symptoms of the dreaded Fae pink eye infection, and will thus be confined to the nursery for the rest of our visit. The *scathach* admits that both she and *Birgit* are currently experiencing itchy and irritated eyes and predicts that they are also most likely afflicted with the highly contagious bug as well. As Dylan no longer shares the nursery at *Dun Siorai*, having graduated to a room of his own earlier this year, the nanny is hopeful that the little *Mac Nuada* will be well enough to still participate in the day's activities.

In anticipation of the excitement the day will bring, both boys ignore the miserable weather and the tedium of the long-winded, early morning spiritual ceremony. I can't help but wish some of their youthful enthusiasm would rub off on me, because frankly, my feet have gone numb with cold and my nose is like a block of ice on my face. When the last offering is placed in the magical cauldron, a sign that the New Year rites have ended, I literally jog from the sacred grove back to the house in glorious anticipation of a warm fire and a steaming cup of coffee, a secret Mundane treat I have allowed myself here in the Otherworld.

I have three hours of precious "me time" before we leave to attend the Horse Tournament that both *Oisin* and Dylan will participate in. Because of my important role as House *Nuada's* Lady Hostess for today's sabbat events, and the need to return back to my dental practice in the next 36 hours, I've been warned to stay clear of the nursery and the dreaded pink eye plague. I love my children to the moon and back, but the idea of three hours of complete, uninterrupted freedom is a gift I rarely receive. Sipping my smuggled Blue Mountain coffee, I mentally send what

I hope sounds like a sexy message of seduction to my Eternal Mate with a detailed description of how I'd like to spend these next few private hours.

It seems to take an unusually long time for my Tax Man to answer, and when he does, it's not the hot and spicy response I was hoping for. *"'Tis a tempting offer, Love, but I'm afraid I donna' have the freedom of time ta' spend neked' with ya' right now. I am workin' with Oisin and Dylan on handlin' their rides for today's competition amidst such slick and icy conditions. I'm also hopin' that Ole' Darragh the Saddler can come up with some extra straps ta' keep our lad's wee slippery feet from slidin' in the stirrups, but the type that will still meet the event's strict rules. We are on a particularly tight timeline today. I'm sorry ta' admit that I expect I will be tied up here until the competition begins. A raincheck, perhaps?"*

"Sure, Tax Man, a raincheck it is. Will I see you before the competition?" I ask.

"'Tis not likely, Love. Perhaps ya' shad' plan on taking the carriage on yar' own over ta' the tournament grounds. I will meet you there," his Lordship advises.

"Okay. That's what I'll do. If anything changes, let me know. And if at any point you think its unsafe for Oisin and Dylan to ride, I'm expecting you to withdraw them no matter how much they whine and complain."

"Aye, Love. Ya' have ma' word on it."

I feel the connection between us end; no doubt my husband anxious to get back to whatever it was he was doing before I interrupted him. I consider a short nap when there is a knock at the door to our family quarters, and I open it to find my bestie, dressed in her *Samhain* attire and holding a bowl of choice apples and nuts.

"A blessed *Samhain* to you, Lady *Nuada*," Mel says.

I throw my arms around my dearest friend. "What a wonderful surprise! I didn't expect to see you until the bonfire this evening. Come on in and visit for a while," I offer. "I just made a pot of Blue Mountain."

"Sounds heavenly," she says as she hands the bowl of fruit to me. "From my parents, wishing you and his Lordship a happy New Year."

"That's so thoughtful of them. I'll have to visit with your folks when we return to Salem," I reply. I've known Mel's parents as long as I've known my best friend, and without fail they have treated me like family despite my solidly Mundane upbringing. We were always friendly, but after Declan used *Riail an Tiarna* (The Lord's Rule) to grant Duncan and Mel's wishes for a traditional Fae handfasting in the *Nuada* sacred grove despite the objections of both Duncan's parents and the House Mages, Michael and Rhianna Sparks never missed an opportunity to let Declan and I know how much this act of courage meant to them.

I pour my friend a cup of coffee from the pot on the sideboard, a magic-born flame underneath keeping it warm, while Mel makes herself comfortable in a chair across from mine. I notice, not for the first time, the dark shadows under her eyes, testimony to the lack of sleep that haunts her nights. I consider whether or not to bring up a touchy subject, but being good ole' "Nosey Rosie," I ask anyway. "Are you up to talking about the Scotland trip?" I ask as I hand her the coffee mug.

She takes a sip and nods her head. "I suppose there's no reason not to tell you." She sighed, then continued.

"The information we received proved to be true. Unlike the last two unfounded rumors, the young *Sidhe* woman in Edinburgh actually did exist and is currently five months pregnant. She told us the baby was the result of a holiday fling in Phuket, Thailand, a Mundane French lad she met in the hotel bar. It was a three-day whirlwind 'romance,' but on day four, the man checked out without so much as a courtesy goodbye. When she returned home and realized she was pregnant, she tried googling the name he'd given her and the company he said he worked for, but there appeared to be no such person or company. The woman assumed everything she'd been told by the Frenchman had been a lie. Now, she was just trying to figure out the best path for both her and the baby. Her mother is a widow, and totally Mundane. It was the woman's deceased father who was *Sidhe*. House *MacCool*, I believe she mentioned."

"House *MacCool* is a pretty powerful clan," I interject. "They trace their bloodline back to the legendary *Finn MacCool*."

"I'm aware," Mel replies. "The woman has already been contacted by several prominent House members, including Lord *MacCool* himself. They feel it would be best for the child to be raised among its own people, but the expectant mother says she has no desire for a life in the Otherworld. She's only crossed the Veil with her father a handful of times, and none of them have been in the last eight years. Her mother, on the other hand, wants the woman to raise the child in Scotland, free of any of what she calls 'that evil Fae influence.'" Mel put her mug down on the table next to her, then drew up her knees and hugged them, a pose I've seen her take a million times when she's feeling especially distressed. "I feel for the woman, Rosie," Mel continues. "It's a no-win situation with everyone pulling her in a different direction. I'm not sure I'd know what to do in the same situation."

"You did let her know that you were interested in adopting the child as well, right?"

"Of course. We were completely honest about our willingness for an open adoption if that was what she wished, or a closed one, if she felt it was the better option for her. She thanked us for our transparency and flexibility, and promised she would let us know what she'd decided, but truthfully, Rose, I didn't feel very positive about the whole thing. I know any financial dealings over adoptions are prohibited by *I Idirian* Sacred Law, but you know how things work among the Ruling Council. If that child is truly House *MacCool* by blood, there's little chance of any other House couple adopting that baby."

My bestie is right. When it came to bloodlines, the Fae, especially any that could trace their heritage back to the ancient kings and heroes, would not easily give up one of their own. This was a situation I didn't believe would ever work out in Mel and Duncan's favor. Not if a Ruling House was involved. "I'm sorry, Hon. I know how difficult it is to keep your hopes up when there seems to be so few options. Declan and I both have the word out that we know a loving *Sidhe* couple of House *Nuada* looking to adopt. You never know who might know someone who knows someone. It's still in the realm of possibility," I say, hoping I sound more optimistic than I feel.

"I appreciate that, Rosie. You and Declan are so

supportive of us, and I want you to know it means the world to Duncan and me both," Mel replies, her voice cracking, followed by tears of grief.

We both end up with a case of the weepies, rocking and hugging each other until all the current tears are shed, and when Mel leaves to join her husband for lunch, a sense of gloom hangs over me, a not-so-auspicious start to the New Year cycle.

I suppose it would have been naive foolery to believe the rest of the day would go any better than the morning had. I'm not nearly as superstitious as my *Tuatha de Danann* spouse, but even I could tell the Universe was not blessing us with a particularly lovely *Samhain* sabbat.

Despite the on-going awful weather, the Ruling Council had decided to go ahead with the *Comortas Capall* (Horse Tournament) as planned, a decision I thought was utterly ridiculous and proved that the male Lords didn't give a hoot about anyone else's discomfort or safety when so -called "tradition' was involved. This included my sometimes insufferable, pig-headed Eternal Mate, who handed me an extra lap blanket and patted my hand as if I were a child when I complained about the weather conditions. For most of the afternoon, all of *I I Idir,* at least the supposed "lucky folk" not down with the dreaded "pink eye," suffered through bouts of sleeting rain and chilling wind that chafed any exposed skin. The only ones joyful about this damnable Horse Tournament were the vendors selling hot drinks, warm food, and cozy lap blankets.

As to prove the point to my husband that continuing on with this competition was a bad idea, House *Nuada* ended up faring very poorly, an unusual outcome for a clan so utterly devoted to horsemanship. Only two adult House members even placed in any of the afternoon's events; our Duncan taking third place in the Bareback Match, and a senior stable hand by the name of Festus O'Malley, placing second in the 500 Meter Race. Because of the freezing temps, poor Dylan was forced to wear riding gloves, a first-time attempt for him, and thus rendering him unable to guide his pony as well as he might have bare-handed, while *Oisin* was disqualified in his 200-meter race for leaving the gate a mille-second before the start whistle sounded. It certainly didn't help matters that *Mairead* Beckett, with whom my eldest son had a love/hate relationship, took home a blue ribbon in the Jr. Division steeplechase race, an outcome that had Dylan sniffling under my lap blanket.

At the end of this miserable interlude, none of the Fitzpatricks were happy campers, though some of them were more ill-tempered than others, specifically our resident teenager who complained loudly and bitterly that he had been "robbed of his opportunity to take first-place in the 200 by judges who had it out for him because of his Elven heritage." Any sympathy my husband might have held for the boy's bad luck vanished with *Oisin's* raging on about the prejudice against him, especially in such a public venue where other people could hear him.

I could tell by the set of Declan's jaw that his Lordship was quite perturbed over his younger brother's poor sportsmanship along with his disregard of Ruling Council protocol regarding competition. My mate held his tongue until we arrived back at *Dun Siorai*, but then laid into the boy without bothering to offer the privacy of his office.

"Ya' have gone and shamed this House, *Oisin* Fitzpatrick *Nuada,* with yar' childish public tantrums," his Lord stated in that cold, calm voice I don't much like hearing from him on any occasion, and especially not when dealing with the children. "'Tis plain bad luck and insufficient trainin' that caused yar' harse to bolt too soon, and not any feelin' of ill will the judges hold far ya.' We ken' work together on a method ta' combat a 'quick start' befar' the next competition, but I am left unsure what ta' do with yar' constant need ta' make the worst possible choices. I have been mar' than patient with ya' brother because we are kin. Had it been anyone else embarrassin' this House in the manner ya' did today ya' would be truly feelin' the painful sting of yar' bad behavior."

This whole scenario is spinning out of control right before my very eyes. *Oisin* seems to be physically shrinking in stature with every harsh word my husband throws at him, and the boy's hands are furled into tight fists. I take a few steps toward the child in an attempt to act as a buffer while perhaps cuing my Tax Man that his own behavior is over-the-top, but the look the teenager sends my way stops me in my tracks. Because it is nearly sundown, and my tooth fairy magic is awake, I sense the absolute rage in the child's aurora as well as in his eyes, and goddesses help me, it's downright scary. Even Dylan has gone behind the sofa to hide, and I try to understand how we got to this point as a family.

Oisin turns his attention back to his elder brother. "Do yar' worst, *Nuada*. You donna' frighten me. Have me whipped if you are so inclined to do so. Everyone knows you are jealous of me... envious of Elven magic that is ten times stronger than yar' *Sidhe* own."

MISSING 32

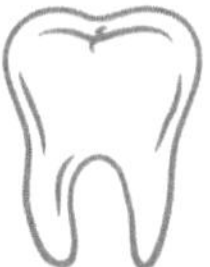

Big Dog Words Have More Bite Than Bark

THE BOY'S words hung in the air between the two brothers, almost like the magical energy behind them had turned the sounds into something thick, dark, and syrupy. My Eternal Mate was so still it seemed as if he'd turned to stone, and for the breath of a moment, I wonder if *Oisin* had possibly spell-casted him. Then I saw the muscles of his throat contract, and the words, though calm, sounded tight and emotional. "When have I ever laid a hand on you in anger, boy?

Oisin looked away and didn't reply. He couldn't answer Declan's question because there had never been a single time since the day the boy came to live with us that we ever saw fit to use any type of physical punishment with him. The Fae still strongly hold to the old Mundane proverb that sparing the rod would result in spoiled, unruly children. Once out of toddlerhood, most Otherworldly parents don't coddle their offspring. Because I grew up Mundane, and Declan was so adamant about not being the harsh parent both his were, perhaps we had been a wee bit…indulgent with the boy, undoubtedly trying to work through the wounds of his difficult entry into the Universe. I desperately wanted to believe *Oisin's* recent bad choices were simply the result of adolescent growing pains. Yet something seemed off about this current scenario, and the realization that I had even considered the possibility the kid had used dark magic towards my husband testified to my misgivings.

As if to mirror my thoughts, Seamus, *Oisin's* faithful terrier, jumped from his dog bed and took a place at the boy's feet as if standing guard, something I hadn't seen the canine do in such an overtly protective manner in nearly four years. The kid paid no mind to his dog's vigil, but I observed that Declan took notice of this oddity as well, that expressive left eyebrow of his twitching up and then back down. There was definitely something odd going on. A weird vibe in the air.

Then, before I could contemplate it any more, the tension in the room shifted, as if someone had suddenly opened a window, letting the stress out like acrid smoke on the wind. Even Seamus relaxed, his little furry body appearing to "stand down." It was Declan who broke the silence. "Ya have no answer far' me, brother?" he asked.

Oisin stared back at my mate with no expression, his face a blank canvas lacking any specific emotion, which to my mind, was one hundred times more concerning than the ornery teenage one I was used to seeing. "Nay, ma' Lord. We both know ya' have never struck me in anger or punishment. But 'tis yar' right ta' do so, and I accept my fate if that be it," he says matter-of-factly. "'Tis the way for we persecuted *Dökkálfar.*"

Because Declan is…well…Declan, a man who prizes honesty and family loyalty above most things, the kid's blandly pragmatic answer feels disrespectful and flippant in a situation where my husband believes he is being honest and heart-felt. If *Oisin's* goal was to push the Tax Man's emotional buttons, he hit his mark. "Feckin' hell, boy!" his Lordship swears as a pair of crystal candlesticks on the mantle explode. "I have tried evera' way I know ta' reach ya. Ta' make ya' feel like ya' belong ta' somethin' bigger than yar'self. However, these past few months it feels as if I am tryin' ta' *capall a tharraingt síos staighre* (pull a horse down the stairs). The Tax Man switches to the Old Language, a sure-fire sign of how really upset he is. "*Troidann túi gcoinne mo threorach chun túa thabhairt go fireann Nuada ar bhellach do shinsear aguscaithd'oidreacht Dökkálfar mar sciath le do chinniúint a sheachaint* (You fight my lead to bring you to *Nuada* manhood in the way of your ancestors, and wear your *Dökkálfar* heritage like a shield against facing your future)! Equal amounts of *Sidhe* and *Ljósálfar* blood flow through your veins as well as the *Dökkálfar,* boy! 'Twould appear that out of misguided stubbornness you seem to have chosen to ignore that part of the story."

It's obvious *Oisin* is not the only one capable of pushing emotional buttons. My husband's words stab at the boy's conscience, apparently enough to force a reaction. The lad spoke through clenched teeth, but it wasn't difficult to feel his anger, or to read the fiery red blaze of his aurora. "How ken' I forget, Lord *Nuada,* when at every turn someone reminds me of it? In either world, I am a freak whom no one wants. 'Tis all I'll ever be."

"Oh, *Oisin*…Sweetheart…you know that's not true!" I take a step towards the boy to offer comfort, but my husband's voice in my head stops me. *"Please, Love, I am beggin' ya'. Let me handle this as I see fit. I believe we are at a turnin' point with Oisin. As his older brother and his Liege Lord, 'tis ma' duty ta' carry him inta' manhood."*

For a brief second, I think about ignoring my Eternal Mate and doing what I think is right. In my Mundane-educated opinion, I don't think this has anything to do with the dawning of any so-called *"Sidhe* manhood." I believe *Oisin's* behavior of late is a natural reaction to his early childhood trauma, buried for years and now re-surfacing as his need for independence grows. It's a logical assumption, but I have first-hand experience of things incorrectly assumed. It's a hard fact that I have little experience with the adolescent development of *Sidhe* males, and in this case, that's a huge stumbling block towards my understanding of this conversation. For better or worse, I err on the side of caution and stay put with my mouth closed, letting Declan lead this family circus. And, as I have mentioned before, it's not in the *Sidhe* parenting "handbook" to cosset Fae children, especially one as old as *Oisin.*

"Yar' correct, *Oisin.* You will never completely shake the stain of yar' bastard birth from your path. Nor will ya' be able ta' deny yar' bloodline, as it is plainly mirrored in the planes of yar' face," his Lordship counseled, his words like scorching arrows aimed at a confused child. "It is yar' character and deeds that will decide who *Oisin* Fitzpatrick

Nuada truly is. 'Tis high time far' ya' to put yar' childish excuses and become the man the Universe has meant far ya' to be."

It was a completely honest little pep talk, even if I thought the phrases used were a tad harsh. The conversation should have ended neutrally at that point, with both parties wandering off to cool down and contemplate the extremely personal exchange. However, because Declan was Declan, raised in the propagandic atmosphere of The Ruling Council, and *Oisin* was the surly adolescent with unresolved issues he currently was, things went downhill at rapid pace.

When the teenager didn't answer, my husband added, "Do ya' understand what I am sayin' ta' ya', lad? I need ta' know that ya' see this as the watershed of yar' entire future." In response, the kid dramatically rolled his eyes, not unusual for his maturity level, but definitely NOT a good decision. Declan took two steps forward, closing the space between the boy and himself. Lowering his voice, he practically growled at the teenager. "I swear ta' ya' right here and now, and in front of yar' Lady Sister, that ya' will become a true and proper son of House *Nuada*, even if I have ta' drag yar' whinin' ass down the correct path ma'self."

Okay. So maybe this wasn't the Tax Man's greatest parenting moment. In his defense, *Oisin* was his first teenager, and because Declan was his elder brother and not his biological father, maybe the kid was having an especially tough time with my mate's inborn, uncompromising nature. I just knew this scene wasn't going to end well.

The teenager didn't back down, standing toe to toe with his Liege Lord. This close, it was hard to miss the strong family resemblance, though *Oisin* had the muddy gray eyes of his Elven ancestors instead of the green or hazel prominent among the *Sidhe*. "At last ya' speak the complete truth, brother. I am no kin ta' ya'. Ya' don' care how I feel as long as I act the part of feudal serf, bendin' ma' knee in yar' service. Ya' want me ta' become yar' lap dog in the manner of yar' cousin, Duncan, who dances on yar' every word. 'Tis no in ma' nature, neither *Sidhe*, nor Elven. But ya' ar correct, Declan Fitzpatrick. I will walk the path the Universe has laid out, and not the one you have chosen far' me."

Oisin's words stab me in the heart. I understand the boy's wounded frustration, but to drag Duncan into the conversation in such a demeaning way, when said man has been nothing but kind and generous to the boy is especially hurtful. If I feel this way, I can only imagine how upset my Tax Man must be. Thankfully, despite the swirling emotions I'm feeling through our Bond, his Lordship is able to react in the cool, collected way that has made him a voice of reason within the Ruling Council. "Ya' have stated your intentions, as is yar' right as a man. Alas, as of yet, ya' have not reached yar' fourteenth year. When ya' reach the age of manhood, ya' are free ta' set out upon yar' own path. Until that day in December, I remain yar' sovereign guardian and ya' will do exactly as I tell ya, beginning with this vera' evening. I expect ta' see ya' in attendance at tonight's *Samhain* bonfire, dressed in appropriate House colors and not that ridiculous black costume ya' insist on paradin' around in. Ya' will follow all rules of proper protocol."

The kid opened his mouth to protest, but my husband put his hand up to stop him before he can utter another word. "Disobedience of ma' orders will have consequences, none of them at the hand of a whip, but nonetheless, ya' will not much like them, beginnin' with the surrenderin' of *Réalta Dorcha.* If ya' are determined to find yar' own path within the kingdoms of the Otherworld, ya' will find it sorely difficult ta' make yar' way without a harse'. I suggest ya' think carefully."

Réalta Dorcha (Dark Star), was *Oisin's* beloved stallion, gifted to him by my husband when the boy was physically strong enough to handle the sheer power of a Fae equine. Together with the Stable Master, the lad had worked tirelessly to train the animal to an impressive level of skill, and despite the poor showing this morning with a false start, the stallion held great promise for racing and stud value. The loss of "Dark Star" was a huge threat, and the Tax Man knew it. I just hoped my mate understood he was drawing lines in the sand that couldn't be erased.

Still, the warning hit its mark. The teenager visibly paled, and some of his emerging bluster disappeared. It was more than the monetary value of the horse. *Oisin* truly loved his animals, both *Seamus* and *Réalta Dorcha,* and the idea the stallion might be taken away frightened him. It made me not particularly proud of my Tax Man, an emotion I knew he felt from me, but didn't react to. Not waiting for a comment, his Lordship continued with whatever plan he'd hatched in his head. "I will take yar' silence as confirmation that ya' understand ma' position, Brother. Can I assume, then, that I will see you at the bonfire tonight, dressed appropriately, and sheathed in yar' best House *Nuada* manners?"

"Aye, ma' Lord," his younger brother replied without looking up.

"Good. I am glad of it. Ya' are dismissed until this evening," Declan stated, his staid expression never wavering. As the boy turned to leave, Lord *Nuada* added, "Oh, one more thing. I want ya' ta' bring *Seamus* with you ta'night. The poor dog has been cooped up in the estate far far too many hours. He is in need of a good outing."

MISSING 33

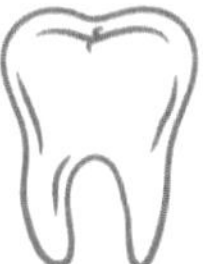

When All Fun is Sapped...

IF I WERE to take a vote among the four Fitzptricks left standing without the affliction of "Rotten Eyes," I'm pretty sure it would come out that none of us were particularly in the mood to attend the *Samhain* picnic and bonfire. The weather was lousy and the mood among my family members was about the same. *Birgit, Niamh,* Liam and Ronin were holed up in *Dun Siorai's* nursery, and from the wailing and whining I heard from beyond the closed door, things were not going smoothly in there either. Even the normally-cheerful, ever-un-flappable *Birgit* sounded cranky. The *scathach* assured me that despite the unhappy noises emanating from my two youngest children, they were all fine and she and *Niamh* did not mind sacrificing themselves to this dreaded bout of *Súile Lofa* (Rotten Eyes) for the sake of House *Nuada* and its Lord and Lady.

I do my best not to roll my eyes at her mellow drama,

lest some type of *scathach* magic allows her to see me through the door. Bacterial Conjunctivitis is a very common childhood disease in the Mundane world, and although its symptoms are very annoying, with proper treatment it doesn't leave any serious lasting problems. However, for the Fae, who never catch human-like colds and viruses, and can self-heal most injuries through magic, *Súile Lofa* was firmly considered a Mundane curse that humans purposely set upon their Fae counterparts. Like the dreaded Norovirus, that awful "bug" we Mundanes call the "stomach flu," the Fae, especially the *Sidhes*, suffered the same symptoms as humans, but, apparently, several times worse. Personally, I thought much of their fear over "pink eye" had more to do with the nasty appearance it caused rather than any physical discomfort. The *Sidhe* were a very vain race of people when it came to their appearances, and the red, gooey, leaking eyes brought about by the disease thoroughly disgusted them.

In all honesty, I would have preferred to trade places with the *scathachs*. I did not relish spending the next four or five hours in the company of three crabby Fitzpatrick males of graduated sizes. The terrible weather and the myriad of food hampers and picnic paraphernalia we needed to take along forced everyone into the carriage for the trip to the grounds of *Crann Bethad* where the festivities were being held. Thus, I was amply treated to Dylan's under-the breath whining that he'd "given up free *milseáin* (sweets) for a stupid horse race and the annoyance of *Mairead* Beckett bragging all evening about her prize ribbon." *Oisin,* of course, said not a word, instead preferring to glare at me while jiggling his left leg so much that the cushion we all were sitting on jiggled along with it.

My loving husband chose to sit atop the carriage with the driver despite icy crystals spraying his face rather than enjoy the company of his disagreeable clan. This was probably a good thing as I wasn't currently speaking to him anyway. After the intense discussion with his younger brother, his Lordship stomped off to his study. I had lovingly tried to follow to offer sympathetic company and was rudely told that "after five years I shad' know when ta' just feckin' leave him alone." I knew that once we arrived at Her Majesty's bonfire, he'd put on the required mantle of calm, collected Lord of House *Nuada*, but currently he was just plain "cranky D.P. Fitzpatrick," and I wasn't in the mood to deal with it either.

The *Samhain* bonfire in honor of The Morrigan's name day was a command performance and no excuse ever made it permissible to not attend, except, perhaps, Dr. Brannigan's mandated quarantine. We arrived at *Crann Bethadh* to a traffic jam of carriages and horses, making getting to House *Nuada's* tented pavilion on the far west side of the grounds a chore. Cook and her crew were there waiting for us, along with Master Tuck, who as of late seemed to be spending a lot of extra time with our lady chef. As the meal was being laid out, Declan and I made our required obligation of visiting all the other Lords and Ladies of the Ruling council, presenting each with a small holiday token which was the norm. As we moved across the grounds, I noted that Dylan had already found the little *Banphrionsa*, the two of them involved in some kind of game of tag with a group of other children.

Oisin had made the company of a group of older teenagers who were busy showing off their knife throwing abilities, a skill he excelled at. I was shocked to see him actually smiling, and I let myself believe that perhaps this evening would end better than it had started.

As usual, Cook had outdone herself. The array of picnic food included all of the traditional autumnal foods, as well as some family favorites, and it didn't go unnoticed that a large number of Lords and Ladies made their customary visit to our pavilion during the time dessert was being served. Cook's apple nut tartlets, with their flaky, buttery crust and just-sweet-enough fruit filling, were the stuff of legends, and anticipating their appeal, our House culinary wizard always made sure there were plenty to share.

Once the music started, the pavilions emptied out, with most people socializing and dancing around the gigantic bonfire. I wasn't surprised to see my husband's *mathair*, Lady *Siobhan*, make her way over to our tent. She had sent word she would be joining us after dinner. What I hadn't expected was that she would drag along my sister-in-law, Lady Meghan *Mac Badh*, a change in plans I didn't relish.

"A Blessed *Samhain* to you, Lady *Nuada*," Meghan purred with a tone of fake sincerity. "As usual, you look a true picture of maternal…satisfaction."

It was not meant as a compliment. What Meghan was implying was that I was still looking post-partum dumpy and lumpy. Normally, I didn't pay a bit of interest to insults regarding my weight, but today being today, I reply with a nasty dig of my own. "And you are looking as lithe and thin as ever, Lady *Mac Badh*. Can I assume, then, that as of yet there is no sign of a Raven heir on the way for House *Badh*?"

Meghan smiled, all perfect white teeth and dimples, a female version of her mother and elder brother. "Not that I am aware, dear Lady, though 'tis not far' lack of trying. His Lordship and I stay drunk on the love of the newly handfasted."

"Oh nice. I know exactly what you describe, but perhaps tenfold stronger," I boast.

My Eternal Mate, who hasn't even bothered to greet his mother and sister rises from his seat. "If ya' ladies will excuse me, I still hope ta' make my traditional *Samhain Siúlóid Machnaimh* (*Samhain* Walk of Meditation) befar' the woods are crowded with 'Wilding' revelers." He leans down and kisses me on the cheek. "I will return and join ya' for the last dance, ma' Lady," before turning and heading for the dense wooded area beyond the festival grounds.

I consider my current options; stay and endure the scathing tongues of Dragon Mama and her murderous daughter, or pretend I'm on a spiritual quest and join my husband in the woods. It's not even a contest. "Lady *Mathair*, if I could gratefully ask you to keep an eye on Dylan for a short while, I'd also like to make my own *Siúlóid Machnaimh*." I point to where Dylan is sitting with *Mairead* Beckett at a small table eating one of Cook's famous tartlets. Seeing me, the little boy lifts a hand to wave to me.

In return, my sister-in-law literally snorts her derision, and my husband's mother raises that annoying one eyebrow at me. "Come now, Lady Rosalinda, 'tis no secret that yar' not much far the practicin' of the Old Ways. If this is a ploy ta' *rendez-vous* with yar' mate on a sabbat known for its rites of fertility, there's no need to fashion silly stories. Go then, Lady *Nuada*, and meet up with yar' mate. House *Nuada* awaits yet another son in its line, and I am happy to watch over wee *Mac Nuada*."

Truthfully, a roll in the woods amidst this frigid weather wasn't foremost on my mind. Plus, the nasty words my Tax Man threw at me this afternoon certainly weren't libido builders. However, if it meant I could escape this current scenario, I was all in for whatever excuse got me out of here. I drop a polite curtsy. "Thank you, Lady *Mathair*. You know me so well. I deeply appreciate your understanding." Then I turn around and hightail it out of the pavilion before anyone can change their mind, and follow my Eternal Mate into the woods.

MISSING 34

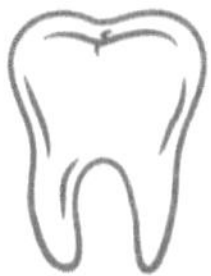

...And The Fox is Trapped

THE BOND BETWEEN US IS, for the most part, always open, so it doesn't take me long to track my Tax Man down. In spite of temperatures hovering near freezing, I find him in the process of removing the last of his clothes, obviously in preparation for shifting. "Oh," I say, not trying too hard to hide my disappointment. "I didn't know you planned on shifting for your meditation. I thought I'd walk with you, but I can head on back if you want to be alone."

Because the Bond is open, I can tell he's torn over wanting to be alone with his thoughts and his fox freedom, and not hurting my feelings. He reaches for his pants. "That's okay, Love. We ken' walk ta'gether. I am feelin' broken far' the words I said ta' ya' this afternoon. There is no time that I wad' no want ya' next ta' me. I shad' not have said that I did."

"Can we still walk together if you're in your fox form?"

I ask, his melty, heartfelt apology making me more open to dealing with furry Declan.

"I suppose," he offers. "I ken' try ta' pace ma'self so that you ar' able ta' keep up with me. But are ya' truly comfortable with witnessin' me in this form, Lass. I know this has been difficult far' ya' ta' accept."

"Does it make me a little weirded out? Yes. Absolutely. But if this ability is part of who you are from now on, Declan, then I will learn to love it as much as the rest of you. It just might take a little time," I reply.

He pulls me to himself, still standin' there only in boxer briefs, hands still where paws will shortly be, and kisses me. "I love ya', Rosie Parker. From every breath I take." Then, he shucks off the boxers, arms and legs shifting right before my eyes. Lord *Sionnach Rua* points a paw toward the path. *"I'm needin' ta' run, Rosie Lass, and stretch my legs. Is that okay with you? I will meet ya' where the bend meets the road."*

"Sure, Sweetie. You go ahead. I'll catch up." I watch as my Eternal Mate scampers through the wooded underbrush, and through the bond I can feel his absolute joy at being free from the responsibilities that weigh him down as Lord of House *Nuada.* He stops along the trail to smell the dark earth and the wet leaves with a sense of exuberance I've rarely seen in the five years I've known him. I smile at the thought that this might be how the Tax Man was as a small child when suddenly, those pleasant reveries are shattered by the sound of a metal clang and a piercing wail, almost like a woman's hoarse scream.

In my head I hear my mate. *"Feckin' hell, Rosie. Come quick!"*

I push through the nearly bare branches in order to follow in the same steps as my husband, and when I find him a quarter mile up ahead, I freeze in horror at the sight; my beloved Eternal Mate's furry self is agonizingly caught between the sharp jaws of a spring trap. Even in animal form, the familiar green eyes are awash in pain, and the grimace Lord *Sionnach Rua* is wearing is a sure indication that he's in serious trouble as blood pours from his hind leg and puddles around his paw.

I drop to my knees and attempt to pry the jaws open, but despite bloody hands and my best efforts, the teeth embedded in my husband's leg don't budge. "I don't have the strength to pull them apart, Declan. Can't you use your magic to escape?" I ask, trying but not succeeding in keeping the panic from my voice.

"I ken' no use magic, Love. The jaws of the trap are made of brass, and embedded in ma' flesh as they are, I am without any magical ability. It's after sunset. Da' ya' think ya' ken' try yar' own magic?"

My magic is weak at the best of times, even when I'm calm and focused. This is not one of those times. I concentrate all my attention on pulling open those jaws, and though they rattle a bit, they don't loosen even an inch. "Oh shit! I'm sorry, Sweetie. I'm trying my best, but it doesn't seem to be working." An idea comes to my frantic mind. "Maybe I can reach Duncan and he can come help us," I offer, as yet more blood pours from my *Mo Shiorghra's* leg and his breathing turns to ragged panting.

"Ma' cousin usually keeps his shields firmly up, but I suppose you ken' try. In the meantime, I'm gonna need ya' ta'

start carryin' me toward Crann Bethadh. Her Majesty's trolls will know what ta' do. Far' whatever reason, the trap hasn't been pegged ta' the ground, so I believe it might be possible far ya' ta' pick me up, trap and all. "

I have less confidence about carrying the weight of a large red fox along with a heavy metal trap than I did about calling for Duncan, but I set my mind to both tasks. Declan in fox form most likely weighs about fifteen or sixteen pounds, while the trap, because of the solid brass jaws, probably clocks in at an additional four or five pounds. Because I'm a "strapping" sort of girl, I could normally handle twenty plus pounds, but this is no ordinary fox; this is my Eternal Mate who, between the teeth tearing at his flesh and the brass acting as a burning buffer to his magic, is in the throes of agonizing pain. And, because we share such a strong Bond, I have no doubt that when I touch him, I will share every physical sensation along with his emotional frenzy.

We are, however, out of other options, and I'll be damned if I let my beloved Tax Man bleed out here in these dark, cold woods. I center myself using every trick I have ever learned to focus my magical energy. Then, I plant my feet, bend my knees, and lift Lord *Sionnach Rua* off the ground, trap and all, and into my arms. As anticipated, my fox-form husband is dead weight and slick with the blood from the jaws cutting into his hind quarters. I struggle to keep him from slipping out of my arms, and hell, that's the easy part. Between my own fear and doubts, and Declan's rising panic and loss of blood, I am mentally overwhelmed, and any focus I hold falls completely apart. I know for a fact that there is no way

I'm going to be able to carry him nearly a mile to the tree fortress that The Morrigan calls home. I need Duncan's help. ASAP. Thus, I need a way to hone in on reaching my husband's cousin. The mage-taught Otherworldly techniques weren't going to work for me in this situation. Instead, I do what I always do when I'm stressed to the max. I sing. At the top of my lungs. Usually in the shower, but I was gonna' have to make these woods a workable alternative.

I draw up a mental image of Duncan Fitzpatrick, then I start humming the tune to one of my favorite shower songs; "Copacabana," by the fabulous Barry Manilow. However, I start ad-libbing the words, a musical S.O.S. of sorts. *"My name is Rosie. We're in the forest. Himself with bright red fur and a tail hanging down to there. We are in trouble, awfully bad trouble. Crann Bethadh is too far. Please bring a strong crow bar."*

I zero in on those few notes and lyrics, repeating them over and over in my head while also picturing our dearest friend. If Declan thinks I am crazy, he doesn't say. Probably because he is too busy trying not to pass out over blood loss. After what seems like forever, with Declan slipping down from arms and inching closer to my knees, I get a response from Duncan. *"Rosie...is that really you, ma' Lady?"*

"Yes! It's me Duncan. Declan is in serious trouble. He's in fox form and stepped in a trap. Hurry!"

"Stay exactly where ya' are, Rosie. I'm on ma' way. Keep this line of communication open far' as long as ya' ken. It will make it easier ta' find ya'."

I do as he asks. I keep singing my little "Copacabana"

ditty, while at the same time willing my beloved husband to stay conscious. I almost die of relief when I hear Duncan's voice. "Rosie? Where are ya', Lass?"

"We're over here," I shout. "Near the big rowan tree."

I hear him crashing through the bushes, and when he sees the state Declan is in, he lets loose a string of obscenities. *"Le cacar androchbhastard a thug seo faoi deara* (Fuck the evil bastard who brought this about)! No worries, Cousin. We will get this feckin' thing off ya' in no time." Duncan, like I had done earlier, attempts to pull the jaws apart with his bare hands, but the brass contraption remains firmly closed around my mate's leg. Following my advice, he'd brought along a crow bar. "When I pry these two pieces apart, ya' pull his Lordship's leg out as quickly as ya' ken. Because of the magical force of the brass, I will only be able to get them a wee bit open far' a vera' short time, so ya'll have to act fast."

"Got it," I replied.

Declan's Second wedges the crow bar's corner tip into a small space where the teeth don't quite align, then pushes down on the tool's handle with his entire body weight. The jaws groan under the pressure, and without worrying about delicacy, I yanked the caught leg up and outward. Lord *Sionnach Rua* lets out a shriek that makes all the hair on my arms stand up.

"Ma' Lord," Duncan called out, "do ya' think ya' ken change forms far' the trip to *Crann Bethadh*?"

Himself doesn't answer, losing consciousness over the pain of the released leg. Duncan scoops up the fox from my arms. "It seems he will have to travel in his fox form. 'Tis probably easier ta' carry him this way, but I have no doubt ma' dear cousin will be ornery as shit to find out I had ta' carry him like a wee *bairn*."

That was an understatement. His Lordship was going to be angrier than a caged beast when he came to. Still, my husband's mood didn't concern me in the least as long as he actually regained consciousness, along with his human form. I had a lot of anxiety over those two possibilities.

MISSING 35

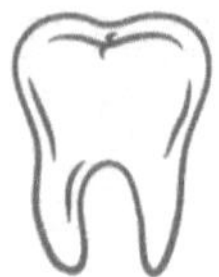

Does He Need a Vet or a Doc?

THE TREK to *Crann Bethadh* was nearly a mile and a half, and despite the chill, I'd worked up a good sweat keeping up with Duncan's quick pace. We are met at the servant's entrance by Doctor Robyn Brannigan, the 26th Merlin, and two high-ranking members of the Royal Troll guard carrying a cotton stretcher. I can tell by everyone's worried expressions that my concerns regarding Declan's current state are justified. "Take him directly to the *othar-lann* (infirmary)," the Doc orders the two Troll guards. "I'll be there shortly."

The guards carefully take my husband's fox form from Duncan's arms and place him on the litter, then off they go to the infirmary, wherever that might be in this giant tree estate. Robyn signals us to follow him, and questions me while we walk. "Can you tell me how this all came about, Dr. Parker?" he asks using my professional title like he always does in serious situations.

"My husband and I were out for a bit of a *Samhain* walk after dinner," I explained, leaving out the part about me wanting to ditch my in-laws. "His Lordship planned to use the opportunity to try out his new ability, so he shifted into his fox form. I was just following along when I heard him cry out in pain. I tracked the sound and found him caught in a spring-hinged, jaw trap. Unfortunately, the jaw part with the teeth seemed to be made out of solid brass, thus hindering Declan's ability to use his magic to escape or shift back to his Fae form."

"Brass, you say?" the Merlin asks. "Are you sure?"

"Aye, ma' Lord," Duncan replies for me. "Pure cooper and zinc. Whoever designed that trap intended for any use of magic to be foiled. 'Tis unlikely it was meant for menacing animals. 'Twas not even pegged ta' the ground by a chain. This was a deliberate attack."

"It does sound suspicious," our Merlin says. "Did you happen to bring the trap with you?"

"Cac (shit)!" Duncan swears. "I should have thought you might want to examine it, but in ma' hurry ta' get his Lordship help, it slipped ma' mind. I will leave immediately and retrieve it."

"That would be helpful, Duncan. Thank you." As Duncan left to bring the wretched trap back, the Merlin turned to me. "Is there anything more you can add, Lady *Nuada?*"

"No, Lord Merlin. Not really, I'm sorry to say. I don't believe his Lordship had any warning that the trap was in his path. By the time I arrived at his side, my husband had pulled himself away from the trap's original spot. But I could tell approximately where it had been by the pile of branches and sticks that had been used to cover it."

The wizard shook his head in disgust. "Just another sign that magic was obviously used to deceive. There's little doubt your mate should have been able to smell the tang of the different metals that made up the contraption, especially in his fox form. The fact that he didn't means a purposeful spell of deception. I'll know more when Duncan brings back the trap and I run a few metaphysical tests."

The three of us stop in front of a non-descript door marked with only a Raven symbol, common to most of the entry ways in the estate. "This is the infirmary, Dr. Parker. Lord Merlin and I will attend to your husband both magically and physically. I have no doubt you want to be at his side right now, but I'm going to respectfully ask that you wait in the east visitor parlor until I come and get you."

I shake my head no with enough force to loosen the decorative combs holding my braids to the side of my head. "I'm afraid I can't go along with your suggestion, Doctor. Respectfully, of course. I go where my Eternal Mate goes. As a medical professional, I understand about not getting in your way. I'll act in a manner befitting my titles, both here and in the Mundane world. I promise, I won't be a distraction."

"It's not your feelings I'm worried about, Dr. Parker. It's my patient's feelings I'm acting in accordance with," he responds bluntly. I must look confused, so Robyn goes on to explain. "We all know how proud Lord *Nuada* is regarding any show of personal weakness. Surely you remember how he hid his suffering at the hands of the North Koreans, almost to it being a detriment to his healing. To be totally transparent with you, my knowledge lends that in his current condition, your *Mo Shiorghra* will be unable to shift back into his Fae form without assistance. The Lord Merlin and I will most likely have to force his change using a combination of magic and mind-altering drugs. It will not be a pleasant experience for him, and knowing Declan Fitzpatrick as well as I do, it would greatly wound his pride to have you, his One and Only, witness such a thing."

Ganging up two against one, Lord Merlin sticks his two cents in. "You know your mate better than anyone in his life, Lady *Nuada*. Do you disagree with Robyn's perception of your husband?"

I can't fight them both, mainly because they are one hundred percent correct. The Tax Man hates for anyone to see any sort of personal weakness, and takes attempts at sympathy in a less than polite manner. The last thing Declan would want is for me to see any outward signs of his suffering. It would hurt him more than any physical pain. "I suppose I can't deny the truth, gentlemen. I'll wait in the visitor parlor as you ask, but you must promise to come get me as soon as you think it's okay for me to be at his side."

"Thank you for being true to your husband's needs," the Doc says." You are truly a gift to House *Nuada*." Frankly, I want to tell him to take his polite, protocol-centered compliment and shove it, but I don't. None of this is Robyn's fault. He's been a good and loyal friend, and I know he has Declan's best interest at heart. Thus, I let myself be drawn away from my Eternal Mate's side by two Troll guards, who deposit me in the east parlor of *Crann Bethadh* with a formal bow and zero words.

* * *

If you believe that I gave in to Doc Brannigan and Lord Merlin's mandate far too easily, then I'll let you in on a little secret. I had assumed I would covertly keep abreast of the situation using the open Bond between my *Mo Shiorghra* and myself. Even in his unconscious state, I was keenly aware that my Tax Man was still physically functioning; his heart, lungs and brain were all ticking along as they should. That's why it was such a complete shock when that open line of communication was completely cut off.

I didn't know which of the two gentlemen were responsible for this travesty to my bonded autonomy, though my money was on the Merlin. Still, I cursed them both using every colorful Gaelic swear word I'd learned in the past five years while pacing the entire length of the Royal parlor multiple times. Needless to say, I was thoroughly embarrassed when I turned around to find *Aoibheann, Crann Bethadh's* head housekeeper, standing in the entrance way with a tea cart. I stutter out a lame apology. "I'm sorry, Mistress *Aoibheann*. That type of language is absolutely uncalled for in the Royal Seat. I'm afraid I'm a bit…overwhelmed."

The housekeeper smiled with sincerity. "No worries, Lady *Nuada*. These are trying times for all of *I Idir*. Her Majesty and the *Banphrionsa* are still out celebrating the

Samhain bonfire. I am to tell you to make yourself comfortable and that the Black Knight will be here to speak with you shortly. In the meantime, I've prepared some hot tea and sabbat sweets for you while you wait."

"Thank you, Mistress. That's very kind of you," I reply, though having to speak one on one with the Black Knight was not on my preferred list of things to do this evening. Any discussion with that man was always intensely stress-inducing and usually came attached to bad news. One thing was for sure; as family holidays went, this one sucked. Big time.

"If I can be of any assistance, Lady *Nuada,* please don't hesitate to ask," the housekeeper says before dropping a polite courtesy and leaving me in my worried solitude.

I was not in the least bit hungry, yet I go through the ritual of fixing myself a cup of tea, lest I offend *Aoibheann's* proprieties. As I drop a sugar cube into my cup, I think to myself that I'd prefer a good stiff shot of brandy at this moment. "I heartily concur, Lady *Nuada,*" says a familiar voice behind. I know without turning around it's the Black Knight. The man's ability to enter a room without making a sound is disconcerting, to say the least. Even worse, is his propensity for poking around in one's head when he's never been invited to do so.

Without a word of apology for sneaking up on me, or taking advantage of my unshielded thoughts, he wanders over to a large cabinet and pulls out an ornate bottle of amber colored liquid. Uncapping it, he holds it over my tea cup. "May I?" he asks.

I nod my acquiescence and Beck pours a good, long finger of brandy in the tea cup, then takes an extra cup and pours one for himself. *"Go Maire sibh an Bhanrion* (Long Live the Queen)," he says, raising his cup and then draining it. I follow suit. The brandy has the pleasant taste of wild honey, but burns like scalding lava on the way down. I can't help but shudder as the liquid fire hits bottom, causing the Black Knight to smile. "Packs quite a punch," he remarks.

"That's putting it mildly. What the hell is that? It tastes sweet on the tongue and then…wowza!" I reply.

"It's called 'Dragon's Fire.' Made from a very rare type of Otherworldy wild honey and fermented pears and grapes. Because the honey is not produced in contained apiaries, it's often hard to cultivate and gather, making the brandy in short supply and very expensive. It fools you with its initial sweet taste, but it's like a missile going down and will one hundred percent knock you on your ass," the Knight explains.

The warmth of the tea and brandy spreads from my stomach to my brain, and I wonder if that wasn't part of the man's plan, though for what reason he'd want me drunk is a question I can't answer. While my brain is still functioning, I ask, "Is there any news on my husband's condition?"

"I'm told that all things considered, he's doing miraculously well," Beck says. "Working through difficulties, but making solid progress."

A flash anger runs through me at the notion that the Lord Knight can see my ailing husband, but I, his Eternal Mate, cannot. Immediately, my husband's superior officer says, "If it makes you feel better, Lady *Nuada*, I haven't been allowed to see him either. I'm going by what I've been told."

Truthfully, knowing the Black Knight was denied entry as well does make me feel better. However, now I'm ticked because, once again, he's taking information directly from my head. Uninvited. Most Fae with *Sidhe* blood lines can communicate telepathically. But general common courtesy forbids jumping into someone's head without consent, and most Otherworldly folk keep their minds shielded when they are not specifically engaged in telepathy. I've always been a bit sloppy with that, my Mundane learnings often making my thoughts an open book. Still, I think it's very rude of the Black Knight to take advantage of this, especially when I'm already so freakin' stressed, and so I tell him so. "You are being most rude and uncivilized, Lord Knight, foraging in my mind without permission. I'm fully shocked that someone of your status stoops to what is basically eavesdropping."

I'm prepared for a piercing stare down and a cold warning in the way I've seen the Black Knight do on many occasions. Instead, he just laughs. "Come now, Rosie," he says, using my given name, "we both know I've been peeking in at your thoughts since day one. It's the nature of the spy game. Frankly, if you don't want uninvited guests in your head, then it will have to be you who puts a stop to it. I have no doubt you're perfectly capable of properly shielding, but for whatever reason, you refuse to do so." He leans forward in his hair, and steeples his finger. "I will say this much, Lady *Nuada*, once you decide to lock up that brilliant mind of yours, you're going to make one helluva' terrific asset."

I'm not sure if I should be pleased at Beck's words, or thoroughly insulted. I don't get the chance to contemplate which side of the fence I sit on because we are interrupted by a flurry of noise and voices outside the door to the East Visitor Parlor and I recognize the scathing tones of my demanding Lady *Mathair*.

MISSING 36

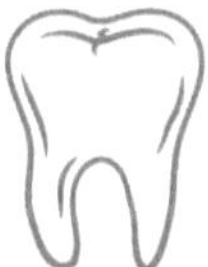

Dragon Mama is Solid as Rock

"Open this door, *a leathphionta amadáin* (you half pint idiots)!" my Lady *Mathair* commands.

There is no subsequent response by the Royal Troll Guardsmen, forcing the Black Knight to answer the door himself. "Lady *Siobhan*, always a pleasure to see you," Beck says as he steps aside to let her in. "What brings you to *Crann Bethadh?*"

My husband's mother glares at him, not an ounce of trepidation over the man's reputation. "Sometimes, Lord Knight, ya' are insufferable with yar' clumsy attempts at humor. You know very well I am a member of the Royal Circle and *Crann Bethadh* is ma' home. Perhaps the more logical questions should be why is ma' son here at Raven's Nest and not at the *Samhain* bonfire where his lordly self should be?" Looking across the room, *Siobhan* apparently notices me for the first time. "There you are, Lady *Nuada*! We have been looking all over far' ya'. My eldest *garmhac* (grandson) is in need of his *mathair*, and here you sit, closeted up with the Queen's Hand of Justice." Turning to Beck, she asks, "What has the *mí-ádh* (unlucky) girl done now, Lord Knight, that you see fit to once again interrogate her without the benefit of familial counsel?"

I'm not sure what bothers me more; having my mother-in-law automatically think I've done something bad enough to draw the Black Knight's attention, or the fact she just called me "unlucky," which to the Fae is no small insult. "For your information, Lady *Mathair*, I'm not in any trouble at all. Secondly, why is Dylan in need of his mother, and if you're here, who is keeping tabs on him?"

She "tsk-tsks" me, a not-so–subtle indication that she believes me to be a neglectful mother. "The *uan beag* (little lamb) has been rubbing his eyes all evening," she explains. "At first thought, I believed it was because of the irritating smoke from the bonfire, but then Lady *Mac Badh* pointed out that the boy's eyes did seem unusually red and watery. 'Tis no secret that House *Nuada* is crawling with a dreaded *Súile Lofa* (Rotten Eyes) infestation. With his *mathair* nowhere to be found, sending him back to *Dun Siorai* seemed most prudent."

"You sent him back alone?" my voice is three octaves higher than normal at the incredulity of her carelessness.

Lady *Siobhan* "tsks" again. "Of course not, *gé amaideach* (silly goose)! I called far' a carriage and sent him back with that *bastaird* (bastard) boy. The child's supposed 'uncail (uncle).' No doubt he is already tucked in bed."

I let my racing heart slow down before answering. "Well, thank you for that, Lady *Mathair*, but honestly, when I left to walk with his Lordship, Dylan's eyes looked perfectly fine to me."

"Ah, yes. Yar' walk with ma' son. It's why I've returned home to *Crann Bethadh* earlier than planned." Declan's mother turns her back to me and addresses Beck. "The entire festival grounds are awash in rumor that Lord *Nuada* has somehow been injured and has been taken back ta' the Raven's Nest for aid. As his *mathair*, as well as a high-ranking member of yar' team and the Royal Inner Circle, I demand ya' make me aware of what is goin' on tonight."

Say what you want about *Siobhan* Donnely Fitzpatrick *Nuada*'s bitchy attitude, I still have to give the woman credit for never backing down to any man. Ever. Truthfully, the only person she wisely minds her manners with is The Morrigan herself. No doubt about it. Dragon Mama is a certified "bad ass," and there have been many times in the past five years I wish some of her steely courage would rub off on me. Not that I'd ever tell her that, and unlike the Black Knight, she's far too protocol-orientated to poke around uninvited in my head, so I believe myself safe from her finding out that I actually do admire her. She would consider it a weakness on my part.

"If you'd like to have a seat, Lady *Siobhan*, I will explain what I am able to," the Queen's Second replied. He picked up the crystal flask and offered her a pour.

"Goddesses, no, Black Knight. I'll take a pass on your Dragon's Fire. I'm in no mood ta' have ma' senses dulled with that wicked concoction," my mother-in-law says. "I'm well aware of yar' tricks in getting tongues to loosen."

Realizing I've been "had," I give the man a genuine

dirty look, which he answers with a congenial smirk before attempting his "explaining" to my mother-in-law. I'm curious to see just how much of the truth he's planning on telling her. "I'm afraid I have some shockingly interesting news, Lady *Siobhan*, regarding his Lordship." He lets that statement hang for a bit, and when Dragon Mama doesn't show any reaction, he continues. "As of late, it appears your only son has shown the ability to shift form."

"Truly?" she asks, the only indication of her surprise is the raising of that crazy family eyebrow. "That is amazing news, Lord Knight. There have been ancient songs and tales that tell of earlier generations of Donnelys havin' the "*Aistriú na Foirme* (Shifting of Form)" magical ability, but it's been over six hundred years since it has actually shown up in the bloodline. Is it one form or multiple," she calmly asks, as if she hadn't just been told her son had off-the-charts magical skill.

"Currently, he only has one shifted form," Beck confirms. "That of the red fox. The Merlin believes it to be his spirit guide. It's too early to know if there will be others, though we are all pleased with the news. Which leads to the reason Lord *Nuada* is here at *Crann Bethadh*. It seems while he and Lady *Nuada* were in the woods, he was taken down by a purposely set spring trap, one suspiciously wrought in brass to stymy his magical energy. If Lady Rosalinda had not been with him and able to call for help, your son's prognosis would be much worse than it is. Both Robyn and my father believe he will eventually make a full recovery, though the whole experience is rather unpleasant. He was in fox form when it happened and unable to shift because of the brass interference. It was required that he be "force shifted" by means not of his own. I am sure you understand what that involves."

Dragon Mama made a sour face. "'Tis most painful, I'm told. Nevertheless, ma' son is *Tuatha de Danann*. He will handle his discomfort in the manner befitting his heritage. May I see him?"

"I'm afraid the Doc has mandated no visitors for the next few hours until his Lordship can…as you say… handle his pain in the manner befitting his bloodline. We will let you know when you can check in on him. Until then, feel free to return to your *Samhain* festivities."

"I think not, Black Knight. I prefer to stay here at *Crann Bethadh* and await news of Lord *Nuada*. Besides, as it gets closer to the time of the "Wilding," I'd prefer not to be out and about mixing with the lustful hordes that will soon take over the grounds."

"As you wish, my Lady." Beck stands and addresses me. "As for you, Lady Rosalinda, it will be a few hours yet until you can be at your mate's side. Perhaps you would like to return to *Dun Siorai* and check on your children. I would be happy to escort you there and back."

As much as I don't want to be too far from Declan, I desperately do need to check on all four children. If Dylan has "Pink Eye," he'll need to be moved to the nursery with the others before more of us are down with the "Rotten Eyes." Plus, if it's going to be a long night like Beck has implied, I'd rather change into something a little more comfortable. As I get older, I'm finding the stays in the

Otherworld corsets to be instruments of torture. "That sounds like good advice, Lord Knight. I gratefully accept your offer of an escort back to *Dun Siora*."

MISSING 37

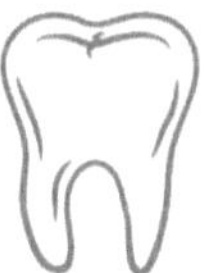

The Black Knight is A Real Ass

I SHOULD HAVE ANTICIPATED that the Black Knight, like my husband, would not suffer a cushy carriage from one place to another. The last time he'd "moved" me he'd used personal magic. But that had been years ago, when I was supposedly "arrested" for the murder of Marcy Kilcrabtree. Theodore Beckett had a reputation to keep as a "man's man," so my trip back to *Dun Siorai* was, of course, on traditional horseback. If this journey had been taking place during daylight hours, I would have been lent a gentle mare from *Crann Bethadh's* well-stocked stables and expected to ride on my own. However, since it was late on a moonless night, with the roads slick and icy, along with the unofficial start of "Wilding Night" being an additional security issue, it was decided that it would be safer for me to share the Lord Knight's stallion instead of riding my own.

We set off across the festival grounds, which at this

time of the evening had emptied out considerably, with couples, older folks and families heading back to their prospective homes. The revelers still left around the bonfire were those gearing up for Wilding activities, and I could tell from the drunken, bawdy songs and unabandoned dancing that it would be a long and raunchy night. I wondered if *Oisin* was out there among the revelers like Declan had believed, and I hoped with my whole maternal heart he would stay safe and make good choices.

The fastest way to *Dun Siorai* was through the more direct wooded paths rather than the stone paved main road which winded its way through the entire glen. I had secret fears I might be asked to sit in front of Black Knight, a position far too intimate in my mind, but thankfully, he helped me take a seat at the back of the saddle with the command that I should be "fully prepared to hang on when necessary."

He wasn't kidding about that. The Queen's Second wasn't of the mind to move at a calm trot and took his horse to full gallop almost immediately. Thus, I was forced to put my arms around Beck's waist to keep from falling off, with my face pressed practically under his armpit to avoid getting pelted in the face with stinging ice pellets as we rode against the wind. Even with my fox capelet between us, it felt entirely too close. I thought to myself that it had been a long time since I'd been this "pressed up" against a male other than my husband, and it felt, for lack of a better word, weird, with all my senses firing off over the strangeness of it; the wrong smells, the wrong sounds, the wrong aura. Maybe because it was after sundown here in the Otherworld, on the *Samhain* sabbat, no less, that I was so sensitive. Whatever it was, it made me uncomfortable, and for the first time since Declan's assault, I was glad that the Bond between us was temporarily closed. I wasn't sure how my Eternal Mate would feel about the situation I found myself in; would he be annoyed that I'd agreed to ride like this or think it was humorous that I was this so freaked out. Not knowing for sure let me believe my darling husband would be completely sympathetic to my lack of choice, and that thought made me less anxious.

Truthfully, I was a bit surprised at the amount of uneasiness I was feeling this evening. In the five years I'd shared my life with the Tax Man, there had been plenty of situations, both in the Otherworld as well as the Mundane, where things had gotten a little "hairy." I had thought I'd done a fairly reasonable job of training my emotions along with my physical self in preparation for the challenges our complicated life brought us. Still, I couldn't seem to shake the level of high apprehension I'd been experiencing since we arrived yesterday afternoon.

As to counter these thoughts, the Black Knight asks, "You okay back there, Rosie?" His using my given name didn't help things.

I blamed myself for his mental intrusion and instantly pulled up a shield to my thoughts "I'm fine. Just anxious to get home," I reply.

"Understandable. We should be there in about twenty minutes or so."

And no doubt we would have been if we hadn't been stopped a quarter mile up the path by a group of masked Wilding revelers, both male and female, who had decided it might be good fun to tease and harass local passersby. "Halt in the name of the Raven Queen whose name day we celebrate on this glorious night!" the tallest of the group commanded. Raising his torch he said, "In her Royal name we ask for a token, a tankard, or a tumble, if the gent and the lady so be inclined. All forms of payment are welcome as we can accommodate lad or lassie," he commented, throwing a clownish bow and a lecherous grin my way. His awkward sway made it obvious he was deep into his cups.

Instantly, I took everything back I'd said earlier about feeling uncomfortable next to the Black Knight. Now, I was one hundred percent glad for his presence in front of me, knowing full well that no one in their right mind would take on the Throne's infamous Hand of Justice. Yes, I've had basic hand-to-hand training, but this was a large group of Fae, obviously drunk and without their normal boundaries. I'd rather not have my skills put to the test right now when my mind and magical energies were so scattered.

"Hmmm," Beck replied, keeping his face shadowed under his hooded cape while giving into the local vernacular. "Ya' say ya' stop us in the name of Her Majesty? And that ya' seek *Samhain* payment in order far' me ta' pass? Do ya' think the lass behind me would suffice as payment?"

WTF? Did the Black Knight just offer me up to these goons?

"Aye, good sir. And yourself as well, with whatever ya' might fancy. We are not a *piocach* (picky) band," their spokesman states. Behind him, his cohorts clapped and whistled.

"Here man, bring yar'selves and yar' torches closer, so the lass and I ken' get a better look at the offerins'."

All dozen or so of them shuffled forward, lanterns and torches held high. It was at that moment that Himself pulled back his hood and smiled at them. "Do ya' like what ya' see, *cairde* (friends)?"

With the light on his face, the party animals got a grand look at who they had had the misfortune to stop. Instinctively, the group behind the man all took a step backwards, leaving their fearless leader to answer for them. The young man pulled off his mask and began to wring it in his hands out of sheer nervousness. "I am most sorry, ma' Lord. we did no' recognize ya'."

"Obviously," Beck replied in that cold, sarcastic tone he's totally mastered. "I believe it fitting that you apologize to the Lady as well. Your comments were most crude."

The man moved closer to me with his light and we recognized each other at the same time. *"Balfour?"* I ask in surprise. The tall man is one of our groomsmen at *Dun Siorai,* specifically the one who handles Dylan's pony, *Toirneach.*

"Is that you, Lady *Nuada*? Aye. 'Tis I, *Balfour*. I am most sorry, ma' Lady for ma' vulgar words. I dinna' know 'twas ya' behind the Black Knight. I would no think, ever, that ma' Lord's lady would be…" He lets his words trail off, knowing full well he was digging himself a bigger hole."

I was thoroughly mortified while contemplating how to

best explain the reasons I was out in the woods during Wilding Night without my husband when Himself interrupts. "Our secret is out, Lady *Nuada*. I don't know how we'll ever live it down," he relates with a perfectly straight face.

Now both *Balfour* and I look at the Knight in complete shock. I am absolutely lost for words, so it's the groomsman who replies to Beckett's ridiculous comment. "Rest yar' worries, Black Knight. And ya' too, dear Lady. Yar' secret is safe with us. We won' breathe a word about seein' the two of ya' tonight ta' anyone." He turned and addressed his friend. "Ain't that right, ma' friends?"

The whole group made a point of giving their word, which in *I Idir* meant absolutely nothing. Rumors would spread all through the town, eventually making their way to the Ruling Council. I wanted to give his Royal Pain-in-the-Ass a good swift kick in the shins for putting me in this position. I vowed I might even do it.

"I appreciate your loyalty, Master *Balfour*. In return, I promise not to relay to Her Majesty that you and your buddies were found to be 'shaking down' unsuspecting people in her name."

"I would be most grateful for that, Lord Knight. Truly, we meant no harm. Just a little Wildin' Night fun. We wad' have let ya' past unscathed. Ya' have ma' word on that."

"I accept your word, Master *Balfour*. And you have mine as well regarding Her Majesty. Now, Lady *Nuada* and I must be on our way. Enjoy your evening."

"Blessed Be, ma' Lord. You too, ma' Lady. Have yar'-selves a fine *Samhain* night as well." And then the young man winked at us with what can only be described as sly cheekiness; and in that moment, all I wanted to do was crawl inside my fur cape and completely disappear.

I made a point of not talking to my escort for the rest of the trip until we reached *Dun Siorai*. Once there, I'm forced to answer his logistical question. "Shall I let you off in front of the main entrance, Rosie, or the less formal one closer to your quarters," Beck asks.

I'm not in the mood to hike a mile back from the main entrance to our quarters so I deem to speak to him. "The servant's entrance will be fine, Lord Knight."

"You're not still angry with me over that little prank back there, are you?" He questions in a tone suggesting that, somehow, I'm at fault.

"Of course, I'm still angry with you! Why the hell did you have to make me look like some adulterous floozy back there? It's insulting! I thought we were…well… at least comrades in arms if not friends." I complained, shucking his offer to lift me down from the saddle, and struggling on my own using the stirrups. Thankfully, I don't fall on my ass getting down.

"We are absolutely friends, Rosie. That's why I feel comfortable enough to occasionally tease you. And frankly, you should be thanking me."

"Thanking you? For what? By tomorrow, everyone in *I Idir* will think you and I were secretly out playing at Wilding Night! How am I ever going to face Maureen after this? And what in the goddess's name am I going to tell my husband!" My voice sounds shrill, which is pretty much the norm when I'm angry.

"Neither of our mates will ever in a million years believe such a thing. Fitz adores the ground you walk on and everyone who matters knows it. And as far as Maureen and myself, there is an absolute connection of trust between my wife and I. It's a necessity in my line of work. I think you're over reacting. The truth of the matter is I've just increased your 'mystique' and raised your social rank ten score."

I stare at the man like he's got two heads. He's got to be the most arrogant partially human being I've ever met! "That's an incredibly arrogant and ridiculous statement, Lord Knight! I don't need help 'increasing my social rank,' from you, or anyone else," I contend.

"Look, Rosie. I don't want to hurt your feelings, but most of the movers and shakers in the social hierarchy simply ignore you. I know neither you nor Fitz care for any of that Ruling Council bullshit, but it's how the game is played in the Otherworld. We are in the middle of a war here. It may not seem like it in the traditional sense, no swords clashing or bullets flying, but the Mundanes, with the help of Callum Fitzpatrick and the traitors still left in *I Idir* and *Asgard*, are this close," he says, using his fingers to measure out the space, "to finding a way to cross the Veil without suffering the usual physical effects. It's only a matter of time until they do, where upon they will promptly move their armies to this dimension with the intention of conquering. I need all hands-on deck, Rosie, actively working here in *I Idir*, as well as back in the Mundane world. You're a smart, witty and captivating woman, Lady *Nuada*, but no one who matters knows it when you hide your light under a bushel. You need to be more...interesting to them. Gossip is like currency here. It's a weapon in my arsenal and I plan on using it anyway I can. That's what true espionage work is all about. Finding your enemy's weakness and using it against him or her. If our little 'misunderstanding' with Master *Balfour* this evening assists in making you more welcome in some elite circles, it's worth a little embarrassment, don't you think?"

His saying people find me "not interesting" most definitely hurts my feelings, but I'll be damned if I'll come out and admit it. "I think you're extremely misguided, Ted Beckett. About me, and the crazy notion that people thinking I'm some kind of insatiable Tooth Fairy sex fiend is going to help you capture my murderous father-in-law. But truthfully, it's been a shitty day and I just want to check in on my kids and get back to my injured husband. Is that too much to ask? For the time being, let's just shelve this silly nonsense, okay?"

"As you wish, Lady *Nuada*," he says, all calm, collected business now. "You go check on your kids. I'm going to take this horse to the stable so he can be attended to, and then I will meet you at your quarters. You can let me know when you're ready to return to *Crann Bethadh*." Beck grabs the horse's rein and turns to head toward the barn, but then stops to add, "Mark my words, Rosie Fitzpatrick. People are going to start treating you differently. You'll see."

MISSING 38

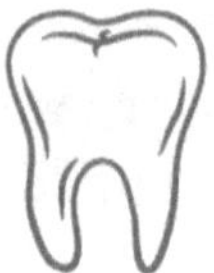

Something Horrid Comes to Pass

BECAUSE IT'S SO LATE in the evening, and an important sabbat to boot, the halls *Dun Siorai* are quiet and empty. That's a good thing. I'm not up for lengthy conversations and probing questions as to why I'm back at the estate and his Lordship is not. If my mother-in-law is correct, and there is apparently a great deal of gossip already circulating regarding a certain Lord's "accident," I'd rather not be forced to talk about it. Unlike the Black Knight, I don't have a plethora of believable lies hanging on the tip of my tongue at a moment's notice.

Our family quarters, which originally belonged specifically to Declan before we met, are tucked away in the furthermost corner of the estate's general living space. The first time I visited *Dun Siorai*, I was put-out by the fact that his parents had assigned him a living space so far from everything else, a reaction I blamed on their negative attitudes toward their only son and heir. It didn't take long for me to re-evaluate that assumption. The location of those suites lent a peaceful sense of calm away from the hustle and bustle of running a place as large as *Dun Siorai.* In addition, the views from those rooms were spectacular and allowed one to see everyone coming and going from the road that led to the main entrance. When our family grew beyond just the two of us, Declan took possession of some adjoining storage areas and enlarged the space, giving us room for a much larger nursery and a luxurious bed and bath suite for the two of us. Even better, there was a small, informal entrance and exit close by, mostly used by the staff, that allowed me the opportunity to save a few steps. Tonight, when I was in a hurry, it was a blessing.

I let myself in, as I knew neither *Brigit* or *Niamh* would be able to answer the door. I could feel the hum of energy attached to the magical wards that sensed it was me attempting to enter, thus allowing the door to swing completely open. "Hello? Anyone here?" I shouted through the entry way. "*Oisin?* Dylan? I'm home."

Silence greeted me, which was unusual, but not alarming. It was late, after all. Perhaps Dylan had gone to sleep when he returned home, and it was likely *Oisin* had returned to *Crann Bethadh* for the Wilding nonsense. I took off the heavy fox wrap, and threw it over the arm of the settee that sat in the front entry way. I headed first for Dylan's room, but found it empty and his bed still made. Then I went straight to *Oisin*'s room off the parlor, only to find it silent as well. Trying not to let fear get the best of me, I made my way to the nursery, telling myself that perhaps both boys had returned home with symptoms of

"Rotten Eyes" and had been relegated to the quarantine of the nursery. I hated waking anyone at this hour, but I had little choice, so I rapped on the door.

Niamh answered, already in bed clothes, greasy ointment covering the lids and surrounding skin of her eyes. "Good evening, ma' Lady. Did ya' have a lovely time at the bonfire?" she asked, covering a yawn with her hand.

"It was lovely as always, *Niamh*. Are Dylan and *Oisin* in the nursery with you?" I ask, working at keeping my voice calm.

"No, Ma' Lady. Were they no with ya' at the bonfire?" she asks, looking both confused and alarmed.

"No," I reply. "We got separated at the bonfire, and my Lady *Mathair* said she sent them home in a hired carriage. She thought they might have showed symptoms of "Rotten Eyes," I explain, forced to leave out key parts of the story. "I checked both their rooms, but they're not there."

"I don' believe anyone besides yar'self has entered the family quarters, Lady Rosie. The way the wards are set, *Birgit* and I would have immediately known if someone had tried to enter, but I suppose anything is possible. Truth told, it's been completely quiet all night," she states. "If anything, I would have expected that *Oisin* dropped the boy off here and went back to *Crann Bethadh* for the Wildin' Night. He's been tellin' everyone who'd listen he was goin' ta' do so. As far' our Dylan, did ya' by chance check the solar parlor? The wee lad loves the magic storybook the Merlin sent him last Solstice. Ken' it be he's listenin' to the old tales and fell asleep in there? It has happened befar' ya' know."

Niamh is right. We keep the precious gift in the solar parlor for safe keeping. Dylan did once fall asleep in there while listening to the magical storybook. The *scathachh* is also more than likely correct about our resident teenager. With the independence he was desperately seeking, *Oisin* probably did go on his own back to *Crann Bethadh.* I just wish I could be sure. My mind now on a single track, I don't even stop to say goodbye to the *scathach* as I race out of our quarters and down to the solar parlor, but something inside tells me my son won't be there. And he isn't. Nor was he in the kitchen where the on-duty scullery maids were helping Cook put away leftovers from the picnic. While Dylan would have no logical reason to be in the formal dining room, or the ballroom, or the music room, I check them all anyway, with no positive results. By this point, my heart is racing and I'm beginning to panic. Could *Oisin* have possibly taken Dylan with him to such an adult event? My sensibilities won't let me think that, but my mother's heart is scared shitless over the alternative.

On my way to the barn and stables I meet up with the Black Knight. Seeing the wild look in my eyes, he stops me. "Lady *Nuada*, what's wrong? Where are you heading to?"

"I can't find Dylan, and there's no sign that *Oisin* ever came home either. The formal clothes in the House colors he and Dylan were wearing at the bonfire are not in their rooms. They're not anywhere, and I absolutely know if my brother-in-law went to the Wilding event, he sure as hell wouldn't go wearing those clothes. I'm heading to the stables to see if maybe they went there. Or the barn. Or perhaps the kennels. *Oisin* had *Seamus* with him."

The head of *I Idir's* security makes a face that doesn't instill calm in me. "You can rule out the stable. I just came from there. Only the two night time groomsmen are there. Are you sure they're not hiding somewhere, perhaps playing a prank? I was good for doing that kind of shit when I was that age," he says.

"No. I don't think Dylan would go along with that. Hide and seek is not a favorite game of his. He gets far too impatient when the other children don't find him right away."

"We'll check the other buildings together. I wouldn't start worrying yet, Rosie. I'm sure they're here some-where at *Dun Siorai,*" he offers, though his body language doesn't quite match his easy words. He is practically running towards the barn and I have to hustle to keep up with him. The two of us search the wooden building from top to bottom, but there is no sign of either boy. As we walk to the kennels, we hear frantic barking that sounds unusually high-pitched for the hunting dogs that are normally housed there.

Beckett reaches the kennels first and turns on the overhead fairy lights, making all the dogs start madly barking. I can still hear that one shrill yap among all the deeper tones. Following the sound, I find a familiar furry face, ginger snoot pressed up against the wire of the kennel. "*Seamus*! What are you doing here?" I ask the agitated terrier. It's then that I recall that I should have noted it odd when the pup didn't greet me when I arrived home. Nor was he in his usual night time location, the cushy wicker basket in *Oisin's* room. Some spy I was going to make, missing such an obvious clue that something was not right. "Over here," I yell, struggling with the extra lock that's been added to the kennel's gate. "It's *Seamus*! I need help getting this lock off."

The Black Knight joins me and is forced to use magic to remove the heavy clasp. Finally released, the dog ignores us both and bolts to the door towards the canine training ring. Inside the ring, *Seamus* turns around to bark at us, as if to tell us to hurry. We find the pup standing next to a circle drawn in the damp earth. Next to the circle are my son's dress boots, the ones he complained were making his feet hurt earlier this evening.

For a moment, all I can do is stare at both the boots and the circle. My confused mind doesn't want to make the connection. The 27th Merlin, on the other hand, is all business, placing his hands on the line, and rubbing the dirt from inside the circle between his fore fingers, all the while careful not to scuff or alter the drawn line. Standing up, he says, "I believe this is a transport circle, Rosie. Someone jumped from here, I can't pinpoint an exact location, but I believe whoever used this circle crossed the Veil in the past four hours or so."

MISSING 39

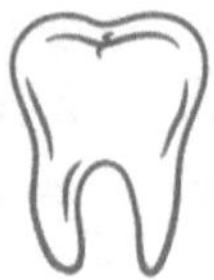

Making Plans To Find the Boys

THINGS HAPPEN FAST AFTER THAT. Beck continues calmly talking to me like my whole world isn't in absolute chaos. My first inclination is to make my own circle and cross the Veil myself. It is after sundown, and being *Samhain*, the Veil is at its thinnest point, so I'd have no tooth fairy problems doing just that. The Black Knight stops me, reminding me that we have no idea where the kids jumped to, nor if they were alone when they did so.

I hadn't considered the possibility that they had been taken against their will. It added a whole new sinister angle to an already horrible situation. "So, you think someone grabbed them?" I ask Beck.

"I didn't say that, Rosie. All I said is it's a possibility. I couldn't get an exact reading from the trace energy elements of how many people were actually in the circle when the magic was called. But the Merlin will be able to do so. He's on his way now."

The words have barely left his mouth when three forms materialized in front of me, obviously breaking protocol by using magic to transport. Upon seeing my husband, I threw myself into his arms. "Oh Declan," were the only words I could stammer out. We clung to each other, me trying hard not to fall completely apart in front of the four men.

"We will find them, *cara is dílse m'anama* (dearest mate of my soul). Ya' have ma' solemn word," he says as he holds me tight enough to be uncomfortable.

"I know we will, Declan. I'm just glad you're well enough to be here," I say, then turn to Doc Robyn. "He IS well enough to be here, right?" I query, knowing my Eternal Mate has, on occasions, disobeyed orders regarding his health.

"Aye, Dr. Parker. His Lordship is doing very well. He should be feeling one hundred percent himself by dawn, though I've recommended no morning runs on that leg for at least a few more days until all the nerve damage is healed."

"'Tis enough about me, gentlemen. What do we know about the disappearance of my son and brother?" Lord *Nuada* replied.

While the three of us had been discussing Declan's injuries, the 26th and 27th Merlin were magically examining the clues left in the circle. After a few minutes of poking at the soil, they both stood up, but it was the elder wizard who spoke. "From what I can tell from the magical energy residue left inside the circle, two people were transported from this spot. It is obvious that the magic used here was by a young practitioner. The boundaries of the spell are sloppy and uneven, as casted by an adolescent who as of yet doesn't have full concentration or focus yet."

"So, it is yar' guess, Lord Merlin, that it was my teenage brother who cast this jump?" my mate queried.

"Undoubtedly so," the 26th Merlin answered. "Furthermore, I feel traces of *Jotun* magic mixed in with the *Sidhe* elements, further proving *Oisin's* hand in this," the wizard said.

"*Jotun* magic? How would *Oisin* even know how to use the Norse elements? We've seen no sign that he's even interested in the Norse old ways," I protest.

"You need to remember that the child is half Elven, Lady *Nuada*, both *Dökkálfar* and *Ljósálfar*. His mother was a powerful practitioner. Undoubtedly, at puberty, his bloodline will have called to him. It is not something he, himself, can even control. That is why the Academy is so important to him. I know for a fact the instructing mages will have been teaching him how to handle the onset of these powerful urges, but he is still a boy, not quite to manhood. It must be very overwhelming to him. When casting this circle, he unwittingly opened the channel to his Elven magic."

"Da' ya' have any idea where they went, ma' Lord," Declan asks.

"As unstructured as the boy's magic is, he would have needed to use a jump he was already familiar with. Setting mental coordinates to a new location would have been too difficult for him at this stage of his magical abilities. Therefore, I can say with relative certainty the two children headed back on the only path they knew. Back to your home in Salem."

"Of course! Duh!" I say, slapping my forehead. "It's the early evening of October 31st back in the Mundane world…Halloween. They went back on their own for that damn trick or treating!"

* * *

Because the keeping of "secrets" is the sacred Fae way, the disappearance of my children, along with Declan's shifter ability and subsequent "accident," is kept to a "need to know" basis. The fact that the trap that "caught" Lord *Sionnach Rua* was made of anti-magic brass, as well as purposely hidden from sight and scent, made it viable to conclude that the device was meant specifically for my mate in his fox form. Since only a few folks knew of his ability, it made the list of suspects small, though there is always a chance that someone, perhaps Dylan or *Mairead*, in their childish naivete, spilt the beans to someone else less innocent. I know how it looks. With *Oisin* using magic to jump to Salem on the same night as my husband's "capture," it makes him a prime suspect. Neither Declan nor I want to believe the boy we know and love is capable of such a thing against his own flesh and blood, but the Black Knight is of a different mind, and I can't help thinking the man's prejudice against the teenager comes from personal experiences of his own childhood.

Only the five of us cross to Salem, my husband leaving Duncan and Lady *Siobhan* in charge of things at *Dun Siorai* until we return. The fact that the Tax Man is at a point where he can trust his *mathair* in such a big way shows just how far they've come in their relationship, though I believe some of their new forged union has to do with their mutual feelings of disgust towards their mate and father, Callum Fitzpatrick, the ole' "enemy of my enemy is my friend" philosophy.

We cross the Veil with ease this time of the year, although I try not to think who or what else can go back and forth using the thinned barrier between the two dimensions. I'm also grateful that Local Lassies Domestic Services, the Fae friendly cleaning company, had serviced my home before we left for the sabbat. I know. It's a crazy thing to worry about at a time like this, but too much of the Otherworld propensity for order has rubbed off on me these past few years, and I rely heavily on Mary Francis McCarthy and her team of experts.

The first thing I do upon landing is rush to the front hall closet to determine whether the Halloween costumes we bought earlier in the month are still hanging there. As expected, they are not. That information, along with the pile of Otherworldly garb left on their respective beds, coincides with our belief that the boys returned home with the intention of completing their trick or treating mission. I relax, just a little, over the knowledge that the two of them are just out cruising the neighborhood for candy, rather than abducted by the Universe knows who.

My relief is short-lived when my Eternal Mate, apparently a much better spy than I'll ever be, notices a few missing items from *Oisin's* room that leave unanswered questions. First off, though his House mandated attire from earlier in the day is there, the knee-high, custom-made leather boots, a Solstice gift from Duncan that the boy dearly loves, are missing from the pile and no- where to be found in the room. The boots are not really anything that would go along with his chosen ninja costume, so that leaves us more than curious. Nowhere in the pile do we find the teenager's dirk, nor the leather sheath I made for him years ago for a toy sword that now houses the Fae style knife that's universally carried, a throw-back to the "Old Ways." The idea that the boy is carrying around a knife with him for trick or treating is more than a little disconcerting. It's also Declan who first notices that a photo of all eight of us taken on a recent vacation to Cape Cod is missing from its frame on the boy's bedside table. Also gone is a gold-plated house key that we gave *Oisin* when he jumped to our Salem home for the first time. The key is mostly a symbolic gesture, as the house is magically warded for entry, but the kid has always treated it as a special item, with the key having its own little box on his dresser.

The combination of these missing items points to one thing none of us want to admit, yet the practical security officer in Ted Beckett announces out loud. "The kid took the things most important to him. *Oisin's* not planning on coming back home. I believe we have a run-away situation on our hands."

This is more than I can stay calm and collected over. I bite my bottom lip and try hard not to cry because I know it will just upset the others, mostly my husband. But one lone teardrop escapes and rolls down my cheek, and I hurriedly brush it away.

"Try not to worry, Rosie," Beck says. "The Sheriff's Office has dealt with at least twenty-two run-away children this past year alone. Most never got beyond ten miles of their home before we found them, and those few we didn't find were older teens with money and resources. *Oisin* is barely fourteen, and a novice regarding life outside Salem. He has no cash that we know of and no experience with Mundane public transportation. He couldn't have gotten far, especially having Dylan with him," the Sheriff of Essex County explains.

"But why take Dylan with him," I ask, fighting to keep my voice in a range that's lower than a dog whistle. "It makes no sense to drag a five-year-old with you if you want to make a quick get-away."

"Could it be that *Oisin* plans on using your son as collateral? To garnish a ransom of sorts. As we concluded earlier, it's doubtful he has any Mundane cash." The Black Knight asks, always and forever seeing the worst in every single person.

"I don' see ma' brother using my son to gain money. It is not in his character to do so. He loves Dylan and is vera' protective of him. Always has been. That behavior does not seem part of his soul," Declan interjects.

The Queen's Second shrugs, which to me says that he believes my husband is being overly naive regarding his half-brother. I don't want to believe something that horrible about the boy we raised as our own, but nothing about tonight makes sense. *Oisin* has been acting oddly lately. Testing the waters of his independence and turning away from the values he held so dearly. Is it even possible he'd set that awful trap for his half-brother so that he could disappear with our son without immediate notice? I hate that the thought even crosses my mind, and double check that all my mental shields are firmly in place, lest someone pick-up on these traitorous thoughts.

"I don't agree with your thoughts on what's behind the lad's run-about, Lord Knight," his father says. "What you're describing would take a calculated and organized mind, someone who figures he can collect a ransom and easily disappear without facing consequences. A planner. In my dealings with the boy, I don't find him mature enough to think that far ahead. To my mind, I believe he took Dylan with him so that the two of you would be forced to come look for them both. Because of the trauma of his early years, he doesn't have the confidence or faith in the world to believe that if he were to run away, anyone would bother enough to look for him. By having your natural born son with him, *Oisin* hopes you'll come after him, even if he knows he will undoubtedly suffer the consequences of his bad decision. Negative attention can substitute for his feelings of inadequacy over his tragic beginnings and his unknown place in the world."

My *Mo Shiorghra* and I look at each other, and I drop the shield between us. I sense my mate's high level of guilt and anguish over the wizard's words. Our family's last few weeks in Salem have been filled with episodes in which the teenager had lashed out, seeking the negative attention the Merlin had just mentioned. All his actions and our disciplinary reactions did nothing but feed into the boy's anxiety about who he was and what his place might be in our family. It's my husband who speaks the words I can't say. "What ya' say, Lord Merlin, is the good truth. Ma' young brother has tested ma' resolve ta' raise him in traditional *Sidhe* manner on several occasions the past few months. I did not see this for what it truly was. A plea for understandin' and patience. 'Tis ma' fault we are in this situation."

Apparently, our conversation is getting too "psycho-babblish" for the ultra-practical 27th Merlin. "Before we all go blaming ourselves for the kid's bad decisions, why don't we focus on finding the two of them first. Once we have them both home safe and sound, you all can beat yourself up over your supposedly bad parenting skills. In the meantime, keep in mind that teenagers, Otherworldly and Mundane both, make stupid choices based on every dumb thing they think is important at the time. They eventually grow out of it when their pea-sized brains start growing with them. Trust me when I say I speak from experience," the Hand of Justice bluntly states.

"The 27th Merlin is correct in his thinking," his father adds. "Young Theodore was a complete pain in the ass between the ages of twelve and eighteen. It was seven years of me wanting to throttle him and having to hold back."

The comment gets everyone laughing and breaks the tension in the room, and I am grateful to the Black Knight for sharing something I know is painfully personal for him in order to de-rail Declan's guilt train. It's an oddly compassionate action for a man who thrives on his reputation for being heartlessly brutal.

"There's a formal plan of action within the Sheriff's Office for missing kids and probable run-aways, but it doesn't seem prudent for me to put out a traditional 'all-points bulletin,' especially if we're trying to keep this situation hush-hush. It won't help *Oisin*'s future in *I Idir* to have unfounded rumors about his behavior following him as he grows into adulthood. The kid's got enough strikes against him already," Beck says. "Let's map out a search plan with a radius of three miles in each direction. Lady Roxanne is on duty tonight, so I'll have her search further out in the patrol car. I'll also let Kevin know what's going on so he and Father Wally can monitor the kids that come to the church's open house Halloween party. There's a small chance they might end up there, as Kev's Halloween party is wildly popular with the local kids. He and Wally really put on a show over there." A street map of the area materializes out of thin air, along with a handful of colored highlighters. Setting up on my dining room table, the Sheriff starts marking off blocks leading from our home. "Now, here's how we're gonna' break this search down…"

MISSING 40

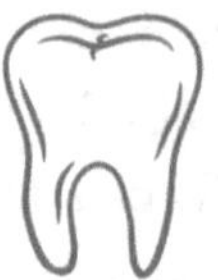

All of the Sorrow, Half of the Joy

THE BLACK KNIGHT sends us out with maps of our assigned blocks and cell phone images of the costumes the two boys are assumed to be wearing. We are thoroughly warned not to make a big deal over the fact that we are searching for missing children, lest we start a full-blown panic in the community during the most popular holiday in Salem. Beck also summons Mel to our house to be there in case the boys return home and to pass out the Halloween candy that has magically appeared in a big bowl next to our front door, all in an attempt to keep things looking "normal." This is the mandate behind our Boss's plan: Act as if everything is perfectly fine. It may be that my children took off on their own in parental disobedience, or it could be something of a completely different nature.

I comb every inch of my assigned blocks, zeroing on every child wearing a black ninja or T-Rex costume.

There are more of those than I could have ever guessed, proving, like the TV commercials boasted, that "everybody gets their costumes at Sal's Carnival of Costumes." In the beginning, I was, perhaps, a bit too pushy in focusing on those two styles of costumes, as a few adults threatened to "call the authorities' on me for "following them." A few parents even recognized me as their child's dentist, with one dad jokingly suggesting I was looking to "nab the candy so it wouldn't rot any teeth." My excuse for being out on Halloween night without my children, while at the same time hunting down kids in certain costumes, eventually became an often repeated, made-up tale about getting separated from my six-year-old son and his teenage uncle, and not being able to identify them because of look-alike costumes. Surprisingly, most people accepted that lame excuse for my intrusion into their little group outings, making me think that when it came to Halloween, most parents lost all sense of logic.

Technically, I'd been now up for thirty-two hours straight, but I was running on pure adrenaline. However, after two hours of wandering the six-block grid that was my section and not seeing a trace of Dylan or *Oisin,* hopelessness began to set in. I'd yet to receive any call via cellphone or mental telepathy that anyone else had been more successful. The streets were beginning to clear of trick-or-treaters, as the city curfew for the traditional activity was 5:30 to 8:00 PM, and my cell phone stated the time as 8:20. As per the Black Knight's instructions, everyone was told to meet back at our home at 8:30 if the children hadn't yet been located, so that an alternative plan could be discussed.

Feet dragging under a heavy heart, I trudged back home, sick with fear for my missing kids and feeling entirely helpless. What was the sense of the people around me having all this magical ability if it couldn't be used to find missing children. While I'm still alone, I have myself a good, solid cry, knowing that I'll be expected to hold myself together when I rejoin the others; that stiff Fae upper lip and all that crap.

Declan is waiting for me on the porch wearing an expression that breaks my heart. "I'm sorry, Love. As I said befar', 'tis all my fault. I was too hard on the boy. I shad' have understood the par' lad was dealin' with more than he cad' bear. I swear ta' ya' on ma' bloodline, I will find them and bring them home."

I just nod and walk past him. I'm in no shape mentally to try and ease his guilt, not when I'm carrying enough of my own. If I had only stayed at the bonfire instead of escaping my mother and sister-in-law to follow my mate into the woods, then maybe I could have prevented what happened tonight. There is the flutter of wings in my head and a familiar voice says to me, *"If you had stayed at the bonfire, your mate would have bled to death in that trap before anyone ever found him. Because you were with him, you still have your Mo Shiorghra alive with you. Trust in the path, little tooth fairy mama. Things will be as they will be."*

Hearing Herself in my head out of the blue startles me and I stop dead in my tracks. Declan, who is behind me, asks "Is somethin' the matter, Lass. You just stopped movin' and came ta' a dead stop."

After living with the Raven Queen in my head for almost five years, the result of a deal I made when my Tax

Man was held captive in North Korea, I've learned that I am expected to keep her "little pearls of wisdom" to myself and not share them with anyone. Even my mate. "No. I'm just tired is all. This is just really hard…to deal with."

"Aye, Love. 'Tis a sorrowful path to walk, that's the honest truth. Yet, I see the others have arrived as well. No doubt Beck has another idea. The man always has a Plan B."

Declan holds the door open for me to enter, but I am riveted to the spot. This time it is to watch a county patrol car pull up to the front of our house. Deputy Roxanne Spinelli Brannigan exits the vehicle and goes around to the other side of the car. She leans in and pulls out a small figure from the back seat. As she turns around, I see the silly T-Rex head hanging down the child's back and a full head of ginger curls. "Dylan?" I screech at the top of my lungs.

The Deputy puts Dylan down and our son races up the front porch stairs and straight into my arms, sobbing his little eyes out. He's not the only one weeping. Declan is wiping at his eyes while I'm a blubbering mess. I can hear Mel sniffling behind me. "Why don't we all go in the house and we can sort this out," Lady Brannigan advises. "We're kind of a spectacle out here and the Sheriff was adamant about keeping this on the QT. I'm sorry I didn't text you people when I found him. Apparently, I must have dropped my cell phone on the road when I was buckling Dylan in the car and never noticed. And per the Boss's mandate, we were radio and telepathy silent, so I just drove over here as fast as I could."

We all shuffle inside, Declan carrying Dylan who is still heavily weeping. "It's okay, lad," his *athair* consoles, "yar' home with us safe and sound." Our son looks up at his father with eyes all red and oozy, and I know, sure as the sun rises, it's not the crying that's making them so. Dylan undoubtedly has a bad case of pink eye, and at this moment, is probably highly contagious.

"Oh, Da! It was terrible. I was vera' scared and then I lost all my track an' tradin' *milseán* and *Uncail Oisin* said we cad' not go back and get some more."

In my joy at seeing Dylan home safe and sound, I had immediately forgotten to ask about *Oisin*, and the guilt of that hits me like a two-ton hammer to the gut. No wonder the boy feels the way he does. It's us. Declan and me. We're the problem. Somehow, we have played favorites with our birth children and the poor child knew it. Immediately, there is again the cawing of birds in my head, but no voice offering guidance, leaving me more confused than ever.

"Where did you find the boy, Rox," the Sheriff asks. "I assume it wasn't here in his neighborhood."

"No, Sir. I was making another drive around the perimeter of Salem's city limits when I saw the boy walking down Bridge Street, the short route near the Salem-Beverly Bridge. I knew right away it was Dylan by the dinosaur costume he was wearing. Plus, there was no reason for anyone to be in that area this late at night. The bicycle and walking paths all close at dusk."

"Bridge Street? Isn't that the same spot where Fr. Kevin found *Oisin* the day he was truant?" I ask, not liking the way this was looking for my husband's brother.

"Dylan, where is your *Uncail Oisin* right now? How come he isn't with you?"

"I don't know, Mama," he answers, then starts weeping into his father's shirt again. I give my husband credit. There's no missing that our son has "Rotten Eyes," and everyone knows Lord *Nuada* is ultra -fastidious about dirt and germs. To his credit, Declan doesn't push Dylan away, instead holding our son closer to his chest and patting his back.

"Why don't we let young Master Dylan tell us what happened in his own words," the 26th Merlin gently suggests. "Can you do that, lad. Tell us all how you came to be walking down Bridge Street?"

Dylan pulled away from his father's embrace and viewed all the people staring at him. They were a rather intimidating group, and the boy shook his head no until his father coaxed him. "Go ahead, son. Tell us what happened. No one is angry with ya'. We were just all vera' worried about ya' and now we are still worried over yar' *Uncail Oisin.* Can ya' be a brave lad and tell us what happened so we ken' bring yar' *Uncail* home?"

MISSING 41

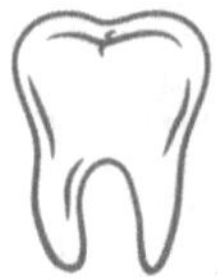

Shedding Some Light On This Terrible Plight

And so began Dylan's story. From what we could piece together from his constant starting and stopping, along with the child's mixed-up tales about which houses gave him what type of treats for Halloween, it appeared that *Oisin* had planned all along to sneak away from the *Samhain* bonfire and return to Salem in order to go trick or treating with his friend. At least that was the story he shared with Dylan. When Lady *Siobhan* commanded that he take his nephew home by carriage, *Oisin* was happy to return to *Dun Siorai* to make his escape because he told Dylan that his magic was stronger near his *"mathair."*

I'll be the first to admit it; hearing Dylan talk about *Oisin* being near his murdered mother gave me the chills, while at the same time, all the hair on my arms stood straight up. Dylan went on to explain that he began pressuring *Oisin* to take him along to Salem so he could go trick or treating as well. His *Uncail* refused, and Dylan threw a fit and threatened to tell *Birgit* and *Niamh*. Instead of going into the side entrance leading to our family quarter as his *uncail* had ordered him to do, Dylan doubled back and followed *Oisin* to the kennels where the teenager was desperately trying to get *Seamus* into a crate so he wouldn't follow him.

"The doggo dinna' want to go in at all," our son explains. "He was bitin' *Uncail Oisin's* pant leg and growlin' sumthin' fierce. Then, ma' *uncail* saw me hidin' by the door, and said if I dinna' go into the house he'd lock me up in a kennel right next ta' his gad' boy." Dylan looked up at his father. "But I was no afraid, Da. Well, maybe just a wee bit scared. I told *Oisin* that I was the *Mac Nuada* and he better not be puttin' me in any dog cage because I would tell his Lordship and then..."

"Go on, wee *Mac*. Finish yar' story," my husband coaxes.

Dylan eyed the Black Knight across from him, then turned and talked softly into his father's chest "I tol' him that the Black Knight would cut his head off with the fearsome *Caladbolg*." Keeping his eyes downcast, the little boy added. "I am sorry far' sayin' such a thing, ma' Lord Knight. I dinna' want him ta' leave me behind."

Most adults, when confronted with such a statement, would assure the child that civilized folk didn't go around cutting people's heads off. But the Queen's Hand of Justice, never one to miss the opportunity to strengthen his "mystique," looked my son straight in the eye and said, "No worries, young *Mac Nuada*. You only spoke the truth.

I do cut people's heads off. But only vera' bad people," he replied with a wink.

Dylan returned the pardon with a wry nod, but I wanted to give the man a good piece of my mind. Buttons to banjos, he was an insufferable piece of work! Seeing the dirty looks I was aiming toward his Superior Officer, my mate changed the subject. "So, then what happened after that, Dylan? How did ya' end up in the Mundane world?"

In between numerous sighs and yawns, our son continued his story. Eventually, *Oisin* relented to taking him along. The circle Beck and I had seen near the kennels was the one the teenager used to move them to Salem, and Dylan left his boots behind because they were pinching his toes. Once back home in Salem, they found their costumes in the front hall closet, changed into them, and began circling the neighborhood while gathering their treats. "It was great fun, Mama," he admits to me, "but then I got ta' thinkin' how ya' might be worried 'bout where I'd gone, so I told *Uncail* I wanted ta' go back ta' *I Idir*. He said he cad' not take me because he was waitin' for his friend, Finbarr Lally."

I literally gasp when Dylan mentions that name. "Finbarr Lally? Again?" I ask. "Who is this pain-in-the-ass-kid? He's a really bad influence!" As before, I feel a vague sense of having seen or heard this name before. Somewhere important, but try as I might, just like the last time, I can't place where I know it from.

"That does seem to be the million-dollar question," the 26th Merlin says. "He seems to be a key player in all of this."

The Tax Man, annoyed at our constant interruptions

of the child's story, prods Dylan to continue. "So, did ya' meet with this Finbarr Lally, Dylan? What did he look like?"

"Aye, Da. He was a vera' tall sort of boy, dressed, I suppose, far' track n' tradin' in a long robe with a hood. I dinna' see much of him, his face was all covered up by the hood, but I did see that he had long white hair. Or maybe that was part of his costume. I donna' know far' sure. Anyways, he made *Oisin* and I walk vera' far. I got so tired, *Oisin* had ta' carry me on his back. Finbarr Lally was no vera' happy to have me along. He told ma' *uncail* 'twas not the right time ta' bring *Mac Nuada* into it. I asked *Oisin* what his friend meant by that, but he told me to hush with ma' talkin' befar' I made his friend angry."

I imagine all the things that could have gone wrong. Of how close we came to losing Dylan. I shudder and squeeze Declan's hand. He squeezes back. *"I know, Love. 'Tis too terrible to even contemplate."*

This time it's the Black Knight's turn to coax the boy along. "So, *Mac Nuada*, how did you come to be walking down Bridge Street? Did this Lally fellow send you away?"

"Not right off, ma' Lord. We went inta' the woods where this friend had a giant bonfire, but no as big as our *Samhain* one in *I Idir*. He was still angry with ma' *uncail* for bringin' me along when suddenly he got a good look at ma' eyes in the light from the fire. He cursed somethin' awful, and told *Oisin* ta' get rid of me befar' they were all infected. *Uncail Oisin* walked me back to the main road and told me ta' keep walkin' until someone stopped ta' help me. I was no happy ta' walk by ma'self in the dark, and I begged him ta' come with me, but he said he had ta' stay with Finbarr Lally. I did as he said, but no one came by until the police lady showed up. I knew she was no 'stranger danger' 'cause I recognized her from the hand-fastin' in *I Idir*, so I let har' put me in the car. And that's how I came home," he concludes, as if the crazy story he'd just told was an everyday occurrence. "Oh. I almost forgot somethin'." Dylan reached inside the front of his dinosaur costume and pulled out a crudely wrapped package. "*Uncail Oisin* said I should give this ta the both of ya."

I unwrap the item wrapped in a brown paper lunch bag and tied with string. Inside, lay the little leather sheath I made for *Oisin*'s toy sword. The sword that had burned up when the boy saved my life. The one he faith-fully carried his dirk in. My lip starts to quiver and I hand the note written inside to my *Mo Shiorghra*, as I don't have enough emotional control to read it myself.

Declan read the note out loud:

> Ma' Lord Brother and Lady Sister,
> I have decided to' take his Lordship's words to heart. 'Tis high time I find my own path as I am called to do by my ancestors, and such path is not found in the sheltered halls of Dun Siorai, but rather out in the world alongside Finbarr Lally.
> Please take care of this for me. Or maybe give it to Mac Nuada when he is older. I won't be needin' it where I'm goin'.
> Yours,
> Buaf

PS I am sorry for draggin' wee Dylan with me. I did no mean for that to happen. If you are reading this, I hope that means he made it home safely. He will be a vera' good Lord someday.

Audience or not, I can't stop the tears that are rolling down my cheeks. Declan's face is pale and still, and Dylan, who understands more than he lets on, is silently weeping again into his father's shirt.

"What a fuckin' mess," the Black Knight growls, not one to mince words or ever worry about dropping an F-bomb. "I'd really like to get my hands on that sonofabitch, Finbarr Lally. Who the hell is that guy? If he's even a 'guy' at all and not some Otherworldly demon of sorts."

"Tis a damnable mystery," the Merlin replies. "And somehow, I don't think we're going to get the answers we need all boxed up neatly and ready to find."

In the midst of my heartache and misery, the wizard's words "boxed up," hit my brain like an arrow from an imaginary bow, clearing the despair in my head. This is followed by the sound of shrill, cawing birds. Like a gift from the Universe, or perhaps I should be more direct and say a personal gift from The Morrigan, Herself, on her sacred name day, I know exactly where I've seen that name before. "Hold on a second," I announce. "I might just have a few of those 'boxed' answers." Without explaining anything more, I jump from the sofa and head toward the garage.

"Rosie, where are you going?" the Tax Man calls out to me.

"Just hold on a sec. I have to find something," I holler back. "Don't anyone go anywhere."

I flip on the overhead lights and cross the garage towards a tall shelf of cardboard boxes, looking for a specific one labeled "Dad's Personal Stuff." It is, of course, on the top shelf, requiring me to pull over a ladder and climb up to reach it. Retrieving it, I carefully crawl back down the ladder and carry the box inside.

The entire group looks at me curiously as I flip open the top and begin rummaging through stacks of old documents and certificates as I try to explain what I'm up to. "These are my late father's personal effects. When he passed, my sister Claire brought all the stuff he had in storage over here because Decan and I had more space to store it. I was supposed to go through it all and sort out the important things, but I found one item in here that made it just too painful to continue, so I just shoved it all back in the box and stored it on the top shelf." I find what I'm looking for; a worn, black leather journal with a gold letter "A" marked on the front. I flip through it, looking for a certain page, and then finding it, I hold it up, explaining, "This is my mother's diary from when she was a young girl. It was among my father's things. I guess he didn't have the heart to throw it away, even if the words inside were difficult to read. In it, my *mathair* describes how she met a Fae boy in the village market of *I Idir*. A boy she fell head- over-heels in love with. A titled boy pretending to be a common farmer, who called himself by the false name of… 'Finbarr Lally.'"

I let my audience put two and two together and watch as the lightbulbs go off in all their heads. "*Oisin* hasn't run-off with some mysterious Fae teenager," I state with greater calm than I actually feel. "He's with his murderous sire, Callum Fitzpatrick."

* * *

Find out what happens to Rosie, Declan, and their beloved family in Book 7 of The Tooth Fairy Chronicles: Toothless Grins And His Father's Sins

MORE FROM SERENADE PUBLISHING

Songbird Series

By Sarah Williams

Songbird

Brigadier Station Series

By Sarah Williams:

The Brothers of Brigadier Station

The Sky over Brigadier Station

The Legacies of Brigadier Station

Christmas at Brigadier Station

Heart of the Hinterland Series

By Sarah Williams:

The Dairy Farmer's Daughter

Their Perfect Blend

Beyond the Barre

The Outback Governess

By Sarah Williams

Primrose Series

By Tanya Renee

Prairie Sky

Prairie Nights

Prairie Fire

Prairie Hearts

Prairie Sound

Prairie Rain

Prairie Prestige

Prairie Roads

With The Band

Finding Direction

Love Notes

On The Edge Of Forever

The Spring of Love Series

By Virginia Taylor

Forever Delighted

Forever Amused

Forever Heartfelt

The Triple Goddess Series

By Ellen Read

The Ancient Fire

Beneath The Mist

For more information visit:

www.serenadepublishing.com

About the Author

Victoria Rocus is a retired educator, accomplished miniaturist, and full-time author living near the home of country music, Nashville, Tennessee, USA. When she's not writing new adventures for her imaginary friends, catering beach parties for mermaids, or finding homes for orphaned dragons, she's building and rehabbing one-of-a-kind dollhouses and accessories, just like her favorite character, Dr. Rosie Parker. Many of her multiple miniature buildings are 1/12 scale replicas of settings from her unique fantasy stories.

Victoria started her writing career as a weekly blogger while still teaching middle school language arts. Now retired from the educational field, she's been able to make writing a full-time adventure, penning several fantasy and romance stories she hopes readers will enjoy with both a sigh and a smile.

Find out more at: victoriarocusauthor.com

instagram.com/victoriarocusauthor
tiktok.com/@victoriarocusauthor

Acknowledgments

In a lot of ways, writing a book series is like going away to summer camp. Though the kid in you welcomes the journey with joyful anticipation, you always still harbor a wee bit of anxiety over the unknown future and worry whether you'll be able to hold it together for as many weeks as your adventure lasts. What makes it a happy, memorable experience are those certain "counselors" and "friends" who help guide you through it, which is not unlike the many people who work to bring a story all the way through publication.

A special "Tooth Fairy Cheer of Thanks" goes to Sarah Williams, "camp counselor" and publisher extraordinaire, who has been instrumental in getting Rosie and Declan's story out into the world. I wish for you marshmallows that never burn and fall off their stick, along with much future success as you grow Serenade Publishing.

Kudos as well to my awesome beta reader team for your genuine feedback and continued support. Whatever the future holds, I know for sure that I will want Carol Peden Fuller, Donna Gentile Ruth, Daniel Caddigan, Kaia Viney, Michele S. Kaspar, and Gail Hoder, along with talented fellow authors and friends, Arla Jones and K.C. Nord, as part of my "Rosie relay team."

A big "two, four, six, eight...who do we appreciate"

sent off to my "campfire friends" who have supported me so wonderfully along the way; Shannon and Ryan B, Dan and Chris C, Steve and Gail H, Roy and Denise P, John and Paula D, Marcia W, Debbie P, Bonnie M, Bill F, Betty M, Lorraine, R, Linda F, Cindy J, Christine M, and everyone who isn't mentioned here by my fault alone and who I will surely remember right after this book goes to press. You guys all win the Tooth Fairy Chronicles "Spirit" award.

To my life-long "bunkmates," my dear family; my husband, Victor, my children Steven, Michael, Allison and Kaia, and my sweet, little "peanut," Valerie James. You make all the days worthwhile, the rainy ones as well as the sunny times. Love you loads! Kiss, kiss. Hug, hug.

And lastly, to all the wonderful and supportive readers who willingly got on the "camp bus" and took the ride with Rosie and Declan. Wishing you guys "a hundred bottles of beer on the wall" and everything good that goes with it. Thank you!